Amber Laura

# Topaz and Lace

Publisher: LitLiber

# COPYRIGHT

ISBN: 978-0-9986608-5-1

AMBER LAURA

TOPAZ AND LACE

Copyright © 2017 by Amber Laura

Cover art by LitLiber

*Book cover model*
Amanda Dornhecker
Used with permission.

All rights reserved. Except for use in book reviews, no part of this published work may be reproduced, copied, edited or republished in any form or by any electronic or mechanical means, either now known or later invented, including but not limited to: photocopying, recording, or downloading and storing, without prior written permission by the publisher, LitLiber. For information on permission, contact LitLiber at business@litliber.com.

This is a work of fiction. Characters, names, places, descriptions, and events are either the product of the author's imagination or are used fictitiously—that is, for the sake of furthering along the wholly imagined story, and perhaps adding a sense of realism to the fantasy. As such, nothing within it should be read as real or actual, in fact or likeness; any resemblance otherwise, to person, place, or thing, is entirely coincidental.

LitLiber

www.litliber.com

# Amber Laura

**Amber Laura** lives in the beautiful, wild country of northern Minnesota—tall pines and birch bark, hiking trails, lakes, and fresh air.
But that's only a technicality; in her imagination, Amber Laura has lived all over the world. She considers it one of the best perks to being a writer: easy, cheap travel. Well, that and the oddball characters she meets along the way....

Visit her blog at www.litliber.com.

Topaz and Lace

## Other Novels by Amber Laura

*Twenty-Seven Tiered Almond Cake*

*After She Fell*

*Redesigning Her*

*Slightly Delayed and Somewhat Haphazard*

## Other Short Stories by Amber Laura

*Of Things Unsaid*

*Calling in the Tropes*

*The Kiss Fix*

*Up Here With You*

*The Wake-Up Call*

Once More, Again

Amber Laura

*From one love story to another, this book is for you:*

*Chad, for holding my heart.*
*Amanda, for holding my hand.*
*And mom—for holding me together.*

*I love you. Forever. Without you, I wouldn't be me.*

Topaz and Lace

# TABLE OF CONTENTS

INTRODUCTION
CHAPTER ONE
CHAPTER TWO
CHAPTER THREE
CHAPTER FOUR
CHAPTER FIVE
CHAPTER SIX
CHAPTER SEVEN
CHAPTER EIGHT
CHAPTER NINE
CHAPTER TEN
CHAPTER ELEVEN
CHAPTER TWELVE
CHAPTER THIRTEEN
CHAPTER FOURTEEN
CHAPTER FIFTEEN
CHAPTER SIXTEEN
CHAPTER SEVENTEEN
CHAPTER EIGHTEEN
CHAPTER NINETEEN
CHAPTER TWENTY
CHAPTER TWENTY-ONE
CHAPTER TWENTY-TWO
CHAPTER TWENTY-THREE
CHAPTER TWENTY-FOUR
CHAPTER TWENTY-FIVE
CHAPTER TWENTY-SIX
CHAPTER TWENTY-SEVEN
CHAPTER TWENTY-EIGHT
CHAPTER TWENTY-NINE

# INTRODUCTION

Abigail Hastings stared out the window at the empty roadway before her house. "Well, she's gone," she said softly.

"Yup," her husband said, coming to stand beside her. Throwing an arm over her shoulder, he brought his wife up close to his chest.

Abigail sniffled. "I wasn't sure at the last minute if she'd get in the taxi."

"Me neither."

"I kind of hoped she wouldn't."

He laughed. "I know."

"She's never left home before," Abigail told him as if he weren't entirely aware of this fact.

"No."

"Not even for college," she murmured. "She was always just down the hall from us."

"It's only two months," Edward reminded his wife.

She nodded. "Yes."

"It'll be good for her."

She sighed. "I suppose."

"She needs to spread her wings."

"So you keep saying." Her voice was mildly accusing. "I still think we should have brought her to the airport."

Edward chuckled. "Then I'd have had to worry about you."

"Me?" Abigail pushed at his chest. "Embarrassed I'd make a scene?"

"No, convinced you'd have found a way to get on that plane with her."

Abigail laughed then. "Probably you're right."

"I usually am."

"Oh, hush."

Edward squeezed her to his side. "Hey. It'll be good for us, too."

"Yeah..." but she didn't sound convinced.

Edward turned her in his arms. "I promise you. It's for the best."

She wiped at her eyes. "I hope so."

# CHAPTER ONE

Grabbing her suitcase off the spinning baggage claim carousel, Cassie took a deep breath. Her stomach quivered as she looked around the swarming airport. Men in pointed boots and weather-beaten straw hats paraded past her, southern drawls and colorful sayings peppered the air, accompanied by the secreting smell of hot, humid sunshine. Standing out like a sore thumb, Cassie grimaced at her own conservative pantsuit with its pale pink shirt.

"Welcome to Pantula, Texas," she whispered unsteadily to herself. Although that wasn't quite true. She wasn't in Pantula. That was some ninety miles away yet. Still, the sound of her voice was a comfort in the sea of strangers milling around her.

Hauling her luggage with her, Cassie shouldered her way into the crowded waiting area. Tall, floor-to-ceiling windows offered a grimy view of the parking lot outside.

"Cassandra? Cassandra Hastings?"

Lurching at the sound of her name, trying to ignore the hustle of bodies pushing past her, the squeal of wheeled cases scraping noisily against the polished floor—Cassie turned to see a short, wiry-looking gentleman walking determinedly toward her. He was older, nearing sixty she guessed, stooped in posture and with a shock of uncombed white hair, the uneven lengths of which were spiking out of his head in all different directions.

She felt her fingers tighten against the handle of her suitcase as he came up to her. Smile at the man, Cassie. Smile. But her lips were trembling so hard she couldn't be sure she wasn't actually grimacing instead. Propping her suitcase beside her feet, Cassie held out a hand expectantly. "Yes, hello and you must be—"

"Samuel Tompkins," he supplied, engulfing her hand in a rough, warm shake.

Cassie smiled shyly. Dr. Samuel Tompkins didn't look anything like she'd imagined. And as he would be her immediate supervisor throughout the duration of her externship, she'd had cause to think about him frequently the past few weeks.

"Indeed, indeed!" he continued. "Pleasure to meet you and may I say, you look just as lovely as the picture you sent." He shot her a dazzling smile. The photo in question, forwarded to his office for the very purpose of identifying her in this bustling place, had been taken this last spring of Cassie smiling into the camera on the steps leading up to her college courtyard.

"Thank you…" Cassie murmured nervously and then, as an afterthought said: "And, uh, please, call me Cassie." She felt like puking all over his neat denim shirt, but she was relatively pleased with the steady undulation of her voice.

He smiled impishly. "Cassie. I like that. Well, nice to meet you, Cassie—"

"You as well."

"On behalf of the staff at the Tiamango Veterinary Clinic, welcome on board," he offered with a smile.

She smiled crookedly. "Thank you." The words came out shyly.

Dr. Tompkins looked down at his watch, nodding with satisfaction. "Your flight made good time. At this rate, we should be in Pantula by five o'clock."

Cassie nodded absently. Pantula, Texas, the small, bite-sized town where she'd complete the last of her coursework requirements before she'd receive her degree as a doctor of veterinary medicine. Pantula, Texas, the final stop before college graduation. With a population boasting more heads of cattle than people, Cassie could only imagine what she'd find when they arrived.

Land. Lots and lots of open, brownish-green land, with cows and horses, goats and rusted out fences…and not much else. Cassie had done her homework. She'd looked up every available image of the small town she could find on the internet. She'd checked out the animal population. All her findings had come back unremarkably the same: old, quiet, and filled with livestock.

A seizure of nerves settled in her stomach at the thought. She actually felt her foot take a step backward before she caught herself.

"Have everything you need?" Dr. Tomkins asked, interrupting her thoughts.

Cassie nodded gratefully. Drawing in a difficult breath, she answered him. "Yes. I think so."

"Then shall we?" he asked kindly, but he was already steering her toward the exit.

Stepping outside, Cassie felt her stomach shift. Her life had turned decidedly foreign in the last couple of hours…

Think of the Peterson Veterinary Hospital, she reminded herself forcefully when her legs seemed stuck to the pavement. A meditation of sorts, images transposed themselves before her eyes. In exchange for the half-full parking lot loaded down with four-wheel-drive vehicles, instead, Cassie saw a large, rectangular waiting room with lightly padded chairs and an animal scale tucked to one corner. Concentrating hard, she could almost see the sleek lines of the receptionist desk, the copper veins on the quartz countertop; smell the clean, sterile odor of the examination rooms with their speckled tile and white counters with black tops...

Smiling a little more naturally then, Cassie felt her stride loosen. Thoughts of the Peterson Veterinary Hospital always steadied her focus. She'd been practically guaranteed a job there after graduation. One of the veterinarians would be retiring soon and, after a brief internship there last fall, the owner had all but assured Cassie the position was hers.

She only needed to complete this one last externship.

That's why she was here, after all, right? The Peterson Veterinary Hospital.

"That and good old fashioned peer pressure."

"What was that?" Dr. Tompkins asked, turning back to look at her.

"What?" Cassie's face burned. She hadn't realized she'd spoken that last part out loud. "Oh. No-nothing," she assured him quickly. Tucking her chin into her chest, she stared down at the ground, following him toward an impossibly large, white pickup truck.

"It's quite a ways into town yet," he reminded her as he unlocked the doors. "Feel free to doze off if you'd like," he invited before hopping inside.

Mortified at the mere thought, Cassie hurriedly assured him that wouldn't be necessary. But as the truck turned out onto the open stretch of highway, she felt her stomach muscles convulse. Staring out the side window, she couldn't help the small wash of homesickness that settled in the pit of her stomach. Gone were the usual bisecting lanes of major highways and freeways, the sight of copious fast-food chains and strip malls. Instead, her eyes met nothing but passing prairie.

She was a long way from home. Clamping her hands firmly between her knees, she battled with the nerves that always accompanied the start of clinical rotations with the oppressive sense of emptiness located outside her view.

So on second thought, she did close her eyes—to bloat out the sudden moisture there or to keep from seeing the reality of her new view, she wasn't sure. An unknown exhaustion crept over her person. She felt her neck fall back against the headrest. Breathe, Cassie. Just breathe.

It's okay. It's oka—

The anxiety and nerves of the past twenty-four hours—intermittently spent packing and pacing and then saying goodbye—finally catching up to her, Cassie felt her body slump against the seat, her ears growing numb to the rattle of the engine. Her feet felt tethered to the floorboards. Three miles out of town, with her head bobbing fitfully against Dr. Tompkins shoulder, Cassie fell asleep.

Waking with a jolt sometime later, she felt the truck tires bounce along a particularly rutted stretch of road. Jerking upright, she quickly ran a hand over her mouth. How long had she been out?

Turning toward Dr. Tompkins, she blushed. "I am so sorry...!" she stuttered, her face hot. Great first impression, Cassie. Drooling all over your boss. "I guess I was more tired than I thought," she grumbled.

He waved her apology aside. "No worries. I'm used to long road trips. By the end of your stay with us, you will be too." He laughed at his quiet joke.

Gazing out the windshield, Cassie checked out the passing scenery. Surprisingly lush, green grass stared back at her. Miles and miles of it, broken here and there by the dotted appearance of a cow, a lolling hill, or a patch of mesquite trees. It was both beautiful and remote.

"Where are we now?" Cassie asked.

"Close to home, about five minutes this side of the city limits. You had yourself a good little nap there, darling!"

Cassie bit her lip. But the nap had been good for one thing, at least— the return of her perspective. At least she no longer felt the overwhelming urge to vomit. A little more in control of her emotions, the terror of the newness around Cassie faded a little.

Shifting her attention back to the window, she resumed her inventory of the landscape. The isolation of just minutes ago was transforming, intersected now with agricultural buildings—holding pens and a hay loft, sundry barns and riding arenas and outbuildings dotted the earth.

As the truck sped across the gravel road, Cassie spied something else. A little ways off and to the left of this massive ranching operation, standing regal and refined, was an equally impressive red brick home. As the truck rambled forward, Cassie got a better look of the long, paved driveway leading up to this breathtaking farmstead, at the end of which stood a grand wrought-iron entrance gate. Splayed in prominent display across the top of the ornate fixture were these words: McDowell Estate.

Following her eyesight, Dr. Tompkins spoke up: "Impressive, huh? Well, don't worry you'll get the chance to check the place out proper"— of course, he was referring to the animal compounds—"and it won't disappoint. The McDowell's run a prosperous cattle ranch here in town. Heck, it's getting so busy with all them heads soon they'll have us on retainer!" He guffawed again. "In fact, we'll be stopping by there tomorrow...."

Dr. Tomkins kept talking but Cassie didn't manage to take in a single word of it. What in the hell had she signed herself up for?

# CHAPTER TWO

The decision to come to Pantula had, like so many life-changing decisions, been born on the breath of impulsivity. Cassie had been sitting in the college community center with a group of friends when the topic of senior externships had been brought up. At first, she'd only been passively listening, her focus bent on the homework spread out in front of her. But before long, the excited chatter happening overhead had stolen her attention.

Jenny was applying for a marketing position with some firm out in Boston. Abby was looking at a publishing house out in New York, Marissa a playhouse out in Minneapolis. No one had bothered to ask if Cassie was applying for anything outside the city. There was no need. Of course, she wasn't. She'd stay home and find something local, just like she'd done last year and the year before that.

Thinking back on it now, Cassie wasn't entirely sure what had prompted her. Only, in that moment, she'd felt left-out. Or, perhaps, she'd felt like she was missing out. On something vital. The glow of her friends' faces, the expectant, animated talk of it all. She'd felt boring by comparison.

She had her future all nicely planned out. She'd graduate, move to an apartment in town, and join the Peterson clinic as their youngest veterinarian on staff. That dream had seen her through countless late-night study cram sessions, it had echoed enticingly in her ears when she'd cried off on Saturday night partying with her friends. It had carried her through tough exams and ditched dates.

There had never been a thought of moving away. Of exploring other options. She had it all figured out. Her friends had been right not to ask about her travel plans. Cassie wasn't applying for anything outside the city. What would have been the point?

Which was perhaps the most damning fact of all.

And that's when Cassie had heard herself speaking: "Dr. Seymour was saying something about a spot available at an animal clinic somewhere out in southern Texas." At the inclusion of her voice, all other talk had immediately ceased. She wasn't sure who'd been more surprised at hearing this announcement—them or herself. "I'm thinking of checking it out."

"Where in Texas?" Marissa had asked.

Cassie had bit her lip. "Well, I'm not actually sure," she admitted.

"So you applied?" Abby asked, her large blue eyes staring straight at Cassie.

"Well, no, not yet," Cassie stumbled. "I'm still only just thinking about it."

A chorus of understanding "oohs" and "hmms" had accompanied her statement. No one believed she'd actually do it.

She'd gotten their attention only to become the butt of everyone's joke.

To cinch the matter, Jenny had reached across the table, patting Cassie's wrist. "Well, good for you anyway, hun. Take a look. No harm no foul."

"Yeah, that's great," Marissa had chimed in. "You'll have to let us know how that goes...."

All of which had more or less sealed Cassie's fate. Getting up from the table some twenty minutes later, she'd rushed down the labyrinth of hallways that made up the college campus until she'd gained the outside entrance of Dr. Seymour's office, where the applications were waiting.

"What does it matter, anyway?" she'd muttered staunchly to herself, grabbing for the forms. "You know where you're going. Your future is set." All she needed was to complete this one last rotation. One last school term. "Here or there, makes no difference."

Besides, didn't everyone say college was the time for making big moves? Well, fine. She'd do that. And afterward, she'd be able to merrily cross that item right off her to-do list. No regrets.

And that's how she'd wound up at the Tiamango Veterinary Clinic in Pantula, Texas.

\* \* \*

It was barely seven o'clock when Dr. Tomkins—who'd assured Cassie she could call him Sam, as everybody else did—pulled up outside the entrance to the vet clinic. The lights were all off inside.

"Closed for the evening," Dr. Tomkins assured her. "But we do offer twenty-four-hour service. Everybody shares the on-call duty."

Cassie nodded absently. If the building was closed, what the hell were they doing there? She didn't have long to wait.

Jiggling a pair of keys out of his pocket, Dr. Tomkins, er, Sam, tossed them to Cassie.

She stared down at them nonplussed. They were giving her keys to the building?

Seeing her look, Sam asked: "They did tell you that a room would be supplied throughout your stay here, right?" He sighed. "Please tell me you didn't book yourself a hotel for the night?"

"What? Oh, yeah," Cassie assured him. "They told me."

"Good." Then, with his head, he gestured toward a set of exterior stairs, just visible on one the side of the building. "That's it."

Cassie followed his gaze meekly. "What's it?"

"The apartment. It's right up there."

And when she craned her neck upward, Cassie could just see a door appearing at the top of the second story of the building.

"It's above the clinic?"

"Yup." He laughed. "Makes it easy, huh? No problems with traffic on your morning commute."

Cassie sincerely doubted that would have been a problem anyway, having spied some of the town as they'd driven past, but she kept that thought to herself. Curling the keys inside her palm, she spared him a quick smile. "Easy," she murmured.

"Well, I suppose. I'll let you get yourself settled in for the night. I'm sure it's been a long day," he told her.

Taking this as her cue, Cassie reached for the door handle. "Right. Well, thank you for coming to pick me up," she offered politely.

"Hey, no problem," Dr. Tomkins said. He laughed. "Now scoot."

Heaving her bags out of the back of the truck, Cassie did as she was bidden.

"See you in the morning," Sam hollered out the driver's side window. "Eight o'clock sharp."

Cassie waved in response, her feet already climbing up the metal staircase. It was only as she gained the second-floor landing, inserting her key in the door's lock that she heard Dr. Tomkins' truck slowly back out of the drive.

Turning on a light switch beside the door, Cassie set her luggage on the ground as she looked around her. There wasn't much to see. Thick hardwood flooring seemed to run throughout the place. A small kitchenette was perched just off to the left—and it was small, the length of which spanned no more than three large strides from end to end. The limited space afforded little more than three cupboards, an industrial-sized sink beside an electric stovetop, and a small, slightly dented refrigerator. The other side of the room was occupied by a plaid couch that would've looked right at home in a frat house and a rocking chair that clearly belonged in a nursing home. Hodgepodge wasn't even the word.

Worse, the air permeated with the vague scent of wet dog fur.

"Never mind," she assured herself, "It's hardly forever." Walking determinedly toward the only other door in the place, Cassie pushed it open. Blinking in surprise, her eyes met a massive four-poster bed positioned in the middle of the room. That had some promise. Other than an old bureau shoved up against one wall and a door leading to the adjoining bathroom, the room was bare.

So, it was pretty much like the rest of the place.

Setting her suitcase on top of the bed, Cassie took a deep breath. Silence seemed to seep out of the very pores of the walls.

At the sudden buzzing of her phone, Cassie reached into her back pocket. It was her mother calling. Taking a deep breath, Cassie answered.

"Hey, mom."

"Have you arrived?"

Cassie rolled her eyes. She'd texted her mother when the plane touched down, but she should have known that wouldn't be enough.

"Just got into Pantula."

"And? How is it?"

Cassie ran her bottom lip against her teeth. "Well, I haven't seen much of the town…and the clinic was closed for the evening."

"Did they put you up somewhere nice?"

Cassie squinted. She tilted her head to one side. "Well, I get my own apartment," she hedged. "So I guess that's pretty nice."

"Oh! That's great."

Cassie sighed. "Yeah."

Her daughter's lack of communication noted, Abigail said: "Well, I'm sure you're tired. I can let you go if you'd—"

"No!" Cassie swallowed. "I mean, I'm not too tired to talk."

\* \* \*

Surprisingly enough, Cassie slept well that night. She'd thought she'd toss and turn in the unfamiliar surroundings, her stomach knotted up as she waited for her first day of training. But at six o'clock the next morning, she woke up relatively refreshed to warm sunlight filtering through the bedroom blinds, and the annoying cackle of birds singing from somewhere outside her window.

Slowing pulling herself up against the headboard of her new bed, Cassie mentally braced herself for what was coming. New people, a new place, knowing absolutely nothing. Shimmying out of bed and bounding into the bathroom, she felt the familiar flock of nerves returning. Looking in the bathroom mirror, she made a face at her reflection. Her thin blonde hair traveled in waves halfway to her elbows, and her large green eyes glowed back at her brightly. Too brightly.

Horses. Steers. Bulls. Pigs. Holy shit. Cassie swallowed back initial panic. It was only the first day. That was all. It was just new. It's not like she hadn't worked on large animals before. She'd sailed through all of her other clinical exams. Granted, there had always been a teacher beside her, and a whole host of other students nearby, and no one had expected her to know what she was all about! Closing her eyes, Cassie only prayed the livestock she encountered that day would behave in exactly the manner as written about in the pages of her college textbooks.

Turning the faucet on, she jumped into the shower. The warm drum of water spraying over her tense body helped put things into perspective. Dr. Tomkins would be there. It's not like she would be going out on her own. Plus, she'd reminded him yesterday that her experience with large animals was limited only to what she'd learned in school. A girl from the city, she didn't have the inherent know-how of someone raised in a more rural setting. All to which he'd only smiled, assuring her that he would soon put that to rights. Then he'd simply changed the subject, seeming unconcerned about her lack of confidence.

Cassie would be just fine. This was only an externship, for goodness' sake; a learning opportunity. It's just that, during all of her other clinical practicums, she'd felt, well, a little more familiar with the material. Stepping out of the shower, wrapped in a large white towel, Cassie padded back into her bedroom. Heading straight for the closet, she pulled out her favorite pantsuit. She always felt a little braver when she wore it. By then, it was already time to head downstairs.

* * *

After a whirlwind tour of the Tiamango Veterinary Clinic (which had left Cassie gasping for breath; the place wasn't just mammoth it was state-of-the-art), and an even faster introduction to the staff, half of whom Cassie had already forgotten, Dr. Tomkins lost no time sweeping her out to his waiting truck.

"I figure the best way to get started is just to get started," he informed her as he backed out of the parking lot.

"You'll have plenty of opportunities to inspect the place more closely at your leisure. But today we've got a heavy case load."

Cassie nodded.

"Remember that ranch we saw coming into town yesterday?"

Cassie nodded again. "The McDowell Estate?"

"Good memory," he said. "Yup, that's the one. Our first stop of the day."

"Okay." She wasn't sure what else to say.

"Sleep all right?" he asked conversationally, turning the truck down a country road.

Cassie smiled. "Yeah. Yes. Thank you, Dr. Tomkins. Just fine."

Dr. Tomkins grinned. "No need to be so formal around here—and speaking of that, I told you, you can quit with all the Dr. Tompkins nonsense. Sam will do just fine."

Cassie smiled. "I'll keep that in mind, Sam." She wrinkled her nose. That didn't sound right. "Dr. Sam?"

He laughed quietly. "Better."

Coming upon the imposing entrance of the McDowell ranch, he threw Cassie a quick look. "We're here to check on the well-being of a couple pregnant horses." Eyes pinned straight ahead, she nodded sharply. He smiled. "Hey, first days are tough. I remember. Try to loosen up a little. It's going to be fine."

Cassie rolled her neck a little. "Right."

"It's not like I'm going to leave you alone," he said, unintentionally repeating her earlier sentiment.

Cassie felt the butterflies in her stomach cease a little at the words. "I know."

Dr. Tomkins' slapped a large hand against the rigid line of her back. He laughed again. He had a merry laugh. "That's the spirit! Now, stretch a smile on your face," he ordered. Turning up the long drive toward the barn, he added a bit more ominously: "And don't, for the love of God, let Brannt see your nerves! He's likely to be worse than the animals if he does."

Before Cassie had time to question that cryptic remark, the seasoned veterinarian had already thrown the truck in park and was busy making his way down from its high seat. With nothing else for it, Cassie followed after him. Rounding the back of the truck, she watched him lean inside to retrieve something.

A portable ultrasound machine.

Cassie breathed a little easier. She knew exactly how that machine operated. She was acutely aware of why and when a transabdominal ultrasonography would be performed on a horse. Feeling a little more confident, Cassie smiled. She was still in the midst of this self-congratulatory praising when the barn door ahead of them opened.

A tall, lanky man emerged from its darkened depths. His face was momentarily shadowed under the brim of a straw hat as he started towards them. He had a long, slow stride that nicely matched his long, lean legs. Even though he wore only a pair of faded blue jeans and a blue and red flannel shirt, Cassie got the impression of elegance and authority wafting from his general demeanor.

When he drew nearer, Cassie felt her stomach pitch. He was gorgeous.

"Sam," he drawled in greeting, tipping his hat at the pair of them. His eyes were a startling grey.

Dr. Tomkins returned this with one of his large, toothy grins. "Good morning, Brannt—"

"Who's this?" he asked, and though he cocked his head toward Cassie, his eyes never once left Sam's. The words were soft but nonetheless, there was something dangerous, almost predatory in the innocent question.

Notching her chin up, Cassie refused to accept this blatant snub. She could speak for herself, thank you very much. Her voice rose quickly in response. "I'm Cassie Hastings," she supplied calmly enough. Holding out her hand, she worked up a game smile. *Don't let him see you sweat.* "It's a pleasure to meet you." Dr. Sam's warning echoed firmly in her ears. Who was this Brannt? The ranch foreman? A horse trainer?

Brannt didn't respond to this show of bravado, but his grip, when he placed his hand against hers, was strong, calloused. Turning his gaze back to Dr. Tomkins, he raised an eyebrow questioningly.

"I told you we'd be taking on a student this summer, didn't I?"

Brannt's face clouded over just slightly before clearing once again. "Indeed you did, I just assumed..." he shrugged, letting his muted disapproval dangle in the air suggestively.

"That I'd be a man?" Cassie challenged.

Brannt grunted. His thin lips compressed into a fine line. "That you'd be older than twelve." Those cold grey eyes raked over Cassie's slight frame, taking stock of her worth. They didn't seem to find much if his accompanying frown was anything to go by.

Cassie opened her mouth—

"Right. Well, shall we take a look at those mares?" Dr. Tomkins asked, beating her to the chase. He seemed oblivious to the strong undercurrents flashing between Cassie and Brannt; that or he just didn't care.

Without a word, Brannt spun on the heel of his boot, leading the small party into the dim lighting of the barn. There, standing smack-dab in the middle of the building's large walkway was a magnificent horse. Just off to her side, holding the huge creature steady, another ranch hand could be seen. The fingers of his gloved hand clutched surely against the sides of her halter, the only things keeping her from running away. Jittery, neighing in agitation, the obviously pregnant horse stomped unsteadily against the concrete flooring, her impressive body rocking uneasily from side-to-side.

Cassie fumbled to an uncertain stop at the sight. Propelled by the firm pressure of Dr. Tomkins hand on her lower back, however, she was forced to pick up her feet once more. But not, unfortunately, before this show of reticence was noted in that silvered stare...

"Let's keep her out here. The stall will be too narrow for the ultrasound," Dr. Tomkins decided. Turning toward Cassie, he pointed toward a rack of horse paraphernalia hanging on the opposite wall. "Cassie, why don't you go grab two ropes and we'll tie her up."

Cassie tried for a casual shrug. She could just spy the length of neon ropes hanging there, directly across the arch of the horse's hips. "Okay." Moving around Dr. Tomkins, she stepped forward. She was just about at the horse's hindquarters when a strong, steely hand grasped her arm, impeding any further movement. Looking up into Brannt's dark face, Cassie stilled.

"Never walk directly behind a horse without announcing your presence first," he cautioned her, placing his hand knowingly across the top of the animal's back leg. "Not unless you want to be kicked."

Coloring darkly, Cassie muttered an apology. "Of-of course," She sent a beseeching look at Dr. Sam. "I'm sorry."

At her pure trepidation, Brannt scowled. "Oh, hell, never mind. I'll do it," he growled, looking disgusted. Without another word, he went to fetch the lead ropes. Quietly dismissing the other cowboy (who had yet to be introduced to the group), Brannt quickly took possession of the horse. "Jesus, Sam where did you get this girl?" With practiced ease, he cross-tied the animal into place.

Cassie snapped her teeth together.

"Quiet you," Dr. Tomkins hushed good-naturedly. "There was a time when you didn't know much about horses, either." Without bothering to wait for the other man's response, the vet locked eyes with a now fully mortified Cassie. "This is Berma," he established. "She's at just over two hundred seventy-five days gestation."

And at Cassie's quick look, added quietly: "This isn't Berma's first pregnancy and she had a difficult birth at parturition last time…"

"We're monitoring the heartbeat," Cassie considered.

"Exactly."

"So it's absolutely imperative she stay calm," Brannt added pointedly.

Cassie raised rich eyebrows. "I'm well aware."

"Are you also aware that horses can sense fear?" he countered.

Cassie smiled tightly. "I assure you, I'm not afraid."

"Try again."

Cassie bit down hard. Whatever anxiety she'd been experiencing earlier was quickly forgotten, replaced with an all-consuming irritation.

"Sam, you will be the one administering the ultrasound, correct?" Brannt clarified. His words only fueled her dislike.

"This time," Dr. Tomkins agreed. Shooting Cassie a conspiratorial wink, he addressed her then: "Give it a few weeks, and then you'll be the one in high demand."

Brannt snorted in response to this.

Cassie had never wanted to slug someone so badly in her life.

# CHAPTER THREE

With relief bordering on hysteria, Cassie watched Brannt walk the second pregnant mare, aptly named Taz, back into the pasture. Though Taz's pregnancy showed all the signs of natural, glowing health, Dr. Sam had argued that it would be foolish not to examine both horses while they were there. Finally, however, they were done. Out of the corner of her eye, Cassie watched Dr. Tomkins pack up the ultrasound equipment, the very act signaling their impending departure.

It had been the longest two hours of her life. And probably the most exhausting. Brannt had been a pill throughout the entire ordeal. After her little faux pas with Berma, his eyes had locked onto Cassie's every movement, desperate to find her doing something wrong. It was no wonder then that she'd fumbled through Sam's questions about influenza and tetanus inoculations, or that her answers to his seemingly endless questions had grown conspicuously shorter and quieter until she was practically a whispering monosyllabic by the end.

Dr. Tompkins, however, hadn't noticed anything amiss. He just kept working, kept talking, confidently walking her through his process, and still, he went on with those questions…

"Cassie," Dr. Sam said, pulling her out of her quiet reverie, "would you mind setting up a follow-up appointment with Brannt while I load up the truck?"

Rounding big green eyes his direction, for a moment words failed Cassie. Misunderstanding her disquiet for confusion, Dr. Sam said: "In my best guess, those horses are nearing nine months gestation. Care to guess what vaccines I'd like to have administered…"

"EHV and rotavirus," Cassie muttered.

Dr. Sam winked. "Exactly. And also, they'll need a rabies vaccine. The disease has been running rampant in this part of Texas lately." He held out his schedule to her.

"Thanks," he said once she'd taken possession of the appointment book—a large, three-ring binder. Reaching down, he grabbed for his supplies and headed for the door. As an afterthought, he called out over his shoulder: "Don't make the appointment for Thursday. We're booked solid, and I have a business function that evening I can't miss.…"

Sighing out a deep breath, Cassie looked down at the schedule despondently.

"Lost?"

Narrowing her eyes, Cassie only just managed not to make a face when she glanced up to see Brannt reentering the barn. Flipping her ponytail behind her shoulder, she ignored this caustic remark. "Sam would like to schedule some vaccinations." The words were clipped, short.

With a look, Brannt took in the schedule Cassie was gripping so tightly down at her side. He sighed. "When?"

With a flip of her wrist, Cassie opened the binder. Looking down, she examined Sam's availability. The rest of that week looked awfully busy. She flipped over to the next page. She had just begun running her eyes down is length when the schedule was lifted unceremoniously out of her grasp.

Cassie threw Brannt a look. "Really?"

Without a word, he deliberately turned the schedule back to the previous page. "It'll have to be this week," he informed her coolly. "I'm out of town the following Monday and Tuesday and waiting longer isn't ideal."

Cassie just kept herself from saluting him. "Is it possible that someone else could stand in for you?" She spoke through tightly clenched teeth. "As we have an opening next Monday?"

"Absolutely not," Brannt said. His eyes roamed over the chicken-scratch constituting Dr. Tomkins' handwriting. He didn't seem to have any trouble deciphering it. Eyebrows pulling into an ominous furrow, he appeared to have reached the same conclusion Cassie had. They were full-up.

Brannt shot her a lowering look. "I don't suppose you're able to work on your own yet?" Cassie took a moment to soak in what sounded almost like a compliment. Was that an invitation? "Sam could get here and have this all done before you'd be so much as halfway through—" his eyes read over one of the clients marked on the page, "the heartworm test for Timmons' sheepdog on Wednesday," he muttered more-or-less to himself.

Well, so much for that.

Ripping the binder out of his conceited hands, Cassie took almost too much pleasure in informing him that, indeed, she wasn't able to do animal rounds on her own. They'd simply have to figure out something else.

Throwing a hand through his hair—thick, dark, almost reddish brown hair, Brannt pinched his fingers against the bridge of his nose. "What about Friday?"

"Scheduled out to six o'clock."

"Make it seven."

She felt a muscle in her face spasm.

"Well?" He nodded toward the appointment book clutched in her hands. "Write it in."

Cassie smiled tightly. Her jaw ached. She really did not like this man. "Fine," she conceded, reopening the schedule with exaggerated care. "I'll make sure to let Dr. Tomkins know." With a tap of her pen, she scribbled down the appointment. Snapping the book shut, her lips furling into something of a smiling snarl, she took a step backward. "Until then."

Tucking the binder against her side, Cassie turned around, her feet marching her straight for the barn door. Dr. Tomkins' truck was parked just outside. Another thirty seconds and she could wash her hands of this man. That was until Friday night.

Ugh.

Head pitched at a haughty angle, in her rush to get away Cassie didn't notice the edge of a plastic horse feeder, tucked and half-hidden behind a stall door, nosing out onto one side of the pathway. Predictably, the toe of her heavy boot knocked into its bulky frame, sending Cassie fumbling in misstep. With a surprised cry, she tripped forward, head-first.

Only she never hit the ground.

Acting on instinct, at her gasping breath, Brannt lunged forward, his arms catching tight around Cassie's stomach. The rough motion sent her body tunneling backward, into direct contact with his own, her hands splaying out against his thighs. Pressed against his front, Cassie tried to get her breath.

"Are you okay?" Brannt asked, his voice oddly quiet.

Cassie found her voice. "Uh, yeah. I think so."

She could feel his heart beating against the back of her head. It was surprisingly slow and even. Nothing like hers. The heat from his body seemed to fuse itself to her skin and, though she shouldn't have been aware of it, though she shouldn't have had the peace of time to notice, Cassie couldn't help but feel the strength in the muscles resting against her fingers, she couldn't help but smell the scent attached to his clothes: spicy cologne, aftershave, the warm sun.

Because despite his manners, Brannt was every bit as attractive a man as she'd ever met.

Though it shouldn't have been, Cassie found something oddly provocative about their position—her fingers against his broad thighs, intimately touching the thick denim of his jeans, the weight of his belt-buckle nestling against the small of her back, the strength in the hands holding her so close…

Springing forward on the thought, Cassie shrugged out of his arms. Brushing off an imaginary speck of dirt, she kept her eyes consciously busy in the silence that followed. Her breath was coming fast and hard, and not just because of her near fall. She had the terrible, lowering impression he knew that.

Whatever. It was just the shock of it all that had got her imagination going. Nothing more than a defense mechanism against an almost unbearable slice of humiliation. That was all. Attraction built on an emotional high (or low).

Shifting in his direction, with a daring she was far from feeling, Cassie lifted her face to his. "Thank you," she offered primly. "I didn't see the bucket lying there." Well obviously. Her lips ticked when he smiled. "Anyway, thank you for, well, for catching me." Eloquence seemed to have deserted her just as surely as her motor skills.

Brannt smirked. "Don't you know, us cowboys handle damsels in distress rather well."

Cassie felt her eyelids flinch. "A back-handed compliment if ever there was one."

Brannt lifted an eyebrow. "Yeah?"

"Yes," Cassie assured him. "You seem to think my gender prohibits me in some way."

"By not letting you hit your head on the concrete floor?"

Cassie squirmed. "Never mind," she conceded. He was twisting her words. "Let's just leave it at thank you and goodbye." Rounding on her booted heel once again, only this time rather more carefully, Cassie made for her second exit attempt.

Gaining the door, however, she stopped. Her right hand pressed itself against the side of the metal structure there. Looking over her shoulder, her green eyes unknowingly pleading, she met his expression. "Give me a chance. I'll be a great veterinarian one day." She smirked. "Even accounting for my particular set of chromosomes."

On that, she left.

"Get everything sorted out?" Dr. Sam asked as Cassie pulled herself up into the truck seat.

Rolling her eyes, she assured him they had.

Dr. Sam whistled. "You'll get used to it. The odd hours, the 24/7 service status. It's the life of a veterinarian. We're on call. Animals, much like humans, rarely adhere to a nine-to-five schedule."

Cassie shrugged. "It's not the hour that bugs me so much. It's the man."

"Brannt can take a little, eh, getting used to."

"You can say that again," Cassie griped. She shot Sam a curious look. "You seem to get along with him well."

"Sure, sure. 'Course I've also known him all these years."

Cassie frowned. "He's worked here a long time then?" There goes her fervent hope that he might up and quit.

"You might say that." Dr. Sam chuckled. "As he owns the place."

"Brannt's a McDowell?"

He laughed harder. "Brannt's *the* McDowell."

Throwing her head back against the cushioned seat, Cassie let out a pent-up cry of frustration. "Well dammit anyway!"

"Hey, at least he was good for one thing."

"And what's that?"

"Worked you clean out of those nerves."

# CHAPTER FOUR

Dusk was settling around town by the time Dr. Sam and Cassie pulled up outside the vet clinic that evening. Office hours were over, but they still had to put away equipment, invoice client services, and organize prep for the next morning. Exhaustion didn't even begin to cover Cassie's current state of being.

Stifling back a yawn, she considered that at least she wouldn't have time to feel lonely. If today had been any indication of what was to come, this externship, with its regular capacity for long hours, would see to that.

Reaching for the appointment book, resting on the truck's console, she headed indoors, her steps taking her quickly to the receptionist desk.

"There's a folder marked INTAKE on the computer desktop," Dr. Sam informed her as he headed for the supply closet. "Just type everything into the correct fields and don't worry about the rest. We'll deal with it tomorrow."

Tired, hungry, and badly in need of a shower, neither of them spoke—polite conversation would only slow them down. The quicker they got through the evening clean-up the quicker they could retire. Shoulders hunched forward, Cassie opened up the spreadsheet and, in the dim lighting, began to slow process of entering in client charts.

Half an hour later, they called it quits. Making her way slowly up the stairs to her apartment, the sound of Dr. Tomkins' truck roaring to the life in the background, Cassie felt her stomach grumble.

Yawning, she checked the time. It was nearly 7:30 p.m.

With a start, she realized she hadn't eaten anything since lunch. They'd been so busy, with two emergency calls thrown into an already chalk-full day, that there hadn't been time to so much as think about food. But now, letting herself into the dinky apartment she'd call home for the next two months, Cassie recognized the hunger pains ripping through her system. She was famished. Though she knew it was unlikely, Cassie looked at the cupboard doors in the small kitchenette. Perhaps whoever it was that'd readied up her room had been kind enough to stock the place with a few cooking essentials: bread, milk cheese...

Eagerly throwing open both the refrigerator door and two small cabinets nearby, however, gave Cassie her answer. No food. The fridge was empty, with only a small box of baking powder staring back at her. The cabinets held two glasses, three plates, and one chipped bowl. That was far from encouraging. Cassie considered that she had two options. The first was to go grocery shopping. This was almost instantly rejected. She was too tired to go prancing up and down the aisles, scouring for cheap meals. That only left eating out. With a weary sigh, Cassie picked up her phone. Opening up her internet browser, she searched for the nearest restaurants in the area.

\* \* \*

Dr. Sam had offered Cassie unlimited use of his work truck during her off hours. Twenty minutes later, pulling up to a place called Betsy's Diner, Cassie felt almost faint with appreciation for his generosity. She also felt faint with hunger. Hair hanging anyhow down her back, she walked inside the brightly lit café. Wearing jeans and a grey sweatshirt, she'd been too focused on getting here to worry over much about her appearance.

It wasn't like she was going to run into anyone she knew.

Grabbing a nearby booth, Cassie slid gratefully into its cushioned depth. A gray speckled Formica tabletop glared back at her from the fluorescent lighting. A shiver running down her back on a tidal wave of second thoughts, Cassie told herself firmly that no one was staring at her, that she needn't feel so conspicuous, so obvious.

Play it cool, girl.

Sure, she was new in town, a veritable stranger, and sure, okay she was eating by herself, and yes, maybe she felt a little uncomfortable in her own solidarity but that didn't mean—

"Good evening, can I start you off with anything to drink?"

Cassie's head jerked up at the innocent question. A girl in a pretty yellow blouse stood beside her table, a telling apron slung low around her waist. She smiled down at Cassie. Her hair, a chestnut brown color, was scraped off her face in a high ponytail.

She looked nice. Friendly. Near to Cassie's own age.

For a second, Cassie didn't feel so alone. "I would love a cup of coffee, please. Black."

The waitress, whose plastic nametag read Rachel, nodded her head at the command. "Sure thing. I'll be right back." Plopping a thick menu down on the table, she scurried off to the kitchen.

Cassie opened the menu but before she could get through the first page, Rachel was back, a steaming cup of coffee in one hand and a thick serving pad in the other.

Pen poised in midair, she asked: "Are you all set to order or would you like a couple minutes still to decide?"

"I can be ready," Cassie assured her quickly. Letting her eyes travel quickly down the page, she picked at random. "How about the tuna melt. Is it any good?"

Rachel's face scrunched up a little in response. "Honestly? Not really."

"Oh."

Leaning forward, Rachel took possession of the menu. Flipping it to the next page, she pointed to one of the food items. "If I can make a suggestion?" she queried helpfully, one finely plucked eyebrow arched in expectation.

"Please."

Rachel smiled. "Then I would say get the Chicken Fried Steak...or the Chicken Fried Chicken if you'd prefer. Best in the state."

Cassie had some serious reservations about that last comment, but she felt oddly compelled to take her word for it anyway. Sadly, this was probably the best conversation she'd had all day. "Uh, sure. Okay. The steak then."

According to the expression on Rachel's face, Cassie had made the right choice. "Great! I'll go put that order in for you."

And, with a final pat of her hand against the table, Rachel was gone again, leaving Cassie to stare down at the empty booth across from her. So awkward. Thumbing through her phone, she tried to look busy but there were only so many gossip columns she could read, so many social media platforms she could log into before she was only scrolling numbly along. Putting her phone down, she focused her attention on the building's décor.

Thin, floral carpet, worn down and ragged in certain areas and badly in need of a shampooing; peach colored paint on the walls, with thick chair rails to break up the otherwise monotonous hue; black-and-white pictures depicting what Cassie could only assume was Pantula's history; antique copper and pewter pitchers, pots, and other kitchen appliances on the shelves running the length of the building... Cassie's fingers drummed a steady tattoo against the tabletop. The rest of the building was more of the same.

Lowering her eyes once more, Cassie's gaze swept over the table's surroundings. She was on the point of reading the ingredient list on the back of a sugar packet—anything to pass the time, when she heard voices talking. Correction: when she heard voices talking about *her*. At least, Cassie thought they were talking about her. Ears perked forward, she presumed the echo was coming from somewhere off the kitchen.

"...isn't that the girl who's working with Dr. Tomkins?" Yes, they were definitely talking about Cassie.

"I think so."

"What's her name?"

"I don't know."

"What do you mean you don't know, she's your table?!"

Long sigh. "I don't usually greet my tables formally. Maybe she'll pay with a card."

"I heard she made a real hash of it today, already has a rep as the vet who doesn't know anything about animals."

"No!"

"I'm only repeating what I heard."

Giggling.

"You should have heard Brannt in here earlier, complaining about it. Said she don't know a horse's ass from his—"

"Shh! She might hear you!" A third voice hissed out then.

"Oh, calm down."

"Wait. Brannt was *here*? When?" The voice, which Cassie now assumed belonged to Rachel, had a distinct whine to it now. "I didn't see him."

"He came in around lunchtime."

"Oh."

"He had a lot to say about her—"

Rachel. "Did he happen to mention if he was going to the rodeo this weekend?"

"What? Oh, I don't know. Probably..."

"Oh. Well, I was thinking I might stop by—"

There was a moment of expectant silence. Cassie was practically leaning out of her booth at this point, desperate not to miss a word.

"I wonder how long the vet will last," the second voice chimed in again. "From what Brannt said..."

"Did he talk about anything else but her?"

"Geez Rachel, I don't—"

The disembodied voice was cut off by the sudden ding of a bell.

"Foods up!"

Scrambling back into her seat, Cassie couldn't quite catch her breath. And just what had Brannt said? Her lips trembling—people were talking about her, laughing at her—Cassie scrambled for her purse. Tears clouded her vision. Digging frantically inside, she reached for her wallet. She'd only just retrieved money from its billfold when Rachel came into view carrying a large plate loaded with gravy.

Coming up to Cassie's table, Rachel halted, the plate suspended in her hand. Her eyes zeroed in on the twenty dollar bill shaking in Cassie's outstretched hand, the blotchy pallor of her cheeks. "Ma'am?"

"I'll take a to-go box," Cassie said, her eyes fixed straight ahead. There was a tiny rip in the seam of the vinyl cushion across from her. She blinked rapidly. "The check, too."

Rachel's face was a kaleidoscope of realization. Her eyes shifted, her mouth making the unmistakable shape of gaping discomfort. "Sure. Of course. Let me—I'll just go get that!" Taking the proffered money, she scurried away.

She was back in seconds, her fingers clumsy as she handed over Cassie's bagged food and change. Her movements were rushed, awkward. "Sorry you have to leave," she sputtered nervously. "Please, um, come back again—"

Cassie didn't comment. Sliding out of the booth, she rose to her feet. Leaving a five dollar tip on the table, she scooped up her food and, with what little dignity she had left, started for the exit. Holding the box protectively in front of her, Cassie never broke stride. It was only as her hand reached out to push the door open that she found herself pausing, much the way she'd done earlier that morning with Brannt. Turning, she glanced back at Rachel, who hadn't moved from the table.

Where she got the nerve, Cassie didn't bother to wonder. She smirked at the waitress. It cost a lot, that show of indifference. "By the way," she called out. "My name's Cassie."

Rachel's mouth dropped open.

Cassie hitched up one corner of her mouth. "Thought you might be interested to know." On that, she shouldered her way outside.

That's when she cried.

She'd been wrong. No matter how busy she was kept, Cassie wouldn't forget for a single second how many hours remained until she could leave this God-awful place.

# CHAPTER FIVE

Cassie's first official week at the Tiamango Veterinary Clinic finally wound to a close. All in all, she considered it had gone rather well. She'd been part of various administrations of tetanus, West Nile virus, and influenza medications; she'd learned some new treatment techniques for arthritis (particularly with Mr. Burns' farm dog); she'd been assigned to oversee lab work consisting of blood chemistry, gas, and fibrinogen analysis; she'd used the radiograph equipment, and she'd seen the damage of torn ligaments. It had been exhausting, eye-opening, and for the most part, seamless.

At least, when Brannt wasn't around.

Flopping down on her bed, Cassie tried not to remember *that* appointment, the last one of the week, the one Mr. High and Mighty McDowell, himself, had insisted upon. If it hadn't been for that one last visit....

If not for that, she'd probably be on the phone with her parents right now, eagerly pouring over everything she'd learned, everything that she'd accomplished. Instead, she was left thinking about *him*, remembering what had happened with *him*. Going over it all again and again in her mind. What was the opposite of seamless? Turbulent.

Yeah, that pretty much summed up the way he made her feel. Turbulent.

The day, which had been grueling from the start, took on a whole new meaning of the word when she and Dr. Sam pulled up to his place. Cassie's nerves had jumped underneath her skin like a livewire. It's just a rabies vaccination, she'd told herself, alighting from the truck. It's just a simple rabies vaccination, she'd repeated over and over again as she'd made her slow, reluctant way up the barn. She'd done countless others just like it within the week. There had been an outbreak of some sorts recently and everyone within a twenty-mile radius had set-up an appointment to have the immunization done.

Rearranging the hem of her blue cotton shirt, Cassie took herself up the short passage, assured only by the bulk of Dr. Tomkins at her side. Stepping inside the well-lit building, Brannt was the first person she saw. Talking to one of the ranch hands, wearing nothing more extravagant than jeans and a button-down shirt, Cassie felt her stomach clench at the sight of him. Despite her baser feelings, she couldn't deny his attractions. The epitomic western horseman—craggy jaw, tan skin, those thick sideburns. Too bad he had that mouth though...

Turning at her entrance, Brannt's lips pulled up sardonically, almost as though he'd read her mind. "Ms. Hastings," he drawled, tipping his hat to her.

"Mr. McDowell," she returned sweetly.

That sterile beginning hadn't boded well for the evening.

It hadn't helped matters that Taz had been all kinds of jumpy about getting her shots. Nervous under Brannt's prickly eyes, it took Cassie almost twice as long as it should have to clean the injection site. His impatience practically thrummed through the building.

"We've got two more of these to do yet," he told her with a checked glance at his watch. "And a whole other horse to catch."

"Ignore him," Dr. Sam instructed quietly.

Cassie tried. Grabbing for the needle, she took a deep breath. Bringing her hand up to the side of Taz's neck, she rubbed her fingers against the spot where she'd be administering the shot.

"What the hell are you doing?"

"It'll help relax and desensitize her," Cassie said, but unfortunately, her words came out almost questioningly.

"No, it won't. It'll warn her that she's about to get a shot, and that'll only spook her," he insisted. Shooting a glowering look at Dr. Tomkins, who was quietly standing behind Cassie, watching her process, he gestured toward the horse. "Care to chime in at all?"

"You're doing fine, girl," the seasoned vet said.

Brannt sighed. "Pinch the skin," he ordered.

"I got it," Cassie assured him. "You just mind that she keeps still."

After that, the rest of the appointment went smoothly. Surprisingly, even Brannt, who usually took it upon himself to find fault with everything Cassie did, remained relatively quiet through the rest of Taz and Berma's care. It was only as the second horse was being led back out of the barn, when Cassie and Dr. Sam's work was finished that things turned, well, turbulent. At the sudden ringing of his phone, Dr. Sam had excused himself, stepping outside to take the call.

Unsure if she should follow behind him or not—she didn't want to intrude on his privacy, Cassie was left stuck. Kicking at a stray clump of dirt, she puffed out her cheeks. "Well," she said, speaking because anything seemed like a better idea than just standing there, silent. "I guess that's it, huh?"

Brannt raised an eyebrow.

"Everything went fine. The horses look good." She felt like fraud talking to Brannt in that manner. He looked at her like she was one, anyway.

Definitely, she should have followed Dr. Sam. "I-uh, I suppose we'll get going then?" she improvised, hitching a thumb over her shoulder expressively. "Unless, is there anything else you need?"

Brannt shook his head decisively. "No, that'll be all."

"Okay. Whelp, have a good night," Cassie offered, tossing the phrase out meaninglessly. She couldn't care less what sort of night he had.

She headed for the door. She'd only taken a handful of steps, however, when she remembered her water bottle and neck towel—necessary supplies in the hot Texas air. She'd taken them out of her bag between treating the horses, tossing them carelessly to the ground in between breaks.

Groaning silently, Cassie pivoted back around. Retracing her steps, she was just in time to watch Brannt walk over to one of the stalls. His gait was slow and deliberate and, as she stood there, Cassie couldn't help but notice how he favored his right side.

Brannt was limping.

With something of a shock, she realized it was the first time she'd seen him move all evening. He'd stood in that one spot—the same spot as when she and Dr. Sam had first entered the building, the very spot he was tromping away from now—throughout their entire visit. He'd never moved once. Craig, the horse handler, whose name she'd finally been privy to learning, had been the one who'd fetched and retrieved the horses, and Brannt had ordered Sam to grab any incidentals they'd needed along the way.

He hadn't moved because he hardly could. With one hand braced against his thigh, she watched him take another excruciating step.

"Are you okay?" The words popped out of Cassie's mouth before she realized she was even saying them.

Spinning around in surprise, the very action clouding his face with momentary pain, Brannt's eyes locked onto Cassie. She shivered at the look in them. "What the hell are you still doing here?"

Cassie nodded toward the discarded towel and water bottle, lying lifeless on the dirty floor. "I forgot those—what happened? Are you hurt?" Cassie cringed. Would her mouth just shut the hell up already? What had possessed her to ask, to care for God's sake? She could only imagine how much Brannt didn't want to hear it.

Sure enough, those glint grey eyes narrowed even further. "Why, are you practicing on people now, too?" He sneered. "God, spare us all."

Cassie's hands pinned themselves against her hips. "You'd be so lucky!"

"You're here to see about my herd. Not me. Let's keep it that way."

"Fine. Sorry I asked—!" Cassie cried, shaking her hands in the air. "God forbid I throw out a friendly gesture of concern."

Brannt's lips twitched. "God forbid, indeed." He took another step, the heel of his boot pitching unsteadily over a loose rock. Cursing roundly, he stumbled. Righting himself, one hand reaching out to lean heavily against the wall, his face whitened ominously in the corners.

"Oh, stop it!" Cassie ordered, "I've seen enough!" Marching up to him, she took hold of one arm. "You don't look fit to stand much less walk," she muttered, guiding his frankly unprotesting body toward a hay bale. "Sit."

"Bossy little thing aren't you?" Brannt hissed, but he didn't argue with her. If the look on his face was anything to go by, he was too distracted by the pain to do anything more strenuous than concede. Even ornery, cantankerous cowboys had a breaking point, it would seem. A thin film of sweat was beading out underneath the lining of his hat.

Cassie threw him a look. "What happened?" she asked again, glancing down at his injured leg. Her eyes widened. There was a dark, wet patch staining through the denim of his jeans—just to the side of his calf. "Jesus! Are you bleeding?"

Brannt looked down. "Aw hell!"

\* \* \*

Scooting quickly out of the barn, Cassie made quick work getting to the truck. Naturally, the vet clinic didn't cater to human patients, but there was a first-aid kit in the glove compartment: band aids, antibiotic creams, ibuprofen, that sort of stuff. And Brannt clearly needed something. His leg looked bad.

It had taken some effort, and more than a little cajoling, followed by flat-out threatening, but Cassie had finally convinced him to show her the wound. It was a long, deep gash. Winding down his leg, the limb was already an ugly, angry shade of purple. Stupid man, he'd been content to let it heal on its own, never mind the mud and dust and dirt of his daily profession.

Dr. Tomkins was just finishing up his call when Cassie breezed out the door. "Ready to go? That was the Ashburn farm. They've got a lame horse on their hands. I told him we'd swing by on our way back."

Cassie stopped and stared at him blankly. "We can't go. Brannt's hurt!"

Dr. Tomkins scratched his head. "What?"

"Clearly he isn't going to see a doctor and, well, we're here…It's pretty bad."

"What happened?" Dr. Tomkins asked, worried then.

Cassie's arms gestured wildly. "How should I know?" She shook her head. "Something about a tractor blade, a damned idiot mechanic, and that's where he lost me."

Sam nodded. "Hazards of the occupation."

Cassie grumbled. "Now you sound like him. He cut his leg half-open Sam." That was perhaps an exaggeration. "It needs attention."

Dr. Tomkins smiled. Cassie didn't see it. "Does it require both our help?"

"No," she said slowly. "I don't think so."

"Can you be finished in half an hour or so?"

She didn't like where this was going. "Yeah. I guess…."

"Great," Dr. Tomkins enthused. "I'll run over to the Ashburn farm while you stay here and see to Brannt. I shouldn't be long."

Cassie's eyes grew wide. "You're going to leave?"

"No need for the two of us to stay," Dr. Sam replied, opening up the driver's side door. "You said so yourself."

"But...but," Cassie stuttered.

He was going to leave her here. With him?

For an entire thirty minutes!

Swinging himself into the truck, Sam rolled down the window just long enough to pass Cassie the required medical aides before tossing out a quick goodbye and putting the vehicle into reverse. Standing there, Cassie watched her only means of transportation chug itself down the gravel drive. Without her.

Turning back to the barn, she swallowed thickly. Brannt was in there. Hoisting the supply kit firmly against her hip, she slowly walked forward.

# CHAPTER SIX

When Cassie reentered the barn she was pleased to see that Brannt had, for once, taken her advice. He was still sitting on the hay bale where she'd left him. Unfortunately, he didn't look any too pleased about it.

Walking up to him, Cassie looked searchingly around the building.

"Well? Let's get this over with. I've got things to do yet," Brannt growled when she hesitated.

Cassie rolled her eyes. "We can't very well do it here," she said. "It's too dirty...."

Brannt made a sound from low in his throat. "It's a barn lady. This is as sanitary as it gets."

"Yeah, I'm sure it is..."

Brannt snorted.

"Isn't there someplace else we can go, somewhere that's a little, eh, more sterile? I need to make sure the wound is properly cleaned," Cassie informed him.

And that's how Cassie got her first look inside the stately home at the McDowell Estate. Granted, Brannt hadn't been overly welcoming about his invitation, but then again, he wasn't overly welcoming about anything. As he so grumpily expressed, since she wasn't going to stop pestering him until she got her own way, fine, she could doctor the leg in his kitchen. Was she satisfied? Slowly, without offering to help, knowing it would be rudely rebuked, she walked beside him up the long drive and onto the back porch of his impressive home.

Catching the farm door behind Brannt, Cassie's eyes made quick work of the room as she stepped inside: stained concrete countertops, butcher block island, shaker cabinets and thick stone flooring, covered here and there with faded rugs. The room was as expensive as it was spotlessly clean.

Pointing toward a ladder-back chair pulled up to one side of the eat-in island, Cassie made her voice stern. "There. Sit down," she instructed.

"Give the lady an inch..." Brannt muttered.

Cassie gave him a look, and with the wave of her hand said: "Pull up your pant leg." And while he slowly, laboriously shifted the fabric up over his knee, she organized the supplies—a warm towel doused with antibacterial soap, tweezers scoured with hydrogen peroxide, antibiotic cream, and gauze.

"This going to take all day?" Brannt queried, barely held patience coloring his words. "I wasn't kidding when I said I have things to get accomplished yet tonight."

"Oh, shove it," Cassie muttered, bending down to examine the injury now. "The longer you sit here squawking at me, the more time I'll be wasting, thinking up snappy comebacks."

Brannt laughed softly. "I thought women were supposed to pride themselves on multitasking—Oh…!" With a hiss, Brannt finally shut up when Cassie placed a cool rag against his leg. Luckily, the bleeding had more-or-less stopped. Unluckily, the cut was coated with dirt and debris.

"Sorry," Cassie called out belatedly, looking up to watch a white-grimace flash across his face. "Yeah. This may hurt a little bit."

"I caught that for myself," Brannt responded tightly, but beyond that, he remained tight-lipped as Cassie cleaned the area. With steady hands, Cassie carefully pulled out a couple slivers of wood and one small pebble before applying the cream and then dressing his calf.

It was as she was doing this that Brannt spoke again, his voice shattering the silence that had grown like a veil over her ministrations. "So," he asked, clearing his voice. "What made you want to become a veterinarian?"

Cassie worked hard not to lift a sardonic eyebrow at the question. She seriously doubted he actually cared. Probably, he just needed a distraction. Whatever. It was better than having him snip at her, she supposed.

Shrugging, Cassie tried to remain indifferent. "The short answer? Because I love animals. I'm extremely interested in their health and well-being, in discovering the ways their bodies work—particularly because they can't tell us themselves." She kept her voice low. "And, I don't know, I've always felt this connection to them. Animals like me and I like them."

Brannt seemed to take this at face value. "But you don't know a lot about them."

Cassie shook her head despairingly. He clearly wasn't about to let that go. "You mean livestock? I'm not as accustomed to dealing with steers and bulls and whatnot, if that's what you mean." She put the cap back on the antibiotic cream. "Though I still know a lot more than you'd like to think."

"You're not from around though, are you?" That sounded genuine.

Cassie shook her head. "'Fraid not."

"The country?"

"City born and bred."

He whistled softly. "Why Pantula?"

Cassie considered the question. "Lots of reasons. None of them of any interest to you, I'm sure." She was quiet for a moment. "And anyway, what better way to round out my education?"

He nodded. "Knowing horses is practically law around here."

Cassie smirked. "Then I guess y'all have a lot of teaching to do before my two months are up." Her pronounced drawl made him chuckle.

"I reckon so."

Cassie peeked up at him impishly. "What made you decide to be a rancher?"

"Turnabout is fair play, huh?"

"Something like that," Cassie remarked dryly, as she wrapped the ace bandage around his leg. Her fingers felt the warmth of his skin through the gauze. It had a strange effect on her.

Brannt leaned back against his seat. "It's the family business."

Cassie nodded, but when he didn't go on, she looked up. "Yeah? And?"

"And what?"

Letting out a sigh, oddly disappointed with that wildly pragmatic answer, Cassie shook her head. "And nothing."

"Let me guess, that's not romantic enough for you?" Brannt mocked. "Not grand and exciting, is that it?"

Cassie felt her face flush. Her fingers worked fast. "I didn't say—"

"What were you wanting to hear," he ridiculed, his voice lowering: "that I, too, feel a kinship with animals, that my relationship with horses is often stronger than that of my men?"

There was something in the deep timbre of his voice, in that almost defensive tone, that had Cassie glancing up again. Her eyes were wide with understanding. Her mouth trembled as she answered. "Yes…"

He scoffed. "Grow up, Cassie."

She actually felt her neck snap back at the unexpected council. Her fingers tightened on the gauze. "Pardon me for asking," she muttered.

"Ask a stupid question…" he singsonged.

Cassie shook her head tiredly as she tied off the last of the gauze. The finished product was far from neat, but at this point, he should be glad she hadn't fed him the roll. "This was a bad idea."

Brannt sighed. "Pouting, Cassie?"

"No," she assured him, putting the first-aid equipment back in the bag. "Just learning my lesson."

"Aw hell," Brannt muttered. "I don't know. I just never wanted to be anything else, I guess." He shrugged eloquently. "It's never occurred to me to wonder why, that's all."

Cassie didn't say anything for a moment. Then she nodded. "Okay."

"Okay? That's it."

"That's it," she repeated. Then, wiping her hands together, she looked for the antiseptic cream. It was on the bar stool beside Brannt. "Hand that to me?" She asked. Glancing his way, Cassie surprised a funny look on his face—a narrowing of those silvered eyes, a ruddiness in those high cheekbones. But, before she could do more than wonder at the meaning behind that expression, it changed, replaced once more with his usual countenance: mild impatience and annoyance.

Without a word, he handed her the ointment. Scooting back on her knees, Cassie opened one of the bag's zippered compartments to place it in. As she did so she watched, from the corner of her eye, as Brannt's hands went up to the grip the edges of the chair. Before she had enough air in her lungs to shout, he was already lifting himself up and bounding to his feet.

Thoughtless, stupid man.

Understandably, the hard landing jarred his injured leg and she stared, horrified as his knee buckled under his not-insignificant weight. She saw the flare of anguish pull across his mouth, the wince in his eyes....

Without thought, the tube of antiseptic cream falling from nerveless fingers, Cassie jumped to her feet, the length of both her arms circling around his back as she did so. Throwing his body firmly up against hers, Cassie braced herself for the thudding impact—and for the second time since they'd met, she found herself pressed tight to him.

His breath whispered across her forehead as his hands went to steady themselves against her shoulders. Cassie's chest, snug against his, shook with the force of her amplified breathing. Her fingers lay flush across his broad back.

Looking down at where his body touched hers, Cassie felt a pinch in her stomach, felt a ripple zip down her waist. Her breathing was coming a little too fast.

"Hey."

At the soft command, Cassie's eyes, wide and misty, lifted.

"You can let go now. I'm fine," Brannt assured her. One side of his mouth lifted.

Dropping her hands like branded things, Cassie fumbled back a step. She felt vulnerable suddenly, naked under his gaze. Fighting back a blush, she brushed her fingers down her thighs. She hadn't said a thing, but it felt like she'd told him everything....

"I bandaged your leg, I didn't heal the stupid thing," she shot at him.

Brannt smiled. There was something mischievous in that look.

Opening her mouth, Cassie decided she didn't want to know what he was about to say in response to that. "Look, you should probably stay off your leg for a couple days. I'm sure you won't though—"

"You're right about that,"

Cassie frowned. "Fine. Whatever. Have it your way."

"I usually do."

Now it was Cassie's turn to growl. "Stubborn ass," she mouthed.

Brannt's smiled faded. "What did you call me?" he asked softly, taking a single, slow step in her direction.

Cassie cleared her throat. She would not be intimidated. With a tilt of her chin, she said louder this time: "I called you a stubborn ass."

"Is that so?" He took another step forward.

"You got a better adjective?" Cassie challenged, a little breathless at his proximity. Towering overhead, Brannt was mere inches away from her. She hadn't realized how close he'd gotten. If he took one more step she'd be in his arms. Again. Cassie swallowed thickly.

"Impulsive, perhaps," he threatened, his eyes raking over her slightly parted lips. He leaned one hand down against the island, leveraging his body over hers. "Reckless even…" his head dipped ever so slightly forward.

Cassie's chin trembled, her eyelashes lowering, brushing delicately against her cheeks. Her body thrummed with anticipation.

"Is that so?" She said, mimicking his words from earlier. Her voice was mostly breath.

Brannt's words slithered across sensitive skin: "…Yeah, that's so—"

The sudden sound of a pickup truck rumbling noisily up the driveway stopped Brannt short. The loud interruption, cutting through the hushed, heavy air worked like a proverbial bucket of cold water, dispelling the moment.

Both heads turned to look out the kitchen window as a beat-up old white truck ambled into view, the words Tiamango Veterinary Clinic painted across its side.

Sam was back.

Brannt muttered something dark under his breath. Cassie considered it was probably for the best she couldn't make out the exact words. Taking a fumbling half-step, her eyes darted nervously toward the back door. Her fingers tugged unconsciously at the hem of her shirt. "I, uh, I better—that's Sam," Cassie muttered inanely, nodding needlessly out the window. "I should go? Yeah. Yeah, I'll just—" Spinning on her heel, the medical supplies forgotten in her rush to get away, her words left hanging limply between them, Cassie didn't wait for Brannt's answer, her feet flying toward the back door, her legs racing down the porch steps.

"How's the patient?" Sam asked, walking up to meet her halfway. Brannt, thank God, hadn't followed behind her, preferring, it seemed, to stay indoors for once.

"Fine. He's fine," Cassie said hurriedly, her arm steering the vet back the way he'd come. Her gaze was locked on the safety of the work truck. There it was, her only means of fleeing. Reaching for the passenger door, she pulled hard on the handle. "Can we go? I'm tired."

If Sam found her behavior odd, he didn't comment. Instead, he merely clambered up onto the driver's seat. "Sure thing."

Head hung low, Cassie barely dared to breathe until the truck turned off that damn country road.

If it hadn't been for that one last visit…! Plowing her face into her pillow, Cassie screwed her eyes tightly shut, her body sinking morosely into the quilted blanket covering her bed. Turbulent. Brannt made everything turbulent. Her first official week with the Tiamango Veterinary Clinic had come to a close. What a way to go.

# CHAPTER SEVEN

Stretching in the early morning light, Cassie slowly slipped out of bed. It was Saturday, her first day off. Though it was barely seven o'clock, the sun was already bright behind her lacy bedroom curtains, already warm in this southern part of the state. Bouncing into the bathroom, Cassie wondered what happened in Pantula on weekends. Translation: she wondered what in the world she would do to occupy her time. She wasn't due back in the office until eight a.m. Monday morning. Besides a phone call to her parents, the day stretched endlessly before her.

So she took a long shower and unpacked the last of her bags. She washed her bedding and changed her clothes twice—hell, she even stooped to vacuuming the immaculate curtains hanging in the living room window. But by ten o'clock, she'd run out of ways to fill up her morning. With nothing else for it, she slipped down the stairs of her apartment toward the veterinary office, where the keys to Dr. Sam's work truck could be found hanging up behind the front desk. Grocery list in hand, because what else did she have to do, Cassie walked in through the main door.

Billie Jo Greene, the building's receptionist, smiled in greeting as Cassie stepped over the threshold. The Tiamango Clinic was open every day of the week, and technically every hour of the day.

"'Morning Cass," the blonde secretary drawled. In her early thirties, Billie Jo was everyone's best girlfriend. She brought in baked goods every Monday, stitched up all Dr. Sam's work shirts, and made time each afternoon to enquire about how Cassie was getting on in Pantula.

"Morning, BJ."

The receptionist looked at her curiously, skeptically. "You're not on call this weekend?"

"No." Cassie nodded behind her at the trucks keys, which were dangling on a hook underneath one of the shelves. "Just came to grab these."

"Lucky girl," the receptionist said, swinging around to grab them off the rack. "It's going to be a busy day. Kicked horses, lame bulls, Coggins...." She laughed good-naturedly. "My senses are already on high alert."

Cassie gave her a strange look.

"The rodeo may be good for business, but it's bad for the nerves."

"Rodeo?"

BJ nodded. "Just be glad you'll escape all the shenanigans around here."

"There's a rodeo here, in Pantula?"

"You bet. The Tiamango Rodeo is an annual tradition in these parts…oh!" Billie Jo said, interrupting herself, big eyes hot on the younger woman's interested stare. "Are you thinking about going to it?"

Cassie shifted. She dropped her eyes. "I don't know. I mean, I wasn't planning on it. I didn't even know it was happening. Not 'til just now that is," she rambled.

"You should definitely go," BJ enthused. "Have you ever been to a rodeo before?"

Cassie shook her head.

BJ smiled a full-wedged smile. "It's really fun!" Smacking her palm down hard against the laminate counter, presumably for good effect, she listed off the benefits: "Bull riding, saddle bronc, barrel racing…gorgeous cowboys!"

An image of Brannt, in his faded jeans and long-sleeved shirt, that cowboy hat pulled low over his brow, floated unwelcome across Cassie's mind….

"You should really think about it," BJ continued unabashed.

Cassie hitched up one shoulder defensively. "Maybe."

"Well, if you decide to go, give me a call. There's a group of us heading over tonight. I'm sure we'd love to have you join us!"

Cassie felt herself relenting. It *would* be nice to do something. And, at least BJ's invitation meant Cassie wouldn't have to do it alone. "Okay. Yeah, I'll think about it."

"Good. Now, get out of here and go enjoy this lovely day," BJ ordered warmly, waving Cassie toward the door.

She glanced down at her grocery list. Fat chance.

"You know what," Cassie said, turning smartly on the thought. She smiled at BJ. "I would love to go with you to the rodeo. If you really don't mind."

"Absolutely," BJ said. "I'll pick you up at five."

\* \* \*

Cassie closed her eyes, trying to pinpoint exactly what that smell was perforating the air around her. Hay. Dirt. Manure. Wrinkling her nose, she took another whiff. Yup. That was definitely calf poop.

Fluttering her eyelids open once more, she looked behind her where the rodeo arena stood: the bucking chutes, located in the rear of the massive round enclosure, heaved with the weight of agitated bulls, while down on the opposite end a pack of mid-sized steers grazed lazily in their metal pen. In the middle of it all stood a considerable riding arena, the dirt professionally packed and leveled. The Tiamango Rodeo Stampede Grounds.

Turning her head straight once more, Cassie locked her gaze on the white food truck parked before her, its overhead sign promising the best hot dogs this side of the Mississippi. Digging out her wallet, Cassie quickly placed her order with the teenage attendant there. She wasn't really hungry but food had seemed like the best excuse at the time.

In hindsight, she wondered if she hadn't made a mistake, agreeing to come here tonight. Besides BJ and one other veterinarian from Tiamango—Dr. Andrea Coleman, who Cassie had spoken less than a handful of words to since starting at the clinic, she didn't know a single person. Surrounded by virtual strangers at an event she knew absolutely nothing about... Worse, she was stuck with a group of girls who, excluding Cassie, all knew one another well and who, still excluding Cassie, were all good friends with another and who, you got it, excluding Cassie, all lived and breathed roping and steer wrestling and whatnot—

She'd tried. For fifteen minutes, Cassie had sat on those incredibly hot metal bleachers, squeezed between Billie Jo and some black-haired girl named Meghan, a frozen smile stitched on her face as she listened to their inane, anonymous conversations:

"Did you hear that Josh and Melinda Wilson slept together?"
"No way! I thought she hated him?"
"There's a fine line between attraction and hatred!"
"Gross! Josh is such a man-whore."
...
"Have you tried out that new restaurant in town yet? I guess they make a mean biscuit and gravy plate!"
...
"My horse threw a shoe again last night."
"Damn girl. I bet your farrier loves you."
"He ought to. At this rate, I'm personally keeping him in business."
...

And on and on they'd gossiped, leaving Cassie with nothing to say and no one to talk to; silently she'd sat there until, unable to take it anymore, she'd quickly stood up, informing the group she was going to grab herself a small snack—no, no, don't get up, she'd pleaded when good manners had brought them all to their feet, she'd just be a moment. They could stay where they were. They didn't want to lose their spot, or whatever.

Now, grabbing up her food order, a paper boat holding a plain dog with a bag of potato chips, Cassie hunted around for a good place to sit and quietly eat her meal. She just needed a couple of minutes to herself. Then the rodeo would start and she'd have something else to occupy her attention, besides the humble reality of just how alone she truly was. Fifty-two days until she'd depart from this sleepy little town.

"Oh my God, it's you. Thank goodness. I've been looking for you—!"

Cassie froze at the unexpected statement, aimed directly at her. Juggling her purchased dinner carefully in her hands, Cassie studied the girl who'd come marching over to stand in front of her, effectively blocking Cassie's path.

Cocking her head to the side, Cassie narrowed her eyes. Wait a minute…she knew her. It was the waitress from Betsy's Diner.

"Rachel," the girl supplied as if reading Cassie's thoughts. "I'm not sure if you remember me. Uh, we met a couple of days ago? Well, we didn't really meet per se…" she babbled on nervously.

Cassie smiled. "Yes, I remember you. It's nice to see you again."

"Is it?" Rachel asked pensively, her forehead crinkling in consternation. "I certainly hope so. I've felt so bad! Truly, you have no idea—!"

Cassie raised both eyebrows eloquently. Rachel was a talker.

"I've been working up the courage to search you out and apologize but, as fate would have it, here you are!" Rachel took a deep breath, her body sagging a little with the effort.

"Here I am," Cassie murmured for lack of anything substantial to contribute.

"I am just so sorry about the other day at the Diner. You know, about what was said?" Rachel prompted, solemn now.

Cassie nodded. She remembered all right.

"Honestly, we didn't think we were being overheard. If we had—" Rachel shrugged. "Well, anyway, please know it wasn't meant to be malicious, what we were saying. We weren't meaning to talk about you behind your back. We would never speak about our customers in that way," she swore a little too fervently.

Cassie highly doubted that.

"It's just, we don't get many newcomers to Pantula. I guess we're curious about you." Her eyes flicked down to the ground. "But I'm sorry if we made you feel uncomfortable, or unwelcome."

"It's fine," Cassie said quietly. "I appreciate your apology."

Rachel sighed dramatically. "Is there any way we can start over again?"

Cassie made a nervous sound. Rachel was staring at her so seriously. Too seriously. "Of course, we can start over again." What the hell else could she say?

"Oh!" Rachel threw a manicured hand over her heart. "I'm so glad to hear that. Thank you for being so understanding. And I promise, in the future, if I have a question about you, I'll go straight to the source, okay?"

"Okay," Cassie said uncertainly. Good God, the way Rachel talked the questions might prove unending! Holding up her hot dog, Cassie gestured toward her dinner. "I—uh, if you'll excuse me I was just on my way back to the rodeo stands…." which condemned Cassie to return to Billie Jo and her posse of friends earlier than expected, but on the flip side, it also offered an unarguable conclusion to this unnerving little tête-à-tête.

"Sure, sure." Rachel nodded eagerly. "Who did you come here with anyway?" she asked, refusing to take the hint. Aligning her steps with Cassie's, she seemed determined to walk with her the entire way back into the rodeo grounds.

Cassie sighed. She wasn't sure which was worse: feeling like an outsider with BJ or a freak show with Rachel.

"Oh. Ah..."

"You didn't come alone?" Rachel's eyes were wide in her head.

"No. No, some friends from work invited me." Friends may have been a strong word. Cassie felt a wave of sweet relief as they neared the bleachers. Only a few more feet and she could beg off. On second thought, BJ's friends could ignore her all night. Silence had never seemed to blissful.

"Where are you seated?"

"Over by the..." Looking up, Cassie's words trailed off. Standing straight ahead of her, his back to Cassie, arms resting loosely against the rungs of the cattle holding pens, stood Brannt McDowell.

Of course, he would be there, she thought, her lips curling into a snarl. God, couldn't she go one day without tripping over his presence? At least he hadn't seen her, his attention focused on the group of cowboys standing beside him at the timed-event boxes.

Ducking her head, Cassie sped up her steps. The last thing she needed tonight was another run in with Brannt and his oh-so-steely glare.

"Whoa, slow down. The rodeo hasn't even started yet," Rachel panted, trotting to keep up.

But Cassie's legs only pumped harder—hell, at this rate, maybe she could outpace Rachel, as well. Cassie was almost past him when a sudden loud bang ricocheted off the metal pens in front of her. Startled, her body jerked at the sound, her head snapping backward instinctively—

"Hey, calm down," Rachel teased. "It's just one of the steers." She motioned to one of the brown-coated animals detained inside the enclosure, which'd clearly just kicked his hoof against the metal rails surrounding him.

"Yeah, don't worry, Doc," a voice called out. "He can't get out."

Amused laughter, coming from the stands behind Cassie, arose quietly at this anonymous statement. Clearly, her start of surprise had been noticed. Groaning inwardly, she could practically feel heads turning in her direction.

"Just remember," another voice from the crowd rang out, the masculine timbre vibrating with humor. "They're more afraid of you than you are of them!"

More chuckling.

"And I thought we were bad at Betsy's," Rachel commented quietly.

"Moo!" Someone bellowed. Apparently, her reputation as the vet who doesn't know anything about animals had spread.

Head held high, Cassie turned to meet her tormentors head on—she wasn't interested in being ridiculed before a bunch of strangers, of having it overheard by clients of the Tiamango Veterinary Clinic, most of whom would undoubtedly be in attendance. It was a small group of people (this section of the stampede grounds wasn't nearly as popular as down by the bucking stocks); no more than twelve or so good-natured smiles stared back at her. She didn't recognize any of them, except…was that Mr. Tubbs? Dr. Sam and she had gone to his farm two days ago to check on a sick Billy goat.

Oh God. With that reminder came the unfortunate memory of her stuttering surprise when she'd looked down to see the animal eating her shoe laces.

Cassie straightened her shoulders. "I'm not the least bit frightened," she informed them, her voice coming out an unfortunate shade of prudish. "Thank you, anyway."

With that, she turned on her heel, but she wasn't quick enough to escape hearing:

"So, is she really as green as everyone says?"

"Maybe we should switch over to Dr. Riley for the summer."

"There's a thought."

Tears threatening, Cassie forced her legs forward but nothing could have prepared her for what happened next.

"Hey. Hastings—!"

Blinking hard, her shoulders pulled ramrod straight, Cassie turned around, a ferocious smile pinned on her face. She should have known Brannt wouldn't be able to resist joining in the heckling. Shifting her gaze, Cassie made her eyes travel up to his face.

Ambling towards her, Brannt didn't bother to lower his voice. "Glad I saw you," he said. "I want to double check that we're all set for Berma's transmitter appointment."

Cassie set her teeth. Here it was, his big chance.

When she didn't immediately respond, he raised his eyebrows. "You'll be there with Dr. Sam for the suture, right?"

"Yeah. I'll be there," she admitted dully.

"Good," he said.

Cassie's head snapped back. Wait. What?

A wicked gleam entered Brannt's eyes. "I'm sure I don't have to tell you how imperative it is that this foaling goes smoothly?" His voice carried to the waiting crowd. "And she responds to you well. Fact is, I've never seen her stand so calmly for anyone else."

Cassie gaped at him.

Brannt looked downright devious when he added: "I need you there, Hastings."

"I'll—I'll be there," she assured him, feeling her face flush. If she'd thought she was getting attention from the townsfolk earlier…

He nodded curtly. "That's all I needed to know."

Cassie goggled—she had no words.

"Hey, Brannt." At the sudden peal of girlish laughter, Cassie blinked. She'd almost forgotten about Rachel, still standing beside her. But now, turning her gaze toward the other girl, Cassie saw the brunette twirling a piece of dark hair around her finger.

He nodded solemnly. "Rachel."

She smiled hopefully. "Are you going to the dance after this?"

Cassie watched the big man squirm. It was amazing. She hadn't thought he had it in him to be uncomfortable about anything.

"No, I don't think so."

"Oh." There was no doubt about it. Rachel's face dropped, that one-word answer filled with disappointment. "I was thinking it might be fun…"

Brannt nodded. "Yeah?" Before he could say anything more, the rodeo announcer's voice boomed over the loudspeakers, welcoming everyone to the 37th annual Pantula Texas Rodeo. Cassie swore Brannt looked relieved at the interruption. Coolly now, he said: "Looks like the show's about to begin. Better find your seats, ladies…"

Cassie didn't need to be told twice.

# CHAPTER EIGHT

Cassie watched the performance through a blur. Clowns, cowboys, ropes, broncs...they all passed by in a distorted haze. She couldn't focus long enough to watch the men moving rhythmically on the backs of rank horses and wild bulls; nor could she remember the times of the copious women zigzagging up and down the arena as they glided around barrels; the team-ropers quickly nabbed and stretched steers, but she saw all this with unseeing eyes.

Brannt McDowell had single-handedly saved her sorry reputation with this small town.

He'd given his personal stamp of approval on her capabilities as a veterinarian.

He'd practically dared anyone to disagree with him.

And it had worked. At least three people had come up to her since the start of the rodeo to apologize for their behavior.

"We were just ribbing you, boss," one of the men had said. "I hope we didn't hurt your feelings..."

"It was all good fun. No harm meant, Ms. Hastings," offered another.

"Of course we love having you here with us. We need more veterinarians in the world, I always say," Mr. Tubbs assured Cassie, standing chastised beside his wife, who kept apologizing for the town's lack of hospitality.

"We are Southern folk," she insisted. "That's what we do!"

All to which Cassie had nodded eagerly, insisting that she could take a joke, that all was good and forgotten. Blushing hotly, she was both immeasurably pleased and embarrassed by all the fuss.

"Keep this up," Andrea, the other veterinarian with Tiamango said, "and I won't have any clients by the end of the week." She laughed softly at her own little joke.

Cassie tried to smile. "I don't understand..."

"Brannt's word is kind of law around here, haven't you noticed?"

Oh, Cassie most certainly had.

And stupid idiot that she was, during Brannt's little pep talk routine, Cassie had remained practically mute. She'd been too stupefied with wonder to speak up, to confirm that his so-called faith was justified.

When the rodeo had finally dwindled to a close, she shot out of her seat like a bullet, quickly calling out her goodbyes to Billie Jo and Co., her eyes searching through the throng of bodies, desperate to pick out one specific pair of dark blue denim jeans, one very distinct straw hat on that arrogant head of hair—the brim of it slightly dented. She needed to talk to Brannt—preferably without an audience this time.

She needed to thank him properly. She needed to—she wasn't sure what she needed to do, but she was positive she needed to do it with him.

There!

With relief, Cassie's eyes fastened to his tall, commanding form. He was standing in the same place as before…leaning casually up against the cattle chutes. With the clarity of hindsight, she wondered if the steers and calves used in tonight's performance hadn't come from his ranch. It would explain his decision to plant himself near the return alley.

Fetching up beside him, Cassie tried to act natural, waiting patiently as he finished telling a story to the cowhands standing eagerly beside him, eating up his every word. Cassie mentally rolled her eyes. Did everyone in this tiny town fall all over themselves trying to impress the man?

When Brannt finally stopped to take a breath, Cassie seized her opportunity. Placing her hand gently over his arm, she waited for his head to twist in her direction; surprise flickered in those incredibly grey eyes when he did.

"I'm sorry to interrupt," Cassie said in preamble, her voice low and quiet, "but I just wanted to say thank you—you know, for earlier," her voice dropped, the words coming out low, the only show of privacy she was awarded.

Brannt's face pulled taut at the words, his cheekbones and that hard jaw seemingly etched out of stone. His eyes flitted from her to the men still standing around him. At his look, they made quick work of dispersing, the air laced with abrupt and awkwardly executed goodbyes until Brannt and Cassie were left alone.

The man didn't even have to speak for his commands to be followed. Good grief.

Turning to face her, his back shielding them from further prying eyes, Brannt gave Cassie the benefit of his undivided attention. It wasn't pretty. "Just do me one favor, okay?" His voice mirroring her hushed tones, Brannt didn't seem any more interested than Cassie in gaining the looks of any passers-by. "Don't make me regret it."

This time it was Cassie's eyes which filled with surprise. Sucking in a tough breath, she couldn't help but wonder where was the man who'd staunchly, publicly backed her talent and capabilities? For there was no confidence in those hard words, no camaraderie in that cold request, just more layers of resentment and skepticism, and more room for doubt. She should have known.

"Oh, I'll do my very best not to," Cassie hissed. Planting her hands firmly on her hips, she jutted her chin up a notch or two. "And just so you know, what you said earlier, I never asked you to interfere. I certainly don't need you to fight my battles for me. After all, enemies don't make great allies, do they?" she scoffed. "I thank you for what you said, but let's be clear about one thing: I don't owe you for the endorsement."

This was absolutely not the way she'd planned this conversation going.

Brannt's head tipped back ever-so-slightly on this impassioned speech, and the most annoying of smirks managed to sneak its way across his wide, thin lips. "Well, well, well. You're tougher than you look Ms. Hastings."

Cassie's eyebrows rammed together. "Is that why? Why you said what you did…? You thought I couldn't stand up to those people? What was that, your white knight routine?" She snickered.

Brannt smiled wolfishly. "I see it was unwarranted."

"Unasked for, too," Cassie assured him.

Brannt's smiled tightened a little at the corners. "By all means, accept my sincere apology. I won't make that mistake again. Enjoy your evening," he entreated. Then, with the briefest tip of his hat, and a chilling smile, he sauntered off, leaving Cassie standing there, all alone, a slave to her thoughts.

Brannt had thought she needed saving. The knowledge was as irritating as it was unnerving. Despite everything, he'd stood up for her. Why?

Unbidden, the image of Brannt from yesterday evening, his body pressed up close to hers in the quiet confines of his kitchen, flickered across Cassie's mind. His body leaning over hers, their breath mingling as they stood toe-to-toe, his grey eyes sliding down to her lips…. If Dr. Sam had been only a couple minutes longer—

Her stomach clenched at the thought.

"What were you guys talking about?"

At the unexpected question, Cassie whipped around, her startled, guilty eyes flying up to gauge the uncertain expression playing out on Rachel's face. How long had she been standing there, lurking in the background? And why? Cassie felt a wave of unease settle over her person. The girl was perhaps taking this 'starting over' thing a bit too seriously.

Shrugging, Cassie tried for a careless response. "Me and Brannt? Oh, nothing much."

Rachel raised a questioning eyebrow. "Yeah?"

"Just work stuff," Cassie mumbled, unnerved by that stare.

Rachel's stiff smile relaxed a little. "Oh. I figured as much."

"Yup." Cassie stuffed her hands in her pockets, rolling on the back of her heels.

"You guys have become pretty close, huh?"

There was something about the way she said that which made Cassie quick to deny it. "No. I don't think I'd put it—"

"Still, he seems happy to have you on board. That's, well," Rachel's voice was thin. "That's something."

"I guess."

Rachel persisted. "The whole town thinks there's something going—"

"Cassie! Girl, wait up!"

Cassie had never been so thankful for an intrusion in her whole life. Peeking her head over Rachel's shoulder, she spied the tall, lanky form of Dr. Andrea Coleman coming after them.

"Andrea," Cassie called with way more familiarity than was necessary. But hey, anything to end this current conversation.

Saddling up to Cassie, Andrea spared Rachel a quick glance. "I hope I'm not interrupting?"

Rachel shrugged. "I was just talking to Cassie—"

"Not at all."

Andrea bit back a smile. Her eyes took stock of Rachel. "Did I hear you say something about heading to the dance tonight?"

Before she could help herself, Rachel's eyes looked longingly in the direction where Brannt had walked off. "Uh. Yeah. I guess so."

"Better get a move on. The band's already warming up and if you don't get a spot on the dance floor now…" she shrugged meaningfully.

But Rachel didn't seem to be in any hurry to leave.

Andrea looked at Cassie. "You going to the dance?"

"I don't think so. Not tonight."

"Yeah. Me neither." She turned pointedly back to Rachel then, who was still standing there. "Well, have a good time, hun."

"Right," Rachel muttered, and with a last, pleading look at Cassie took herself off.

"Sorry about that," Andrea muttered once Rachel was out of earshot. "She can get a little…aggressive sometimes."

Cassie agreed silently.

"I only wish she'd open her eyes and stop all this nonsense. Making a damn fool of herself is what she's doing."

Cassie decided not to comment on that last cryptic remark.

"Me and the girls are headed out to Lucy's to have a couple drinks. You in?"

But Cassie shook her head. Brannt's words still stinging in her veins, she had a feeling she'd be terrible company. "Actually, I've got a bit of a headache."

"And I can just guess who gave it to you," Andrea muttered.

Cassie stared at her.

"I saw you and Brannt talking," Andrea confessed. "And, well, I know how he can be. God love him, he's the absolute devil sometimes."

"I can second that."

"And then Rachel…" Andrea made a production of sighing. "When I saw her corner you just now, let's just say I know a drowning woman when I see one."

Cassie chuckled. "Was it that obvious?"

"Only to a trained eye," Andrea assured her.

In the background, BJ could be heard hollering something about last call. "Oops, better go," Andrea said. "That's my ride."

"Thanks for the interruption."

"No problem. I'll see you in the office Monday."

"See you," Cassie said.

Rubbing her temples—because she hadn't been lying about the pounding in her head—Cassie slowly made her way over to Dr. Sam's truck. Tomorrow she doubted she'd so much as leave her apartment building. She'd seen more than enough of Pantula for today.

# CHAPTER NINE

"...and my roommate is totally awesome," Cassie heard over the phone. With incredible control, she kept herself from yawning. "Her name is Amanda, and she's taken me out to some of the coolest nightclubs. I'm telling you Cassie, the bar scene in Boston is unbeatable."

If her friend hadn't been going on in this same fashion for the last ten minutes straight, Cassie might have managed a semblance of genuine interest, a smidge of enthusiasm or whatnot. As it was, all she could come up with was a faint: "Really?"

Jenny was also doing an externship for school. Only, hers seemed to be a screaming success.

Bitch.

"You would just love her," Jenny gushed. "She's spunky and just, well fun!"

Stretched out on the old red and white plaid couch of her apartment, Cassie tried not to roll her eyes. Jenny was having a simply *fantastic* time. She'd met someone. His name was Brandon; wild black hair, olive complexion, native Easterner. They'd already gone out twice now. Jenny was damn near in love.

Annoyed with herself, who begrudged someone their happiness, Cassie tried to make amends for her serious lack of participation thus far: "Sounds like Boston is definitely agreeing with you."

"I don't ever want to come home."

Cassie, on the other hand, was counting down the days. Thirty-seven to be exact.

"So, how's Pantula or whatever it is you're at?" Jenny asked.

The only thing Cassie wanted to do less than listen to Jenny go on and on *and* on about Boston, was to talk to her about just how, well, blah the southern part of Texas was turning out to be…

Unlike her friend, Cassie's apartment wasn't high-end with walk-in closets, marble countertops, and a balcony overlooking the bustling cityscape. The best amenity the place offered was a VCR stashed under the television set. The springs in her couch were half-dead, and, oh, that's right, half the town thought she was a complete idiot.

"Pantula?" Cassie scrambled for something to say. "It's great. It's really hot." She'd been in Texas for three weeks and that was the best she could come up with—it was hot. Didn't that sum it up rather nicely?

Jenny waited patiently for Cassie to continue. "And?"

"The clinic I'm at is state-of-the-art," Cassie continued lamely. "And the doctor I'm working with is really helpful—"

"Male or female?"

Cassie scowled. She knew where this was going. "Male. And 57 years old."

Jenny sighed dramatically. "Well? Have you run into any hot cowboys then?"

Cassie pictured Brannt. Grey eyes, tanned, chiseled features. Dark hair hidden under that well-worn cowboy hat. Rough, calloused hands... "No. Nope. Not one."

Jenny laughed freely. "Girl, get looking!"

Cassie felt her lips thin. This phone call with Jenny couldn't have come at a worse time. Her only real evenings out had been routinely marred by Brannt in one form or another. And talk of him was just plain confusing. Dr. Sam was probably the only friend she'd really made and he was pushing sixty—and if that fact wasn't humiliating enough, he'd nicely turned down her offer for dinner that evening in lieu of a standing poker night with his pals (because apparently *he* actually had a social life.)

"I'm not sure I'd have time to notice one anyway," Cassie said instead. "I'm kept so busy, my free time is usually spent catching up on sleep." And rereading her textbooks, but that was way too much honesty for this particular conversation. Cassie pretended to look at her watch. "In fact, speaking of that, I should probably let you go. We have an appointment scheduled in half an hour. I should get ready."

That was a lie. Their last patient had canceled. Cassie was done for the day. But if she admitted that God only knew how long this phone call would last.

"Oh." Jenny sounded bummed. Probably, she still had more highlights of her totally amazing completely awesome time. "Well, all right—"

"I'll talk to you later," Cassie promised tightly.

"Try to have a little fun in the meantime," Jenny advised.

"Will do. Bye."

Ten minutes later, slumping down the stairs, Cassie took herself quietly into the vet clinic. After that conversation, she couldn't stand to sit inside her dumpy little apartment one minute longer. She hadn't really decided what she was going to do, but anything was better than sitting there, staring at her four walls, wallowing in self-pity.

Opening the heavy door, the first person she saw was BJ, perched jauntily behind the mammoth front desk. Standing a little behind her, peering over a file, stood Dr. Andrea Coleman.

"Cassie!" BJ smiled in greeting.

"Hey BJ—"

"Need the truck keys?" The secretary guessed knowingly. After all, there was really no other reason for her to be there.

Cassie nodded. "Yeah,"

"Good for you," the blonde said, snatching them off the peg behind her desk. "Doing anything fun?"

"Just stopping by the drugstore."

"The drugstore?" BJ looked offended. "What are you, eighty? It's a free night. You should be out there enjoying yourself."

"Yeah, and no offense, you look like you need a bit of livening up." This dry comment came from Andrea, who'd lifted her gaze from the documents in her hands to stare disconcertingly over at Cassie.

"Looks a bit done in, huh?" BJ murmured, turning to look up at Andrea.

"As my mama would say, she's got the look of a sourpuss."

"A what?" Cassie sputtered, feeling her face heat up.

"That she does," BJ tisk-tisked.

"Guys, I'm right here."

"Of course you are," BJ murmured comfortingly, handing over the keys to Cassie's outstretched hand.

Andrea had the grace to look slightly embarrassed. "Sorry Cass—"

"And I don't look like a sourpuss, whatever that is."

BJ shrugged. "If you say so." She threw Andrea a knowing look (which was starting to get on Cassie's nerves.) "She looks like she could use a drink, if you ask me."

Andrea nodded speculatively. "I know I could." Then she looked over at Cassie, who was no longer sure if she was annoyed or amused by their antics. Her eyes narrowed in consideration. "Well?" Andrea asked, raising one perfectly arched eyebrow. "What do you say?"

"About what?"

"Grab a drink with me?"

But before Cassie could so much as spit out a word, BJ was bouncing up and down in her chair. "Oh, do it, Cassie. Please. For me?" BJ pressed her hands together. "I'm keen to live vicariously through the two of you—young girls out having some cocktails, the glitz, and glamor."

"Oh please," Andrea said with an eye roll.

"Hey, once you have kids you'll understand."

"So?" Andrea asked, turning back to Cassie. "You in?"

Cassie squirmed under that direct gaze, feeling uniquely pathetic. Andrea was probably only asking out of kindness because Cassie clearly looked desperate and lonely. And like a sourpuss, though no one had yet told her what that was...

But, though she'd normally balk at such an obvious act of charity, her conversation with Jenny still ringing in her ears, she found herself nodding her head yes to Andrea's offer. Maybe it would turn out to be a totally awesome good time.

"Actually," she said. "I'd love a cold beer."

Andrea slapped her hands together. "Wonderful." Shoving the file haphazardly back where it belonged, she smiled gamely. "I'm just finishing up for the day, anyway. Give me five minutes?"

"Okay."

"Beej? What do you say?" Andrea asked meaningfully.

The blonde sighed. "I'd love to join you, but as I said...kids."

"All right. Next time," Andrea said before zipping out from behind the front desk, her lab coat already halfway off her shoulders. With a quick backward glance, she added: "I'll be just a minute, Cassie."

Cassie smiled politely. What the hell had she just got herself into?

\* \* \*

Fifteen minutes later, sitting at a high-top table at the rear of a dinky little bar, Cassie felt her spirits lowering. Andrea, assuring her that the drinks tasted better than the décor looked, was up at the bar ordering for them. Racking her brain, Cassie tried to come up with some conversation starters before the vet returned.

Small talk had never really been Cassie's forte and though she and Andrea now regularly exchanged pleasantries at the office, especially after Andrea's rescue service the night of the rodeo, it was never more than a sentence or two in between appointments—

"Here you go," Andrea said, breaking into Cassie's frantic thoughts, and reappearing almost magically before her eyes with two frosted pint glasses in hand. Slipping onto her chair, she pushed one of them toward Cassie.

"Thanks," Cassie said, taking a hurried drink—anything to disguise her lack of conversational skills. But she needn't have worried.

"So tell me, what do you think of Pantula so far?" Andrea asked, setting her drink to one side of the table. She smiled invitingly.

Cassie opened her mouth to speak...

And for the next twenty minutes, conversation flowed naturally between the women. Andrea's first question had led naturally enough to: "You're from somewhere out in Washington, right? I've never been. Must be quite different than the likes of this place..." and following that— "Have you thought much about what kind of practice you'd like to join after graduation?"

So Cassie told her how unnerving it was, being in a small town, where everybody seemed to know everybody's business, how different it was from her northern experience, where people were friendly but relatively quiet about it.

And of course, she told her about the Peterson Clinic. "It's my daily medicine," she informed the amused veterinarian. "I just picture myself there, in my starched lab coat and no matter how stressed-out I am, no matter what mistake I make, I just plow forward." She smiled. "It's where I'm headed."

By the time Cassie had finished talking, the women were well on the way to becoming fast friends. Relaxing under Andrea's chill demeanor, Cassie forgot to be nervous, she forgot to bumble and mumble awkwardly.

"How long have you worked at Tiamango?" Cassie asked, taking the lead for the first time that evening.

Andrea smiled as they received another round of drinks. "It's been a little over three years."

"Did you grow up here?"

Andrea shook her head. "No. I'm originally from Nebraska. I moved here when I got this job. At first, I had intended to stay just long enough to get my feet wet, then go into a larger practice in a bigger city," she admitted conspiratorially. "But then I met Ben." Ben was her husband.

Cassie smiled romantically. "So you stayed."

"Yeah, I stayed," Andrea confirmed. "And honestly, now I can't imagine living anywhere else. Pantula has a way of growing on you," she assured her. "The quiet nights, the June bugs. The slower pace, it's so good for the soul."

Cassie looked out the bar's storefront window. A few stray cars passed on the otherwise empty road. "It's certainly homey."

Andrea took a long pull off her beer. "It is at that. And you're right, in a community of this size, everybody knows everybody. Everyone cares about their neighbor. I've made the best friends of my life in this little town."

Cassie inclined her head in acknowledgment of this, but otherwise, she remained silent.

"Still, there's always room to make new friends," Andrea offered meaningfully.

"Cheers to that," Cassie responded, lifting up her glass.

"You know, I had originally requested to be your mentor," Andrea confessed. Shrugging at Cassie's evident interest, she conceded good-naturedly, "but, of course, Sam is much more experienced than me, so I wasn't all together surprised when he was chosen for the role. He really is the best. You're lucky. A lot of our customers—Brannt McDowell, for instance—practically refuse to even have another vet out to their place!"

Cassie made a face. "God! Why am I not surprised?"

Andrea's eyebrows hitched upward.

"He's such a chauvinistic prince. You should have seen him the first day I showed up at his place," Cassie muttered darkly. "He was such a jerk."

"He's an acquired taste—" Andrea tried.

Cassie snorted.

"I know Brannt can be a little, uh, rough around the edges," Andrea said cautiously. "But he's actually a good guy once you get to know him."

"I'm not sure I'm interested in getting better acquainted," Cassie assured her. "I should have left him to get gangrene. It would've served him right!"

Andrea tilted her head a little to one side. "Say what?"

Cassie explained the story of how she'd doctored up his injured leg. "I suppose I felt compelled to prove my worth. He certainly seemed to need convincing."

Andrea kept her mouth safely shut.

Cassie grimaced. "I may have walked a little too closely behind one of the horses without properly stating my intentions once."

"I see."

She blew out her cheeks. "And I kind of, sort of, tripped in his barn," Cassie admitted, explaining her less-than-graceful exit that first day they'd met. "But I swear, he seemed more worried I'd crack the pavement than my own damn head!"

Andrea snorted back a laugh.

"And at the rodeo…" she scoffed, taking in a large mouthful of alcohol. "Don't even get me started on that."

Andrea's brows furrowed. "He defended you," she pointed out carefully. "How could that have been bad?"

"Afterward, right before you came up to me—"

Andrea nodded slowly. "Right. It did look like the two of you were having words."

"Yeah, we had those all right," Cassie assured her, before quickly filling her in on the details of that ill-fated conversation.

The rest of the evening followed a similar pattern:

"Brannt is such a…"

"Brannt said…"

"Then Brannt…."

Andrea, quietly sipping her beer, let the younger woman spew. For one thing, the girl looked like she needed a good vent. And besides, she couldn't seem to help bringing him up into every topic of conversation presented, no matter how many times Andrea tried steering the talk to a more general nature. For another, Cassie clearly had no idea how much she was giving away with her incessant complaining.

"Everyone seems to think what that man says is gospel."

"Amen," Andrea said quietly.

\* \* \*

The next morning, sitting over breakfast with her husband, Andrea relayed the previous evening's events. "She sure had a lot to say about Brannt McDowell," she supplied innocently over a bite of cereal.

Flipping down the newspaper he held in his hands, Ben stared over the pages at his young wife. "No," he said mildly. Placing the ink-riddled daily on the table, he stared at her meaningfully. "I know that tone in your voice…"

Andrea blinked. "What tone?"

"The one that says you're up to something."

Andrea shrugged. "What's that line from Hamlet? Girl protests too much."

"A loose translation," Ben replied drily.

Andrea flapped her wrist. "Oh, whatever. You know what I mean. Cassie's antagonism is simply a cover to disguise her real, not-so-adverse, feelings. I'm almost sure of it."

"So?" he retorted.

"So? I think it's reciprocated. You *know* Brannt," she accused, and Ben did. As the business manager for the McDowell Estate, something Andrea had deliberately kept from Cassie, Ben had more than a passing awareness of the man in question.

"Yeah? And the only time I've heard him mention her name, the air turned blue," Ben returned dryly.

Andrea waved this away. "He picks at her, sure, but he's oddly protective of her, too. You saw how he stood up for her at the rodeo. Didn't it seem a little strange, just how much he minded what everyone was saying, especially to a girl he's worked so hard to supposedly dislike?" she insisted. "Besides, Cassie mentioned some other things...." she intimated suggestively. "It got me thinking, that's all. He's different around her. And weren't you just complaining the other day that he's been unusually preoccupied? I think I know why."

Ben gave his wife a level stare.

"So sue me for being curious," Andrea said laughingly. "I like her, Ben. I really do."

He just shook his head. "You're going to meddle, aren't you?" He sounded resigned to her answer.

Andrea smiled. "Just a helpful nudge, that's all."

"Such as?"

"Nothing much really," she assured him sweetly, swirling her spoon in its bowl. "I just asked Cassie if she wanted to go horseback riding with me on Sunday. She said yes."

Ben gave her a look.

"Okay," she admitted, "Yes, fine, maybe I neglected to mention that we board our horses—"

"At Brannt's ranch?" Ben finished for her.

Andrea grinned impishly. "Yeah, that."

# CHAPTER TEN

Bright and early Sunday morning, Cassie found herself being jostled about in the passenger seat of Andrea's truck; the warm sun beating through the open side window played havoc with her loose ponytail. But then, what did she care? Dressed in a pair of faded blue jeans and thin cotton shirt, she hardly had cause to complain, merely tucking the stray hair behind her ears. She was going horseback riding.

She hadn't been on a horse in years. She'd told as much to Andrea, but the other woman had merely waved aside this information; not to worry, she had the perfect animal for Cassie to ride. An older horse, well broken, named Friar. Cassie would be just fine.

Winding down one dirt road after the next, Cassie hadn't paid much attention to Andrea's driving but when the vet turned down an all-too-familiar country lane, Cassie's body hummed into sudden, shocking awareness. Her eyes narrowed on the speedometer when she noticed the truck slowing down. Cassie wasn't sure where Andrea lived, but she was almost certain it wasn't down that particular stretch of gravel. As far as she knew, the whole of the property boarding the north side of the roadway belonged to one, sole ranching outfit—and it wasn't the Coleman's.

Sure enough, at the sight of the front gate to the McDowell Estate, Andrea's hands turned the steering wheel to the left. Nosing the large vehicle up the driveway, her eyes stared fixedly straight ahead, outright refusing to meet the heated expression radiating off Cassie's face.

"What are we doing here? This is Brannt's house," Cassie sputtered as Andrea veered toward the barn.

Andrea flashed Cassie a quick, guilty, look. "Oh, well this is where we keep our horses. Ben and I don't have a whole lot of land yet..."

Cassie felt her jaw clench. "Oh?"

"Didn't I mention that?"

"No. No, you did not."

Andrea played at innocence as she put the truck in park. "Oh. Well, no matter."

Sitting there, Cassie was hard-pressed to undo her seatbelt. What if he was there, inside the barn? What would he say if he saw Cassie?

Would she be expected to scale one of the large beasts with his mocking eyes watching her the whole time? Hives jumped to attention across her skin at just the thought of it.

Andrea, however, seemed to have no such qualms. She was already out of the vehicle, her steps taking her purposely toward the barn. Looking back over her shoulder, she motioned for Cassie to follow suit.

"This way!" she yelled.

Wincing at the sound, desperate not to attract undue attention, Cassie scrambled out of the truck, her steps leaden as she shadowed behind her newfound friend. Please, don't let him be in there, she prayed with each imprint of her booted feet on the ground.

Let him be out in the pasture.

Let him be up at the house.

Let him be in town.

Watching Andrea crack open the door, Cassie squared her shoulders as she came up behind her.

Let him be out of town...out of state.

Let him be...

Cassie's prayers had evidently fallen on deaf ears. Standing to one side of the large complex was none other than the very man she'd so desperately wanted to avoid. He didn't turn around at their entrance, his arms loaded down with a saddle which he easily threw over the back of a horse standing tied up beside him.

Cassie's fingers went up tug her ponytail back in place, her fingers frantically smoothing the hair in place.

"Hey, Brannt!" Andrea called, sidling up beside him.

Shifting in her direction now, Brannt smiled fondly at the tall, raven-haired veterinarian standing so trustingly beside him. "Morning Andrea," he greeted warmly.

Cassie ground her teeth together.

"Thanks for catching the horses for us," she said and then, with an almost apologetic glance, added: "You didn't have to saddle them, though..."

Brannt shrugged. "Fifteen minutes of more riding time this way."

Cassie felt cheated watching their interaction. He wasn't ever that nice to *her*. He didn't smile that way at *her*. He would never think of being so generous...

Jerking her eyes away from the evidence of Brannt and Andrea's friendship (which only seemed to highlight his own lacking reception of her), Cassie let her gaze wander around the building. Two other horses could be seen, each secured behind custom-built stalls, and each sporting leather bridals around regal heads, and carrying ornately designed saddles across their broad backs.

Wait a minute.

That didn't add up.

Two saddled horses in the stalls. One half-saddled horse tied up beside Brannt. Two plus one equaled...three? Three horses. Cassie.

Andrea. And...And Brannt? A cold, hard emotion settled in the pit of Cassie's stomach. Why were three horses saddled?

Please let the third horse be saddled for a ghost rider.

Or, let Brannt be headed off in the opposite direction.

Even better, let him be just getting back in, done for the day.

Let him...

"You saddled three horses?" Andrea asked, her voice echoing off the walls. She'd apparently come to the same mathematical quandary as Cassie.

Brannt grunted as he tied the cinch firmly underneath the horse, which she'd just heard Andrea address as the one and only Friar. "Yeah. With the excess rain we got in March, there've been some pretty extreme washouts in certain places. And over in the east, areas of boggy marsh and ground depression have made for some treacherous travel," he grunted. "If you don't know where you're going...?" He shrugged, letting the sentence dangle in mid-air. "It's not safe for the two of you to go alone, without supervision."

Cassie's eyes grew large in her pale face. "Treacherous?" she squeaked, the first word she'd said since entering the barn.

Glancing up, Brannt looked over at her then, taking in her stiff posture and ashen face. His mouth made a grim line, but otherwise, he seemed matter-of-fact when he answered: "Only if you went alone, which you aren't."

"Who's the lucky escort?" Andrea teased, diverting Brannt's attention.

He shook his head. "Me."

Cassie wanted to faint.

Throwing a triumphant look over her shoulder, Andrea smiled at Cassie. "Best tour guide a girl could ask for. What did you have in mind for us?"

Brannt rechecked the cinch. "Oh, I don't know. I thought I could take you to Rock Ledge. As I recall, you were quite enchanted with it?"

Andrea sent Cassie another charmed look. "Perfect! Oh, Cassie, you'll love it. It's absolutely beautiful country."

"It's not part of the ranch that's currently submerged in water, is it?" she couldn't help asking.

Brannt laughed. It had a rich, deep sound. Cassie was surprised by it. She hadn't known the man capable of such a sound.

"Rest assured Ms. Hastings, it's perfectly intact...and dry."

Cassie felt her cheeks heat up at the words.

"Are you sure you can afford the time to take us out today?" Andrea asked politely when Brannt untied the horse, his hands working the bridal in place. "I mean, we'd really appreciate having you but we don't want to be a bother...?"

Cassie held her breath. She wasn't sure what answer she hoped he'd give.

But all Brannt said was: "Let's get going, huh?" Twisting to look at Cassie, he nodded up at the gelding beside him, whose reins were now held fast in Brannt's hands. "Cassie, you first."

"Me?" Cassie asked stupidly. She looked around the tall, well-lit barn. "You want me to get on him in here?"

"Why not?" Brannt asked with a curious raise of his winged eyebrows.

Cassie shrugged difficultly. "I don't know..."

"Well, come on," he said impatiently.

Cassie made her way reluctantly to where he stood. From the closer vantage point, Friar's back looked a long way up. "Just climb on, huh?" she asked no one in particular.

"Yup. Put your left foot in the stirrup and swing your other leg over."

Cassie reached up, one hand settling firmly on the saddle horn, the other curving around the edge of the back of the seat. Bending her knee, she tried to reach her boot up to the thick U-shaped stirrup but she couldn't reach, the toe of her boot falling just short of the mark. Hoisting her hands higher on the saddle, she tried again, to no avail.

Brannt looked mildly amused at Cassie's flailing attempts, but she did her best to ignore that. "Here," he said, coming to stand beside her. "Place your boot in my hands instead." Locking his fingers together, he made a makeshift foothold for her to step on.

Cassie looked at him dubiously. "Just do it, Cassie," he insisted, his voice ringed with untold irritation—he was a man used to being listened to. "That way, I can give you a boost up."

Feeling foolish, Cassie did as she was told.

"Ready?"

Cassie nodded tightly.

"Lift up!" Brannt ordered and, within seconds, Cassie felt her body rising effortlessly up in the air before landing snuggly against the high-backed seat. Feeling his hands drop their hold on her foot, Cassie quickly snaked the toe of each boot into the stirrups hanging down at the horse's side. The last thing she needed was to slip off the other side. Keeping her eyes lowered, she carefully avoided Brannt's eye.

After all, who's heard of a large animal veterinarian that can't get on a horse?

Luckily though, Friar seemed content to stand still while Brannt and Andrea went to retrieve and mount their horses. That would have just been the icing on the mortification cake if Cassie's horse had decided to take off on her. But alas, Friar didn't seem to have any such inclinations.

"Ready?" Brannt asked, leading his horse from the stall. With the gracefulness of practice, he swung himself up into his saddle. Without waiting for a response, he led his horse forward, walking gracefully out of the open barn door and into the ensuing pasture. Andrea trailed after, close on his heels.

Cassie's horse, however, remained exactly where he was. Trying to urge him forward, Cassie met with quiet resistance.

"Uh, guys?" She called out when he refused to move.

"Give him a nudge with your feet...click with your tongue to make him go," Andrea called over her shoulder.

Cassie did as she was told but Friar remained unfazed. "Go, Friar," she whispered, feeling foolish. He flat-out refused. She clicked her tongue. He swung his head lazily from one side to the other. She prodded his side with her foot. His hide made the slightest quiver and then nothing.

Sitting there, Cassie could feel tears stinging against her eyes. Trying again, the heel of her boot pressed up tight to his thick side, she prayed one more time.

Please go. Please just go.

But, as had all her other pleas that morning, it went unheeded. Friar lowered his head back to the floor.

Frustrated out of all proportion, Cassie felt her chest tighten, her stomach knot. Perfect. Just perfect. She got the defunct horse. She didn't have a clue what she was doing, and there was no way she wasn't being watched, judged by those grey eyes. She could practically feel them burning against her skin. She felt stupid, unprepared. Why had they left her to take up the rear? She couldn't do this...!

Even knowing she was being childish, that it was silly to get this upset, Cassie couldn't help the panic that invaded her senses, the urgency fighting for relief inside her body.

"Please move," she whispered thickly, her chest heaving over the words. "Please, please," she pleaded.

No response.

She didn't want to do this. She didn't want to ride this stupid horse. She should have never agreed to this. A little instruction would have been nice. She hadn't been kidding when she said she'd never really ridden a horse before and now, now...

"Hey," Brannt said, coming up beside her. She hadn't seen him tuck back into the barn. Through a thin layer of filmy tears (tears she hated herself for shedding yet couldn't seem to stem), she watched his tapered fingers reach for the reins lying low across Friar's neck. His arm just barely brushed against her shoulder with the action. "Hold this a little higher in your hands," he said softly. "And go ahead and give him a kick."

Cassie kicked. "See? Nothing happens."

"Harder," Brannt said.

"What if he runs off on me?" Cassie asked, her voice coming out small. She hated herself for that, too.

Brannt smiled and it looked almost gentle. "He won't run off. Friar never runs. Not unless you're wearing spurs. That's why I chose him for you. But, he does need a little motivation. So give him a solid kick and I promise he'll go."

Cassie kicked harder this time...and felt Friar lift his front legs in response, followed shortly by his back. Forgetting herself for a moment, Cassie threw Brannt a dazzling smile. "He's walking!"

"Of course he's walking. He'll listen to you, but *you* have to be in charge."

Cassie nodded mutely.

Riding close beside her, Brannt lowered his voice. "Remember, horses can sense fear. I told you that the first time I met you, right?"

Cassie nodded.

"But I forgot to add that there's no reason to be afraid. Not right now anyway."

"Okay," Cassie mumbled.

"And hey, I'll be here with you the whole time," he said just as quietly, his eyes shadowed by the brim of his large hat. "I won't let anything happen to you, okay?"

"Okay," Cassie said, and this time she sounded as though she meant it, because, all of a sudden, she did feel okay.

Brannt was there. Everything would be fine. This was going to be fun after all. Brannt was there.

\* \* \*

Cassie closed her eyes. Friar moved with easy, undulating steps. The hot sun settled around her body like a sweet-smelling blanket. She felt her body rock softly from side-to-side. Up ahead, Brannt and Andrea carried on a quiet conversation that, just then, didn't require her attention.

In a phrase, it was heavenly.

Opening her eyes once more, Cassie stared out at the landscape. Fields of yellow prairie grass, speckled here and there with long, healthy wisps of bristle and bluegrass stared back at her. And where the pasture evened out in a rough, claylike terrain, little bluestems poked forth in spiky brushes. Trees could be seen way out in the distance, their origin unknown to her foreign eye. Brannt lived on some beautiful property.

"Hey, slowpoke you doing all right back there?" Andrea called over her shoulder, twisting back in her seat to glance at Cassie. She and Brannt were more than five horse-lengths ahead of her now.

Cassie hadn't realized how far back she'd gotten from them. Only, she hadn't wanted to rush along too fast (for the obvious reason that she and Friar were only just getting acquainted) but also because she didn't want to miss a second of the scenery. Brannt's homestead was offering her a slice of Texas she hadn't seen yet, one she doubted she'd be given the gift to catch sight of again. Then again, she also didn't want to get lost. Giving Friar a friendly nudge, she picked up her pace a little.

"Yeah, sorry," she said easily, coming abreast of them now. "I got distracted. It's so peaceful out here."

Brannt nodded quietly, but for once, he didn't seem inclined to challenge Cassie's words. "My brothers and I used to play out in this pasture," he informed them. Pointing toward one of the groupings of large trees, he added: "We used to have a fort out there."

"You have brothers?" Cassie asked, surprised.

Brannt gave her a level look. "It does happen, you know. Parents deciding to have more than one child." His raised eyebrow offered a healthy dose of mockery, just in case his tone of voice hadn't been enough.

"No, I know," Cassie sputtered. "I just...I didn't know you had siblings. Do they live around here?" She strove to keep her voice casual, but for some reason, she was deeply curious.

"Cassie do you have much of our vegetation up North?" Andrea's question was as loud as it was bewildering.

"Uh, some," Cassie offered weakly. Brannt's expression had taken on a hard edge.

Andrea nodded quickly. "Yeah, I remember when I moved here..."

But Cassie wasn't listening. Something had happened. The atmosphere around the riders had changed. She just wasn't sure why. Andrea, usually a chatty woman anyway, seemed almost frenzied in her conversation. Brannt was back to being taciturn, his lip forming a hard, thin line.

"...it's commonly referred to as switchgrass," Andrea said, her voice droning on in her running commentary of Texas plant life. "I don't see any now..." she bit her lip.

"That's our destination. Up ahead." Speaking abruptly, the sound riding roughshod over Andrea's one-sided conversation, Brannt nodded in the distance, indicating a small outcropping a little ways off.

Even his voice was cool, distant. Still, Cassie was relieved for its return. Anything to stop Andrea's sudden, incessant interest in all things flora and fauna. "It may not look like much from here, but when you stand on the edge you can see for miles."

Cassie squinted. No. It didn't look like much.

Andrea grinned, thankfully distracted from her sermon on the finer points of southern foliage. "Oh Cass, you're going to love—" the sudden ringing of her phone interrupted the female veterinarian. Digging the buzzing thing out of her pants pocket, she quickly answered. "Hello? Dr. Andrea Coleman here...."

Neither Cassie nor Brannt could hear what was being said on the other end of the line, but it clearly wasn't good. Andrea's brow furrowed as she listened and then she gasped: "What? Oh no...is he—?" Cassie watched the vet close her eyes with something like pain. "Yes. Okay. I'll be with you right away."

Hanging up the phone, Andrea spoke out loud. "That was Mr. Donald. His horse got spooked by a bear and ran into their electric fence." Her voice out came out in a whisper of despair, marked with heavy disbelief

"Is the horse okay?" Cassie asked though she probably already knew the answer.

Andrea shook her head. "I don't know. At least, the bear didn't attack, but the horse is in bad shape apparently. I've, I've got to go," she said, looking to Brannt as if for guidance.

"Of course," he offered quickly. "Just leave Jinco,"—that was Andrea's horse—"in the barn. One of the men will unsaddle him."

Andrea nodded. "Can you take Cassie back?" she asked then.

"Yes—"

Take her back?

"I could go with you, Andrea. If you wanted?" They were talking like she wasn't even there.

"There isn't time for that," Brannt said, dismissing her words out of hand. "No, you'll stay with me."

"Isn't time?" Cassie asked incredulously. Her hand curled around the pommel. "What are you talking about? I'm right here. It's not like—"

"Don't argue, Cassie," he said, just as though she were throwing a hissy-fit or something.

Cassie turned to Andrea. "I can help," she reiterated.

The other woman grimaced.

"Andrea. Just go!" Brannt ordered, shooing the veterinarian gone with the flick of his wrist.

With an apologetic glance at Cassie, Andrea consented. Turning her mount, she gave Jinco one solid kick, breaking him out into a full run.

"And that, right there, is exactly why she didn't ask you to come along," Brannt told her, his chin motioning toward Dr. Coleman's quick getaway. "So stop feeling sorry for yourself."

Cassie's teeth gnashed together, but even she had to admit that Andrea was making a mad dash for it. Watching her become increasingly smaller in size, Cassie became all too aware suddenly of just how alone she was with Brannt, of the abrupt intimacy of their isolation.

Clearing her throat, she fought for aloofness in composure. "Listen, since Andrea had to leave…" she shrugged pointedly. "I'm sure you have better things to do. I don't want to hold you up."

There was no denying the starch in her words.

"Sulking because you feel left out?"

"No," Cassie returned. Except that wasn't quite true. There was a small, albeit unreasonable, part of her that was a little put-out at Andrea's desertion. No one had even considered that she might be able to keep up. It had been a foregone conclusion from the start that she couldn't possibly make it back to the barn. That had stung a little. "I just don't want the scenery spoilt by the company," she improvised.

"Come on," was all Brannt said. "We're almost there. It would be pointless to have come all this way only to miss it at the end." With a deft motion, Brannt sent his horse walking again. With no choice for it, Cassie prodded Friar to follow suit.

"Since you brought it up," she informed him coolly, "I'll have you know that besides that one small hiccup in the barn, I haven't had any problems with Friar."

"So you're an old hat at it now?" Brannt mused.

Cassie pursed her lips. "No. But would it kill you to give me some credit? I've already admitted that I don't know much about ranch life, but I'm trying. You could at least notice my redemptions too."

Brannt lowered the brim of his cowboy hat. His eyes were shadowed underneath the wide top. "Oh, I notice all right."

Cassie's mouth moved but no words came out, which was probably for the best. She wasn't sure how to respond to that. She was still trying to sort it out when they gained the top of Rock Ledge.

Bringing Friar up alongside Brannt, Cassie stopped to gaze out before her. "Wow," she breathed, her eyes taking in miles upon seeming miles of green grass here, barren, cracked soil there, smatterings of trees, fence lines, small dots that Brannt assured her were Hereford bulls, and the smallest sliver of grey-white glinting water before it widened out into a creek.... "This is all your land?"

"Yes."

"You must be so proud," she said softly, forgetting herself for a moment.

Brannt looked down at her. "It's a lot of responsibility and frequently more work than fun. Something's always breaking down, or flooding, or any other of a hundred things." He sighed deeply: "and I wouldn't want to be anywhere else. This land has been in my family's name for over two hundred years."

Cassie let her eyes rake over the picturesque view once more. Neither of them spoke for a moment. "Thank you for taking me here."

Brannt grunted. "Thank Andrea," he insisted gruffly. "This horseback riding idea was all hers. I'm just the tour guide remember?"

Cassie ground down on her teeth. "Must you make everything so difficult? It was just a compliment, Brannt."

"And I'm all about them," he assured her. "Just as long as they're delivered to the rightful person."

Cassie snorted. "God! Spare me another one of your famous lectures. You are the most infuriating man!"

"I know," Brannt confessed. A light came into his eyes. "I do it on purpose."

"Why?"

"Why? Because you rise so sportingly to the fight." This delicious bit of banter was followed by a devilish wink before he slowly turned his horse away.

Cassie felt her stomach drop.

# CHAPTER ELEVEN

Heading back for the barn, Cassie let out a silent sigh of relief when she spied it coming up in sight. She wouldn't admit it for anything, but her back was getting tight and her legs felt uncomfortably tense in their curved position. Riding horses was tough work, and they'd only been out for a couple hours. Brannt seemed fully at ease on top of his horse, which only acted to highlight Cassie's jostled discomfort.

She had a feeling she would be sore the following morning. (Hell, she had a feeling she'd be sore that evening.) Luckily, she and Sam were staffed to be at the office the next couple days. At least she wouldn't have to worry about hiking through acres of farmland.

Gaining the main pasture, Brannt pulled his horse up to a stop. Friar, the ever-faithful lemming, came to an almost immediate halt, as well. Alighting gracefully, Brannt quickly grabbed his horse by the reins before coming over to hold Friar while Cassie clumsily climbed down.

Bracing her hands carefully against the pommel, she felt her right leg swing over the hefty saddle, the rest of her body sliding down awkwardly in sequence. But, alas, finally her feet touched solid ground.

"Oh!" she cried out at the impact. Smiling sheepishly, she shot Brannt an amused look. "Are my legs supposed to feel like this?" Flexing tired muscles, Cassie laughed faintly at the bowled texture of her inner thighs. Walking a straight line seemed like an impossibility just then.

Brannt didn't bother asking Cassie to explain that statement. "Feel like rubber, huh?" he asked softly.

Cassie grinned up at him. "Yes." Her smile slipped, however, when she made to move. Her legs buckled. "Oh!" she cried out again.

"Steady there," Brannt murmured, stepping forward to place a protective hand on her upper arm.

Stuck with her back against the bulk of Friar and the overwhelming nearness of Brannt, Cassie found it difficult to breathe. She licked at suddenly dry lips. "Sorry about that...I guess I'm sorer than I thought." She tried for a laugh. It came out like a squeak.

"I shouldn't have kept you out so long," Brannt argued, silently handing her Friar's reins.

Cassie smoothed the leather against her palm. "I'm glad you did though."

Brannt eyes softened to an almost liquid grey. "For a rank beginner, you handled yourself well. I almost forgot…"

"That I didn't know what in hell I was doing?" Cassie finished for him, tongue-in-cheek.

A look came over Brannt's face, a mischievousness that she'd never witnessed before. "Yeah," he finally said, his words carried on a husky laugh: "Something like that."

One of them should have moved. Brannt should have taken a step back. Cassie should have shimmied around the side of Friar. But neither of them did. A thick silence permeated the humid spring air. Feeling that proximity, Cassie's eyes searched his face—wondering, pleading.

In reaction, Brannt's own eyes narrowed, the lids drooping down to cover the expression playing out there. The fingers against her arm drew Cassie slowly, ever-so-slowly, nearer. She wasn't sure he was even aware he was doing it. With a stumbling half-step, she drew up to the heat of his body.

"We weren't supposed to be left alone together," Brannt muttered then, the weight of that one heavy sentence sending shivers up her spine. He leaned forward. "I would never have agreed to tag along if I'd known we'd be left alone together."

"Scared of me?" Cassie challenged, but the tone of her voice didn't reflect the confidence inspired in those words.

"Damn right I am," he admitted just before his head bent down to meet hers.

Cassie's eyes fluttered shut when she felt the imprint of his lips. The hand holding her arm slid up to cradle the side of her neck. His fingers flexed there as his lips—his teeth—nibbled against her shaking mouth.

With a soundless sigh, Cassie felt her lips fall open, felt his lips respond in kind. Moaning softly, she felt his tongue skim across the dark recesses of her mouth. Reaching up on tiptoe, her arms encircled his neck, her fingers locking together at the base of it, anchoring her steady. And still, he kissed her.

It was the loud, rude neigh of Brannt's horse, still waiting patiently at his side, which shattered the intimacy of those precious seconds. Lifting his head, Brannt's eyes stared down at Cassie's dazed, shy countenance. Her lips felt raw, her cheeks scratchy from the burn of his slight stubble. Neither of them spoke.

Cassie held her breath. Brannt seemed to be deliberating. Then, his head began to descend toward hers again. "Ah hell," he whispered.

Closing her eyes expectantly, Cassie wanted nothing more than the weight of his mouth against hers…

But Brannt's horse had other ideas. Whinnying again, he shook his head fitfully, the action pulling against the reins in Brannt's other hand.

"Dammit Tagger," Brannt cursed quietly. But the damage had been done. The moment ruined. Cassie watched it happen. Stepping back, his hand dropping possession on her body, Brannt averted his gaze to the stomping animal beside him.

His hat sat skewed on his head, the byproduct of Cassie's fingers mussing up the hair there. But he didn't seem to notice and she didn't have the nerve to reach up and right it. Something had shifted.

Peeking up through the fringe of her lashes, laying heavy on hot cheeks, Cassie observed Brannt's features transform in those ticks of time: his jaw clenching, his eyes becoming a hard, powdery grey. Derision mixed with contempt chased across the features of his face. Brannt may have only taken two physical steps back from her, but it was nearer to fifty mentally...and emotionally.

Wrapping pride around her body like a heavy cloak, Cassie strove for flippancy. "I guess we should get these two put away, huh?" She laughed off-pitch. "They're getting a bit antsy."

Brannt didn't answer her, as he was apt to do. Grabbing Friar's reins out of her nervous grip, he just turned and walked away. Leading the horses to the barn, he didn't bother to glance her way.

"I'll meet you at my truck in fifteen minutes," he said over his shoulder. "Wait for me there."

Bemused, she watched his stiff back slowly disappear, flanked on either side by the swishing tails of his horses, their hooves clicking against the packed dirt and grass, keeping time to his strides.

"And please, spare me the post-modern outrage," Brannt added, gaining the barn doors. He did glance back at her then. "I told Andrea I'd give you a lift home, and so I will." Without another word, he slipped inside the barn, the horses lolling after him.

"Yeah well, I never agreed to be driven anywhere by you," she muttered, but by then he was already out of earshot. Digging her phone out of her pocket, Cassie quickly dialed Andrea's number.

The veterinarian answered on the second ring: "Hey Cassie, what's up?"

"Where are you right now?"

Andrea heard the clipped, almost accusing question with trepidation. "Is everything okay?"

"No, everything is not okay."

"What happened?" Panic echoed faintly across the phone lines.

"Are you still out at the Donald farm?"

"No," Andrea answered quietly. "I was forced to put the animal down. Nothing I could do." It was always hard to euthanize animals; a last resort to an incurable condition.

"I'm sorry," Cassie returned automatically.

"Yeah, thanks." There were only remnants of sadness still in the vet's voice. "Has something happened? You sound upset?"

Cassie's eyes flicked nervously toward the big barn doors. "Can you come and pick me up?"

Andrea wasn't stupid. "Yeah. Sure. I'm just getting back into town. I'll head that way now."

Wiping her sweaty palms against her pant legs, Cassie's eyes stared warily toward the darkened opening inside the sliding barn doors. She strove to keep her voice down: "How long will it take you to get out here?"

"Five minutes?"

"Good. I'll be waiting at the end of the drive."

"Cassie, what's going on?"

"Just hurry, Andrea," she pleaded before ending the call. On some level, Cassie knew she was being melodramatic and that she'd be embarrassed by it later, but she couldn't help herself.

Brannt had kissed her. And she'd kissed him back.

She'd kissed him back!

She could not, *absolutely not*, endure an entire pickup ride into town with him—not after that. She could only imagine the heavy, awkward silence that would ensue. Or worse, his demeaning lecture about how she shouldn't put too much stalk into what had transpired out in the pasture. She could only imagine his mockery and indifference.

Whatever.

Skirting around the back of the barn, Cassie kept her shoulders hunched and her head bent low as she made her way down the gravel drive to the road. She needed to leave. Andrea should have never left her here alone.

Cassie hardly dared to breathe until she saw Andrea's dusty truck coast into view. Standing at the edge of the driveway, she barely let the veterinarian pull the vehicle to the side of the road before she was yanking open the passenger door and clambering up inside.

"Want to tell me what happened?" Andrea asked once Cassie was safely buckled in and she'd pulled back out onto the road, dust flying up behind her back wheels.

Cassie shook her head. "No." Staring out at the long stretch of roadway before her, she shrugged. "He's the absolute worst! I don't know what compelled me to keep riding with him after you left!"

"Did he say something?" Andrea probed gently.

Cassie snorted. "The man doesn't need to. It's the way he looks at you, like an unfortunate speck of dirt dotting the bottoms of his boots."

Andrea whistled. "That sounds…"

Cassie looked at the side mirror. "Can't this thing go any faster?"

"Are you expecting company?" Andrea teased, but she pressed her foot down harder on the accelerator all the same.

Cassie shifted back around, settling in her seat. "No. No, of course not." But still, her eyes took in the rearview mirror. The road behind them was blissfully empty.

"Did Friar knock you into a tree branch or something?" Andrea asked, looking quickly over at Cassie's stony expression.

"No, why?"

"Your cheek. It looks a little red," Andrea murmured, a small smile skirting out at the edges of her lips. But she was smart enough to keep that look carefully concealed.

"Can we talk about something other than Brannt?" Cassie asked. Hearing herself, she grimaced. "I'm sorry," she apologized. "I'm just, that man makes me so crazy sometimes."

"I hear that."

"You too?"

"Ben used to drive me nuts—"

Cassie sent the veterinarian a glowering look. "Don't start, Andrea."

If the other woman was put off by Cassie's mood, she didn't let on. "Mum's the word. Got it."

\* \* \*

Cassie had barely been home for half an hour when an angry pounding sounded at her front door. Through the thin, red-and-blue paisley patterned curtains covering the half-glass panel, she could just make out a pair of wide shoulders and that unforgettable cowboy hat.

Brannt.

Cringing, Cassie sank out of sight, her feet taking her silently into the dark kitchenette. Thank God she hadn't had the presence of mind to turn on any lights.

After Andrea had dropped her off, Cassie bolting from the truck in the same way she'd entered it, she hadn't thought past retreating to the safety of her apartment.

Sparing only enough time to kick off her boots and tear out of her riding clothes, Cassie had jumped into the shower. The warm, steaming water had helped put everything into perspective. It was just a kiss. No big deal.

Only now, those words had come back to haunt her.

Folding her arms defensively across the thin multi-colored maxi dress she'd hastily thrown on, her damp hair hanging in waves down her back, Cassie couldn't quite suppress a shiver of expectation. Biting down hard on her lip, she prayed that Brannt would take the hint and assume she wasn't home. She prayed that he'd leave.

"Dammit Cassie, I know you're in there. Open up!" he yelled, his fists slamming vigorously against the door.

So much for that thought. Sighing out her frustration, Cassie felt her legs shaking, but still, she didn't move.

"I swear to God, Cassie, if you don't open this door—!"

"Go away, Brannt." Instantly, she regretted the impulsive words. She just wanted to be left alone. She needed to think. She needed to figure out what the hell had happened on that ranch. And, most importantly, she needed to figure out how to act like it hadn't mattered—that was paramount of all. She needed to be professional. Cool. Aloof. Brannt was a client, not a prospective boyfriend. *He* hadn't been affected by their kiss. She'd seen that with her own two eyes.

Afterward, he'd been calmly in control, walking into the barn with the horses as though it were a normal, everyday occurrence. For him, it probably was.

Brannt's knuckles rapped all the harder against the wood door. "Hah! So you are home." His voice oozed satisfaction. "Good. Now stop acting like a child and let me in!"

"No!"

"Either you open this door or I will!"

Cassie closed her eyes. Of all the men in the world to kiss why did she have to pick the most stubborn of them all? Still, shaking her head, she recognized an empty threat when she heard one. Did he really expect her to believe he'd break the door down? Come on.

Suddenly, he stopped knocking. Through the thick door, she could just make out a muffled curse, followed by the sound of retreating feet. But it was only at the echo of his heels thundering down the stairs that Cassie let out a shuddering sigh. He'd finally quit.

Moving gingerly into her living room, Cassie sat down on her lumpy couch. Kicking her feet onto the scratched coffee table, she let her head drop back against the cushions. Closing her eyes, she tried to look at the situation objectively.

Instead, all she could see were Brannt's wide, thin lips catching against her own; feel his warm breath as it melted inside her mouth; remember his rough hand as it massaged the back of her neck, bringing her head closer...closer.

A key turned in her lock outside.

Eye's springing open, Cassie had just enough time to gain her feet before her front door was unceremoniously thrust open, with a thunderous Brannt standing over its threshold.

"What are you...? How did you...?" Cassie sputtered, her terrified eyes unable to look away from his dark, angry stare.

Brannt dangled a pair of keys in one angry hand. "I grabbed the spare copy from downstairs."

"But those—" Cassie shook her head confusedly. "How did you get them?"

"I asked BJ for them," Brannt answered her easily enough. "She was only too happy to oblige."

"Those aren't for public use," Cassie moaned, but she wasn't talking to Brannt. She was going to kill BJ. While she made one hell of a receptionist, she was clearly a terrible apartment manager.

Brannt smiled. It was cold, filled with mockery. "Which is why I told her you'd accidentally locked yourself out." His smile widened. "Then she was only too willing to hand 'em over."

"Ah, and you were what, the Good Samaritan in this ruse?" Cassie batted her eyelashes sarcastically.

"Something like that."

"You're a real jackass, you know that."

"Yeah? And you're a little coward," Brannt returned just as quickly.

Curling her fingers together down at her sides, Cassie sneered across the two feet of space separating them. "That's cause for breaking into my house?"

"I didn't break in. BJ gave me a key," he reminded her unnecessarily. "And don't be mad at her either," he cautioned, reading her thoughts. "You could have just opened the door yourself and saved us all the trouble. I told you I'd get in." He grinned cockily.

"But that's just it. I didn't want your company."

"Yeah, I got that when you ran off," Brannt said through finely clenched teeth.

"And yet, here you are," Cassie murmured, waving her arms to encompass his seething form.

Brannt's eyes glittered. That smug smile was eclipsed by cold, hard contempt within seconds. "Well, what the hell did you expect after that stunt you pulled, disappearing like that? No one knew where the hell you'd gone—"

Cassie pulled a face. "And it never occurred to you that I might have simply left?"

Brannt took one menacing step nearer her. "No, what occurred to me is that the bull pasture is just beyond a buffer field next to the barn. If you'd slipped through the wrong fence..." his face tightened. "You ever been stuck in a pen with a bull before? They're mean, ruthless killers, Cassie. When we couldn't find you—" he let the sentence hang unfinished.

"Why does everyone think I'm a complete buffoon when it comes to animals?" Cassie muttered darkly. "Oh, we can't find Cassie. She's probably trying to braid the dangerous animals' hair," she mocked.

It was the wrong thing to say. Brannt all but exploded. "Dammit, Cassie! I had men out there looking for you, putting their necks on the line and for no good reason. If Andrea hadn't texted me... Do you have any idea—?"

In all honesty, she hadn't. Not of all the problems her quiet defection would cause, at any rate. It was a sobering, unfavorable realization, that her childish behavior had created such unnecessary uproar. It was humiliating. "Look, I'm sorry," she responded. "I-I didn't think..."

"You're damn right you didn't think." Brannt scoffed. "And all because of a nothing kiss?" His disdain was almost palpable.

Cassie sucked in her breath. That was exactly the kind of remark she'd been trying to escape. A nothing kiss? It hadn't been nothing to her. "I'm trying to apologize."

"You want people to stop treating you like a damn twit, then stop acting like one," Brannt threw at her, his eyes mirroring his sentiments. "You really are a coward," he said again.

Cassie had had enough. "I am not," she insisted.

"Oh no?" Brannt cut in, his voice unusually soft and low. "Are you sure about that?" And before Cassie knew it, he was across the floor and she was brought up in his hard arms. Before she had time to do more than gasp in surprise, his mouth was already crushing down forcibly against hers.

Groaning, Cassie's eyes stared wildly up at his dark face. Her hands, clenched in fists, were against his shoulders. But his mouth was unrelenting and, though she'd intended to push him away, to pound on his chest, Cassie found her mouth opening, answering the demand of his tongue as it whispered across her lips. She felt her eyes slide shut. His tongue brushed against the top of her mouth, his teeth grazing against her bottom lip.

Fingernails digging against his biceps, Cassie sank into the sensations swirling around her. Her blood was pumping loudly in her ears, nerves jumping against hot, sensitive skin. Brushing up closer, her breasts just grazed against his heavy chest. Her stomach tingled at the contact, dropping, tautening....

Then, without warning, Brannt broke the kiss. Lifting his head, an arrogant, almost challenging gleam entered his eyes. Cassie, yielding and soft in his embrace, carefully extracted herself. She didn't trust that look.

"Wha—?"

Brannt smiled wolfishly. "I have an appointment set with you and Sam for next Thursday." Walking toward the door, his words sounded hollow in Cassie's buzzing ears. Grabbing for the doorknob, he stopped, his eyes staring level with hers. "Or should I just expect your excuses now?"

Cassie was still working up a comeback when he quietly let himself out.

# CHAPTER TWELVE

Cassie yawned tiredly. Looking up at the industrial-sized clock hanging up in the foyer of the Tiamango Veterinary Clinic, she paused to note the time. 8:50 am. Returning to the computer screen blinking before her, she stifled down regret. She had another seven hours to go before the end of her work shift. And it was only Monday.

Pulling up the sleeves of her thin blouse, Cassie placed her hands over the keyboard. She had a lot of data entries to get through. Billie Jo wouldn't be in until noon—one of her kids had a dentist appointment that morning—which meant that Cassie, as one of the few staff members scheduled to be in the office all day, had donned the cap of office receptionist for the interim. Besides, Dr. Sam had insisted, it would only further advance her knowledge of the ins-and-outs of the business. That and neither of the other two part-time front staff members, both of whom were college students, had been available. With school still in session, weekdays were simply out of the question.

Cassie was hard at it, her eyes alternating quickly between the word processing software and a particularly thick file on Melinda Downing's billable services, when the bell hanging above the front door jingled, announcing the arrival of a customer. Smiling automatically, Cassie lifted her head in greeting.

"Hello—oh, hey Rachel," she said. "What can I do for you?"

Rachel didn't answer her at first. Blowing out an agitated breath, the young waitress tried for a casual smile. She failed. The way her lips stretched, it looked like her teeth were too big for her mouth. "Uh, hi Cassie." She swallowed uncomfortably, the fingers of one hand fidgeting against the pocket of her jeans. "I'm glad you're here…"

Cassie gave her a funny look. Of course, she was there. She worked there.

Blushing heatedly, Rachel stuttered, "That is to say, I was hoping I'd catch you in the office today—"

"Yeah? Well, you got me," Cassie returned easily, leaning over the short counter companionably. Clearly, Rachel wasn't here to buy heartworm medicine. This was a personal call. "So? What's up?"

Again, Rachel paused, her eyes skirting around the room, taking in the empty lobby, the uninhabited waiting chairs—their accompanying side-tables bare of Styrofoam cups and candy wrappers.

Watching her, Cassie could actually see Rachel's breathing change, her shoulders hunching defensively, her body reacting—but to what?

"Is everything all right?" Cassie asked softly, keeping her voice down. Not that it mattered. There was no one to overhear. Well, besides Sam, but he was in the back working on some test samples. He wasn't likely to come out here without reason.

Rachel's eyes snapped to attention, landing with a smack against Cassie's curious gaze. Her shoulders pulled in tight. "Is there something going on between you and Brannt?"

Cassie blinked. "What?"

Rachel spoke quickly. "Everyone knows he was at your place yesterday."

Damn BJ.

"And before that, you two went horseback riding together. Alone," Rachel stressed meaningfully.

"That's not exactly—" Cassie shook her head. "How did you even know that?"

"Everyone's talking about it. About the two of you."

Cassie wasn't sure which emotion gripped her harder. Defensiveness or righteousness. Really, where did Rachel get off, standing there and asking over her private life?

Rachel laughed. Actually, it was more of a screech. "Of course, I told them it was probably nothing. I mean, you're only here for a couple of weeks after all. And Brannt is your *client*."

Cassie was slow in responding. "Right."

"But you know how small towns are," Rachel continued, her voice coming out a little too fast. Her eyes narrowed deliberately. "Any potential for drama and everyone is all aflutter with gossip…"

Cassie stared at her stupidly.

Rachel took a deep breath. "You haven't answered my question."

"I'm not sure it's any of your business," Cassie heard herself saying tightly.

Rachel bit her lip. "No, I know. I just thought—listen, I know you don't have a lot of friends here and…" she shrugged. "And anyway, I made a promise. The next time I had a question I would come straight to the source."

Cassie wasn't sure she followed all of that. "Okay."

"So?"

Cassie sighed. "Rachel…"

"Do you like him?"

Cassie knew her silence would only amount to guilt. Cassie desperately wanted to avoid any more public speculation. And if word got around that she had a thing for Brannt—Oh God.

"No." Cassie shook her head vehemently. "Don't be silly. Of course not. Not-not like that." The words echoed in the quiet room. "And we didn't go riding alone. Dr. Andrea Coleman was with us." For part of it, anyway.

Rachel nodded eagerly. Her body relaxed at the words. "Yeah, I figured as much. And I'm sure there's a perfectly valid reason for his being at your apartment," she fished.

"I-I locked myself out. Brannt was helping me...." Cassie cringed. Great, now Brannt had her lying about his so-called heroic gesture of kindness.

Rachel smiled, satisfied. "Yeah. That sounds like him."

Cassie wanted to sink through the floor. "Mmhmm."

Rachel pulled a sympathetic face. "Isn't it terrible how quickly stuff like that can get so twisted?"

"I guess." Cassie just wanted this conversation to end.

"And I should know," Rachel continued. "Until you came along, everyone was wondering when Brannt and I would become an item." She flapped her wrist. "But, like I said, this town sees a private smile or catches wind of a flirty joke and..."

"Good morning, Rachel."

The sudden inclusion of Dr. Sam's voice had Cassie spinning wildly around in her chair, the pen she'd been holding in one hand flying through the air in her surprise.

Rachel, too, looked nonplussed at his silent approach into the waiting room. "Oh, hello Sam," she stuttered, her face coloring delicately. Her eyes seemed to look everywhere suddenly but at the smiling veterinarian. "I was just talking to Cassie..."

"So I heard."

Rachel's face seemed to twitch. "But actually, I should probably get going." She looked at the door. "I don't want to keep you," she muttered. She was already backing up.

Dr. Sam smiled nicely. "Goodbye Rachel."

The girl didn't need more coaxing than that. In the wake of her hastily-drawn exit, Cassie searched for something to say. Just what had Dr. Sam heard anyway? She blushed.

"You two have a nice chat?" he asked.

Shifting uneasily on her seat, Cassie shrugged. "It was nothing really..."

"I'll just bet." His tone was dry, amused maybe, as he came around to one side of the front desk. Leaning up against its high railing, he gave her a knowing look. "Try not to take it to heart."

"Huh?"

"She's been in love with him for a long time."

"What? Who?" But Cassie actually had a pretty good idea on that one.

Dr. Sam laughed. He wasn't fooled by her subterfuge. "Brannt."

"Oh. Yeah..."

"You're competition, Cassie." Dr. Sam held up his hands at the hot denial trembling off her lips. "I'm not saying there's anything behind that statement. But to Rachel, you're a rival. That's why she came in here today. She's testing the waters, making sure there's nothing to worry about."

Cassie tried not to remember the feeling of Brannt's arms wrapping her up close....

"It's not reciprocated, of course," Dr. Sam continued. "At least, not for Brannt. But she's young and naïve and she's still learning how to handle rejection. She thinks she can make him love her back."

Cassie wasn't sure how to respond to that.

"It won't work," Dr. Sam said. "And she'll have to learn that the hard way, unfortunately." He tisk-tisked sadly.

"I didn't know," Cassie offered feebly. Poor Rachel. Brannt wouldn't be an easy man to get over.

"And how could you?" Dr. Sam asked quietly. "She's making a fool of herself and pretty soon Brannt's patience will wear thin. He's been gentle up to now, but you know how hurtful he can be when he sets his mind to it."

Cassie nodded. He could be merciless when he wanted to.

"If he finds out about the little stunt she pulled just now—" Dr. Sam whistled.

"I won't tell him," Cassie hurried to say. She felt sorry for Rachel, despite everything she'd said.

Dr. Sam reached over to pat her on the shoulder. "You're a nice person, Cassie."

"I wouldn't sic my worst enemy on Brannt's temper," she joked.

"Don't I know it," he laughed, turning to walk back down the hallway. "Call if you need anything," he shouted.

\* \* \*

By five o'clock that evening, Cassie was more than ready to call it a night. After BJ had returned from her son's dental visit, Cassie had been released back into Dr. Tompkins' care. While she'd been glad to resume her normal duties, the afternoon had involved a long surgical list, everything from treatment of periodontal disease in Mr. Mumps, a cattle dog out on the Goodridge's farm, to a tricky case involving a cytological examination resulting in the removal of a benign skin tumor in Mr. Martin's sheepdog, through to the suturing of Mrs. Olson's prize pig, who'd run across some loose barbed wire in the field.

The only good thing she could find about it was that it had kept her happily distracted from thoughts of Brannt. And Rachel. That is— thoughts of Rachel talking about Brannt.

Shedding off her surgical garb, Cassie took herself wearily out to the lobby. She needed to confer with BJ about the pig's future appointments. Rounding the corner, Cassie was just in time to watch

Andrea Coleman come into the building through the front door. And judging by the dust covering her face, the sweat sticking to her hair, and the crumpled, half-wet material of her shirt, she'd had an even harder day than Cassie.

"Hey Andrea," BJ called hesitantly. "You look...ah..."

"It's a damn Texas heat wave out there," the veterinarian complained. "Or haven't you noticed?" Honestly, Cassie hadn't. Not really. She hadn't so much as stepped outside since eight a.m. that morning when she'd made the long trek from her upstairs apartment down to the clinic. She'd known it was hot, had heard some of the clients complain, but she hadn't thought much past the inane chatter.

"This," Andrea said, pulling at the damp material of her shirt. "Is the third shirt I've put on today. I soaked right through the first two." She made a face. Taking in Cassie's cool, clean appearance, she pointed an accusing finger. "You lucky bum, you have no idea how good you've had it today. Air-conditioning. Natural shade."

Cassie laughed. "I have to admit, you look a bit rough."

Andrea growled, her supply bag hanging limply from a thin shoulder. "I hope the heat index is out of this world when we get to trade places."

Cassie laughed good-naturedly. "Someone's a bit of a cranky-pants," she said to BJ.

The receptionist howled.

"I just want to go home, take a freezing cold shower, and go to bed. I'm fried. Literally and figuratively."

"Poor baby." BJ didn't sound the least bit upset.

"Save it," Andrea hissed. "Sitting in here where it's all cool and comfortable." She looked disgusted as her gaze switched from BJ to Cassie and back again. "Just seeing the pair of you right now—I hate you both a little bit."

"She gets like this 'round about this time every year," BJ sidelined to Cassie. "I reckon it's that Northern blood of hers."

Flopping down on one of the chairs skirting the waiting area, Andrea sent her a withering look. "Oh, shut up."

BJ laughed gaily. "No chance of that."

"Could you sound a little less pleased with this scathing heat? It's not even June yet."

"Yeah—what's the deal, BJ?"

BJ smiled softly. "I'm just setting the mood, that's all."

"What mood?" Andrea sounded downright suspicious.

"Indulge with me?"

"Think we should be worried?" Andrea asked Cassie.

"Oh, most definitely."

"Look, all I'm saying is it's almost five o'clock which means we can finally open up these!" And, with a flourish, the receptionist reached under her desk to grab out a twelve pack of beer. With a plop, she set it on the counter. "All we need to do now is put this baby on some ice and—voila! Nothing tastes better than a cold drink on a steamy day."

"Jesus BJ, put that away," Andrea hurried to say, her hand flapping nervously toward the adult beverages so proudly on display for anyone to see. "What if a client were to walk in?" Andrea scolded, but her tone was mild in the extreme.

"No problem. Cassie?" BJ asked.

Cassie looked up questioningly. "What do I have to do with it?"

"Actually, I was hoping that you'd take it upstairs to your apartment? Maybe throw it in the fridge for us, keep it chilled just 'til we get done?" Raising her eyebrow suggestively, BJ waited.

"We?" Cassie's voice was frail.

"Of course, we," BJ insisted. "Or weren't you planning on joining us?"

"Excuse me," Andrea interrupted. "When did I say yes?"

"It's roundup season," BJ informed her coolly. "Which means you're basically husbandless for the time being. Of course, you're going to say yes."

"Got it all figured out, have we?" Andrea pursed her lips.

BJ smirked. "It's ridiculously hot outside. My kids are spending the night with their grandparents. And for all intents and purposes, tonight we get to act like we're young and single again."

"I *am* young and single," Cassie reminded them.

"Tell that to half the town," BJ assured her. "They've got odds on when you and Brannt finally make it official."

Cassie felt her cheeks start to swell.

"Oh, don't listen to her," Andrea jumped in. "I'm sure it's not *half* the town." She chewed on her cheek. "It's at least two-thirds."

Cassie choked on a laugh. "You are both terrible!"

Andrea grinned.

"Come on, ladies. What do you say?"

"I'm in."

"Cassie?" Quick as lightening, BJ's eyes turned on the younger woman, their blue depths unrelenting as they stared, waiting…

"Come on, Cassie," Andrea pleaded. "Do it."

"Please?" BJ seconded, her lips pouting. "Don't deny me my few childless moments of existence."

Grinning, Cassie held up her hands in mock surrender. "Okay. Okay! Give it over."

"You're the best!"

"We'll bring the snacks!" Andrea called as Cassie made her way slowly toward the back of the building.

* * *

An hour later, Cassie popped the top of her second can of beer. Stretched out beside her on the lumpy couch, Andrea was busy shoving half a slice of pizza down her throat, and sitting across from them on the old rickety chair, BJ looked more than a little buzzed.

"...Ben said it was the hottest summer he ever remembered," Andrea said, her voice muffled as she swallowed the last of her slice. She and BJ were reminiscing on memories of Texas in July.

"Oh, it was," BJ assured her. Born and raised in Pantula, she'd know. "We spent most of that summer swimming over at the McDowell's, as I recall."

Cassie sat up a little straighter.

Andrea snapped her fingers together: "That's right; they used to have a pool. Ben told me about that..."

"Not just any old pool," BJ informed them, smiling at the memory. "An Olympic-sized pool. Climate-controlled, we kept the water cold that summer—basically lived in it."

"I've never seen a pool there," Cassie said, interrupting them.

BJ's smile slipped. She shared a look with Andrea. "Yeah. They got rid of it."

"Why?"

For a couple beats, her question was met with a heavy, stark silence. Andrea looked down at her lap. BJ sucked in her cheeks: "The pool was for Caleb, the youngest of the McDowell boys. He got a full-ride to college on a swimming scholarship."

Cassie heard the pain in BJ's voice; she picked up on the past tense. What had happened? But Cassie wasn't brave enough to ask.

Andrea took pity on her. "Caleb died his sophomore year in school. He was home on summer break—"

"It was a freak riding accident," BJ murmured, her eyes glossing over with tears. Clearly, she and Caleb had been close.

Andrea blew out her breath. "He and Brannt were out working the fences when they came across a bull which had escaped its pen..." Andrea took a deep breath. "Caleb's horse got spooked and Caleb fell off—"

"He hit his head against a rock on the way down. It killed him instantly," BJ finished, her voice dull, emotionless as her tongue tripped over the words.

"Brannt was there?" Cassie asked, picking up on that devastating fact right away.

BJ nodded solemnly.

"He saw the whole thing," Andrea whispered.

BJ sniffed. "And you know how Brannt is. He's always blamed himself for what happened. Caleb was never as good a rider as Brannt."

"Oh my God! Oh my God," Cassie whispered uneasily. "I can't imagine."

BJ nodded. "Their parents were so broken by that accident—the house, the memories. They couldn't stay." She shook her head. "Moved out to California, I think ...just left it all behind them." Her voice was thick in the telling. "Gave up cattle, gave up everything."

"They've never been back."

BJ grimaced. "Zeke neither."

"Who's Zeke?" Cassie was almost afraid to ask.

"The middle brother. He joined the military right after it happened," BJ informed the room.

"Do they—they don't blame Brannt for what happened?" Cassie asked, aghast.

"Oh, honey no. No," BJ insisted. "That kind of hurt, it changes people. That's all. They left because they couldn't stay."

"Except Brannt."

"Yeah. Except him."

Andrea shook her head. "He had no other choice but to take on ownership of the ranch and the day-to-day operations. It was that or let it all go."

"And he would never do that."

"No."

BJ sounded bitter when she continued: "He was twenty-three years old, freshly graduated from college, and he lost everyone in that summer."

Andrea smiled sadly. "And the first thing he did was have that pool filled."

Cassie swallowed difficultly, her jaw locked tight to suppress the tears she desperately wanted to shed.

It explained so many things:

Why he'd refused to talk about his brothers…

Why he'd gotten so upset when she'd run off the other day.

Why he only wanted the best veterinarian to work on his animals—Dr. Sam knew more about them than even Brannt.

Why Cassie's naivety with livestock made him so uptight and almost angry.

Brannt had buried a brother.

BJ held up a hand. "All right, all right! That's enough sad talk," she insisted, wiping at wet eyes as she did so. "How's about a change of topic?"

Andrea nodded. "Yeah. Something light." Her own voice held the wobble of unshed tears.

"Cassie?"

"Me?"

"Entertain me."

"But no pressure," Andrea teased.

"I want to be on the edge of my seat."

"Rachel came to see me today." The words popped out of Cassie's mouth before she knew she intended saying them. Fighting back a guilty conscience, she reminded herself she'd only promised not to tell Brannt about her drop-in visit. BJ and Andrea were fair game.

Her statement did the trick. Gone was the stilted sorrow of moments ago. BJ leaned forward curiously. Andrea raised an expressive eyebrow.

"Well, now. I wonder why?" BJ murmured dryly.

"You knew?" Cassie asked. News really did travel fast in a small town.

"No, but I'm not surprised, either," BJ answered honestly.

"That girl's got it bad," Andrea said pityingly.

"And he was at your apartment yesterday."

"Yeah, and who do you suppose would've told people about that? It wasn't me. It wasn't Brannt. There was only one other person who knew," Cassie said with a pointed glance at BJ.

The receptionist laughed. "Come to think of it, I may have mentioned it to someone…"

"BJ!"

"What?" She looked innocent. "I just said he helped you get into your apartment." She batted her eyelashes. "And I didn't even mention that he didn't return with your spare key for a whole fifteen minutes." She wiggled her eyebrows. "Last time I checked, it only took five seconds to turn a key in a lock…."

"All right, shut up," Cassie muttered.

BJ grinned. "That's what I thought."

"Keep it to yourself. I don't need Rachel coming at me," Cassie said, only half-joking.

She zipped a hand over her mouth. "I'm a steel vault."

"Oh God."

# CHAPTER THIRTEEN

Cassie was so mad she could've eaten nails. Dr. Sam had left without her!

To think of all the time she'd spent, wasted! Indeed, the past two nights in a row, she'd stayed up well into the twilight hours, pouring through sundry wrangler magazines, scouring through one website article after another, each claiming to produce a bonafide horseman out of the most novice of city dwellers—and in six easy steps, no less. She'd even borrowed the dry-as-dust academic books littering the shelves of the Tiamango Veterinary Clinic, all in the name of self-education, and for what? To be left behind when her presence counted most!

Cassie was done being Pantula's local greenhorn. She was done with everyone treating her like she didn't know a calf from a cow. She was done being coddled, or worse, condemned for her inadequate experience. Armed to the teeth with the newest theories and techniques, she was hell-bent to prove to everyone (and by that, of course, she really meant Brannt) that she knew her stuff, that she was a competent, knowledgeable, and damn fine animal doctor!

And look what happened.

She gnashed her teeth. It had all been for nothing. Because Dr. Sam had left without her.

It had been right there, marked clearly on the computer system: Dr. Sam w. Ms. Hastings @ McDowell E. Thursday, 9 AM.

But it was ten after nine right now, and was Cassie with Sam at Brannt's? No. No, she most certainly was not. She was sitting, stuck, at Tiamango. Abandoned.

After her enlightening evening with BJ and Andrea, Cassie had felt a sudden, unrelenting urge to demonstrate her veterinary prowess to the tall, taciturn cowboy. She was done allowing him to look out for her in some misguided notion of protection. She didn't need his surveillance, thank you very much. She didn't want his concern, rather his respect.

So she'd read and researched, and she'd paid extra close attention, waiting anxiously for Thursday to arrive—waiting for the ticking second hand on the clock. Only, it hadn't worked out the way she'd planned.

It seemed fate had had other plans, because, at the very last minute, just as she and Dr. Sam were preparing to leave, Cassie had been called to the back office. One of the other veterinarians had uncovered a new strain of a particularly violent virus and he'd invited her to observe the test results.

This wasn't an unusual request. Whenever something out of the ordinary transpired, the staff made a point of including Cassie in on the procedure. It was a way to further her experience. She'd always appreciated the gesture before now.

She'd been gone for a matter of minutes—her eyes skimming over the analysis sheet of the infective agent, her brain barely registering the findings held within, her interest hardly held by the submicroscopic parasite...but when she'd retraced her steps back into the main lobby, Sam had disappeared. Asking BJ after his whereabouts had confirmed it.

"Sam? He left a couple minutes ago. I thought you'd be with him?" BJ looked mildly confused. But, at the shocked outrage racing across Cassie's features, that woman had hurried to add: "Don't worry Cass, he'll be back soon. He only has the one visit this morning—"

But Cassie hadn't looked any too placated.

All that study time down the drain. And even worse, a snarky little voice said at the back of her head, Brannt will probably think it was *your* decision not to come, that you chickened out after that kiss.

And that, truth be told, was the real crux of the matter. Cassie's pride couldn't stand for it. Then again, what other option did she have? For starters, Dr. Sam had the truck (i.e. her only means of transportation in this god-forsaken little town, where the phrase 'loaner vehicle' was about as foreign as French cheese). And for another, Brannt had only scheduled a simple fecal egg count, a procedure which hardly called for two people. Even if she managed to get her hands on another steering wheel, careering out there all breathless and excited would only make her look desperate—like some pathetic school-girl, running at any chance to see Brannt.

And really, wasn't that exactly what she was doing anyway?

She was damned if she did and damned if she didn't.

And talking to Dr. Sam about it later, after he'd finally returned, hadn't helped at all. His only reaction to Cassie's quick, terse demand to know why she'd been left behind had been a raised eyebrow and an off-side grin.

"It was only a simple drench Cass, nothing you haven't seen before," he offered mildly and, when Cassie had her mouth open to argue, he wondered curiously: "Was there some reason you particularly wanted to go?"

"No! I mean, no. Not really—" Cassie hedged heatedly. "It's just...."

Dr. Sam patted her on the shoulder. "Well, I promise it wasn't very eventful. Now, tell me about that specimen Simon uncovered!" His abrupt and firm change of subject couldn't be ignored. What else could she do? So Cassie told him what the tests had revealed. The day, which had started with such anticipatory promise, dwindled to a dull, unexciting close.

The excitement, did Cassie but know it, wouldn't start until the following afternoon. It was while she was busy restocking the shelves in the lobby with merchandise that she heard the small bell over the door chime.

It was five minutes to the end of business hours. Dr. Sam was in the lab, finishing up some blood work and BJ had taken off early, leaving Cassie to man the front desk. Turning at the sound, she almost dropped the armload of dog food in her arms when her eyes clashed with a pair of silvery grey ones.

"What…?" Cassie's voice came out no louder than a whisper. Clearing her throat, she tried again. "Brannt. What a surprise."

His look mocked her attempt at casualness.

"I'm sure," he drawled, stepping further into the room. He was such a big, masculine man.

Cassie took a step backward, her legs bumping loudly into the shelving unit behind her. "What are you doing here?" she asked uncertainly.

"Nervous, Cassie?" His eyes raked over the empty room. "Nowhere to run and hide this time?"

Cassie sucked in a breath. "That's not fair," she cried, waving her arms in abject frustration, the animal food shifting wildly in her hold. "Yesterday… It wasn't what you're thinking. I didn't—! Dr. Sam left without me. I didn't even know he'd gone until…" She heaved a great sigh.

Brannt raised a sardonic eyebrow.

"I got called to assist another vet. Otherwise, I would have been there."

"I'm sure."

"Believe me," Cassie spat, tossing the dog food down on a nearby chair. "You aren't that special, Brannt. Just another client as far as I'm concerned. So tell me, why should I run from that?" Whipping back her mane of hair, Cassie lifted her chin up a notch. So take that, she thought silently, as she waited for his response.

It was slow in coming.

Brannt took two steps closer to her. "Feel better now?" he asked, his voice caressing in the stillness of the animal hospital.

Cassie cocked her head to the side.

"For getting all that off your chest," he prompted at her look. His smile widened. It had a menacing, hard edge to it.

Cassie choked. "I just don't want there to be any misunderstandings."

"And I've been carefully put in my place, haven't I?" he asked silkily. Then, pulling himself up to his full height, his expression one of faint boredom, he continued: "Now, if you're finished—" he paused meaningfully. "I actually stopped by for a reason. I need to pick up a gallon of mosquito repellent."

It was the way he said it, with thinly veiled impatience and amusement. His words, their cavalier delivery, made Cassie's passionate outburst something idiotic, uncalled for...a big fat waste of breath and time. There she stood, staunchly defending herself when he clearly didn't care, hadn't given it a single thought.

If she hadn't been so frazzled by his indifference she may have questioned his so-called excuse for being at the clinic. Mosquito repellent? Brannt McDowell, as she was now well aware, did not run such frivolous errands. He had men to do that for him. In fact, his ranch foreman George Jacobs had been by only three days prior to pick up such routine staples. Surely he wouldn't have forgotten something as elementary as that?

But Cassie *was* frazzled. And, quite frankly, she was too exhausted to go another round against his army of wit. So, without further ado, her shoulders drooping, Cassie went to retrieve the requested item before making her way quickly back behind the safety of the receptionist desk. She didn't say a single word to him during this exchange, nor did she proffer up a single token of conversation as she tracked his order on the office computer system. As far as she was concerned, they had nothing further to say to one another.

Unfortunately, her stomach didn't seem to agree because, at that very moment, just as she was typing up his order form, it let out a loud, terrible gurgling sound.

Feeling her face flame, Cassie stared all the harder at the computer screen before her. She'd skipped lunch that morning. It had been a hectic day, what with three emergency calls, and one staff member out sick. Stopping for a quick bite had been out of the question.

She should have known better than to suppose Brannt would let that go.

"Hungry, Cassie?" he teased softly.

Before she could respond, her stomach rumbled again. Bracing a quick hand against the offending body part, she refused to meet Brannt's eyes. "Ever the observant one," she replied tartly. Why must every weakness of hers be shown on such display to Brannt of all people?

"Yeah, me too," he returned surprisingly. Cassie's eyes rebelled, flicking up to catch the expression on his face. He didn't look to be making fun of her. That was a first.

"I couldn't stop for lunch," Cassie confessed, though why she felt the need to confide in him she hadn't the slightest idea.

Brannt leaned elegantly against the high-top counter. "Then you really must make sure you get a proper supper."

There was something predatory in those words. Hurriedly printing out his invoice, Cassie searched for some kind of response. She came up blank.

Brannt, however, didn't seem to be having any such difficulties in that department. "I'm going to call in a dinner reservation at Bev's

Steakhouse for eight o'clock tonight," he persisted at her silence, his tone conversational in the utmost. Until that is, he added: "Join me?"

Cassie's heart kicked hard against her chest, knocking out her breath. "Wh-what?" She couldn't have heard him correctly.

"No misunderstandings?" he reminded her quietly. "Well, here's your chance to prove it. Have dinner with me tonight, Cassie."

\* \* \*

Glancing up surreptitiously from the menu in front of her face, Cassie looked over at Brannt. His head was bare of its usual cowboy hat. Dark auburn hair fell thick and clean across his brow, skimming over the tops of his ears, the ends tickling against the white collar of his shirt. It needed a trim. And yet, it suited him.

Skipping her gaze to the right, she took in the restaurant where they were seated: white linen table cloths on intimate round tables; heavy wooden chandeliers; thick blue and white patterned brocade curtains at the numerous windows; a tall custom-made hostess stand directly across from the glass enclosed double-doors. The room smelled like polish, floral perfume, and sizzling steak.

She still couldn't quite believe Brannt McDowell had asked her out to dinner, still couldn't quite believe she'd said yes, that she was currently sitting down opposite him.

Cassie's head had spun wildly at his invitation, at the quiet challenge laced within it. *Have dinner with me tonight, Cassie.* For the span of a second, she hadn't spoken, the air around the veterinary office growing tense in the aftermath. It hadn't been a question of whether or not she'd accept his offer. She knew she'd say yes. It had boiled down to pride. She couldn't agree to it just like that, could she? That would be too easy, too eager and the smug cowboy didn't deserve either. And yet, she didn't want him to just leave.

It was messy, complicated. Had he not taken her by such surprise, she probably would have done much better, held her composure.

In the end, his penetrating gaze never once lifting from her face, Cassie heard herself saying: "I don't need to prove anything to you, Brannt." The quiver in her voice, however, made a lie of her cool tone. Tearing the invoice off the printer, just to give her hands something to do, she fought for her next line. "But, as it happens, I do enjoy a good steak."

"Is that a yes, Cassie?" Brannt had taunted.

"Yes, Brannt," she'd seethed, talking through the tight grip of her teeth. "That's a yes."

He pushed himself elegantly off the counter. "I'll pick you up at seven-thirty."

"I'll meet you there at eight," Cassie had returned pointedly. She'd smiled sweetly at his quick frown. "As we agreed: no misunderstandings."

He'd rolled his eyes, rather extravagantly, at that. Probably to make her feel like an idiot. It'd worked. "Fine. Whatever. I'll meet you in the parking lot at eight o'clock." With that, he'd left.

Frantically locking up after him, Cassie had hardly had the peace of mind to remember to turn off all the lights in the building before racing up to her apartment. She still had to shower, blow-dry her hair, find a nice outfit, re-polish her nails—and had she remembered to bring those black, patent leather pumps with her from home…?

By the time she'd exited her apartment, Cassie's hair was nicely styled off her face by way of a butterfly clip, the long tresses left cascading down her shoulders and back in an artlessly wavy fashion. She'd donned a blue paisley-patterned knee-length dress, which she'd paired with buckskin cowboy boots. (The shoes had been a wash. Every box and stray compartment in Cassie's small loft had been thoroughly upended in her rush to find them. The result being a mess of clothing trailing from the closet to the bathroom and out to the living room, which had turned up only the lost companion to a pair of socks.) Other than her lips, painted a ruby red, which she'd assured herself matched her summer tan nicely, she'd left her face make-up free. She hadn't wanted to send the wrong signal, after all.

Now, sitting across from Brannt, watching him unobtrusively, Cassie was glad of that decision. He'd traded his usual jeans and button-up shirt for a pair of dark corduroy pants and a white, expertly cut, long sleeved dress shirt. His hair he'd brushed off his face, though one particularly persistent tendril had a habit of falling forward across his right eyebrow. It was doing it now. Cassie would never, ever admit it out loud, but it only made him look sexier.

"Cassie?" Brannt's voice, the insistent quality of it, cut her inspection short.

Glancing up, she caught his patent stare. "Yes?" She had the distinct, lowering, impression it wasn't the first time he'd called out her name just then. This feeling was only strengthened by what he said next.

"Are you ready to order?" Brannt asked, his eyes shifting emphatically to the left, where a black-and-white uniformed server stood, hovering before their table.

Cassie followed his gaze meekly. She hadn't noticed the young man standing there, had been so lost in her thoughts she hadn't seen him approach, hadn't heard him ask if they'd had a chance to decide what they were having for dinner. So now, she looked like an idiot.

"Oh…uh, yes, I'm ready," Cassie stammered, too humiliated to admit that she'd only been using her menu as a cover, that she hadn't read a single word typed on its beautiful stationary. Strangling the edges of it in her hands, her eyes traveled feverishly down its cursive print… "I'll have the 9-ounce New York Strip, please," she announced, reading off the first item her eyes latched on to.

"Would you like any special sauces with that?" The waiter asked politely, not even a hint of expression in the somber question.

"Oh—" Cassie bit down on her lip.

"If I may," Brannt said suavely, only the timbre of his voice conveying his abject amusement at her scramble. Anytime he could see her stumble, damn him! "I would recommend the mushroom hollandaise. It's magnificent here."

Cassie nodded mutely, her eyes focused on the crystal water glass before her plate setting.

"And would we care for any wine tonight?" The waiter asked, his look taking in the open wine list pushed to the left of Brannt's elbow.

"Yes," Brannt assured him before quickly rattling off the particular bottle of his choosing. The name alone would have been impossible for Cassie to pronounce, but Brannt's accent sounded flawless. Even the stuffy waiter looked mildly impressed with his fluency before beating a silent retreat.

"So, you know wines?" Cassie asked curiously. As far as conversation starters, it wasn't the most scintillating, but then again...

Brannt inclined his head a fraction of an inch. "Doesn't fit your description of the common cowboy, huh? My tastes shouldn't surpass that of cold beans and cheap beer, is that about right?"

Cassie felt her body stiffen at the edge in his voice. It had been a bad idea, coming here with him. Why had she thought it'd be any different than all the other barbs? "This isn't going to work, is it?" she asked on a sigh. She pushed her chair back.

"Cassie..." Brannt growled, his voice low and hushed. His eyes swept over the other patrons in the place.

"I should go," she said, the words trembling.

"You'll stay right where you are unless you want to make a spectacle of yourself," he hissed.

"What's the difference?" She laughed humorlessly. "We can't go five minutes being civil to one another." With both hands planted on the table, she made to rise...

"Stop," Brannt demanded, his hand reaching across the table to capture her quickly fleeing wrist. "Sit down for Christ's sake." He exhaled deeply. "Please."

She gave him a beseeching look, but she did as she was told. "I don't want to fight with you anymore."

"Me neither," Brannt said to surprise her. The next words appeared hard for him to say: "I shouldn't have jumped down your throat like that. I apologize."

"We can't seem to help it, can we? It's like we're always looking for the insult in whatever the other is saying."

Brannt considered this. "Then let's call a truce," he offered. "I'll stop being defensive if you will."

Cassie looked at him warily.

"Just for tonight, Cass?" he teased softly.

She shifted. "I'm willing to try if you are."

"My mother taught me about wine."

Cassie blinked at this soft confession, the quick redirection. Biting down on her lip, she kept her mouth shut, afraid he'd stop speaking.

But he didn't. "She traveled to vineyards, organized taste-testing parties, consorted with sundry sommelier. She'd always say: 'I may live with cattle, but I don't live without culture.'"

Cassie smiled.

"She taught us how to appreciate a good bouquet, how to differentiate between vintage and region, how to pair the drink with food..."

And just like that, a sort of enchantment fell over the evening. Brannt talked about wine, about his very first experience on a horse (and how he'd slipped right off the other side of the saddle as he'd attempted to mount the large animal). Cassie told him a little bit about her life back home—her parents and her friends, and the intramural soccer team she played on in the summer, and how she was easily the team's worst player. They laughed over a shared interest in astronomy...and all the while, his hand never left hers once.

# CHAPTER FOURTEEN

The next morning, as Cassie was preparing a sheep dog for surgery, she couldn't quite keep the smile off her face, couldn't quite keep her eyes from glancing over toward her phone. Carefully buzzing the dog's coarse hair, she spoke softly to the sedated creature. She'd been speaking to him all morning, whether he wanted to listen or not.

"I'm telling you, he was different, Ruger," she assured him. Putting the clippers back down on her trolley, she nodded her head decisively. "Open, honest..." She spoke confidentially. "It wasn't supposed to be a date, but I think it was."

The animal rolled its tongue out of the side of its mouth, content for the moment to remain on the table, under the gentle hand of Cassie as she stroked his soft head.

"He held my hand, did I tell you that?" she asked him. "Yes, I did, didn't I?" she realized, laughing softly. "And every now and again, his thumb would reach across and caress my knuckles. I just kept praying my palm wouldn't get sweaty!"

Shaking her head, her mind rewound back to Bev's Steakhouse, back to the evening before. "It was the way he spoke to me. Just vague terms, mostly, but there was something in the way he said things. Something intimate."

Like when he'd asked if she'd visited the town's old drive-in movie theater yet. Apparently, it still ran classics on the weekends. When Cassie had shyly assured him that, indeed, she had not, he'd responded with something like: "Well, we'll have to rectify that fact, won't we?"

"That line could have meant anything," Cassie said to the dog. "Or nothing at all."

That 'we' could have meant the town of Pantula in general, and not her and Brannt in particular; or it may have simply been an offhand comment, something the locals said to out-of-towners, a sightseeing opportunity. "Of course, he wasn't necessarily saying he'd take me to a movie," she commented out loud. Rather it could have merely been *his* opinion (as the second party 'we') that it was something *she*, (as the party of the first) should not miss. "But I don't think so," Cassie murmured softly, her thoughts as scattered as her one-sided conversation.

"And there were other things, too," she insisted. "And, I don't know, they always seemed to suggest something *more*...you know what I mean?" she asked the neutered animal, who'd never experienced anything of the sort.

"And certainly, he'd seemed to be in no hurry to conclude our evening. Which says something, don't you think?"

They'd polished off two bottles of wine before Brannt had finally signaled for the check. By then, Cassie's face had been nicely flushed, her eyes bright with feeling. And though it had been fast nearing eleven o'clock, she'd been reluctant for the night to end.

Gracefully rising from her seat, she'd barely gained her feet when she found Brannt beside her, his hand coming to rest easily against the small of her back as he led her toward the front entrance. Cassie's spine still tingled at the memory of that contact. She'd felt...branded.

She'd been grateful for the support of that hand when, seconds later, they'd reached the hostess stand. She would have lost her footing without it when Brannt suddenly leaned down, his mouth poised beside her ear, his breath sending shivers against her sensitive skin when he spoke.

"If I haven't told you yet, Cassie, you look beautiful tonight."

Ducking her head demurely, she'd peeked up at him through the fringe of her eyelashes. There was a peculiar look on his face when she caught his expression. Something mildly possessive.

"Flattery, Mr. McDowell?" she'd teased softly. "I didn't know you had it in you."

He'd grinned wolfishly. "Nothing of the sort," he'd assured her. "Just stating the facts as I see them."

She could get used to that Brannt.

"Oh, and I almost forgot to mention another thing—" she confided to the quiet animal before her. "As we walked up to the coat check, Brannt ran into an old business acquaintance. I think his name was Jonathon," Cassie mused, thinking hard. She smiled down at Ruger, whose eyes were starting to look heavy in his sweet, white-and-tan face. "Anyway, at first I didn't think anything of it, just reached for my coat as the men said hello and shook hands, but then Brannt turned to me—"

"Cassie," he'd said, sweeping her closer to his side, "do you know Jonathon DuWald? He owns the hardware store down on Main Street."

She'd shaken her head. "It's a pleasure to meet you, Jonathon."

"Jonathon, this is our resident student at the Tiamango Veterinary Clinic," Brannt had gone on to say, keeping the reins of the conversation firmly in his hands.

Jonathon had tipped his hat in her direction, his whiskered face breaking out into a nice, if hesitant, smile. "How do you do, ma'am?" he'd inquired politely, but his eyes were steady on Brannt's face.

Cassie had smiled shyly, but before she'd had a chance to respond Brannt had spoken, his dark eyes sweeping over her face: "Charmed, I can only hope." There was a husky implication in those words, his eyes meaningful as they stared at her upturned expression. "I know I am."

Cassie had colored delicately.

Jonathon had cleared his throat.

"Well, don't let me keep you..." Jonathon's eyes were averted, though there was nothing amiss with his tone of voice. Cassie thought perhaps he'd been hiding secret amusement.

"Have a nice evening," Cassie had managed to say in farewell before Brannt had brushed her steadily out of the building and into the well-lit parking lot.

"He was so protective, almost possessive—but in a good way. It was like he wanted people to know he was with me, and I was with him," she murmured dreamily now. Ruger was snoring faintly by this point. Hardly an ideal listener but Cassie didn't mind.

"Then, well you know the rest," she reminded the animal. After all, it had been the first thing she'd said to Ruger upon settling him in the exam room that morning. The walk outside.

She and Brannt hadn't parked near one another. The restaurant had been so full when Cassie had arrived she'd considered it lucky she'd gotten any spot at all. Now that most of the diners had dispensed for the evening, she'd been forced to see with some dismay that almost the entire length of the lot separated her truck from his.

Her mind had spun. Saying goodbye was already awkward enough in situations like this—and really, how did one define her and Brannt's particular situation, anyway? Was this merely a dinner between colleagues, a ceasefire between sparring partners or...something more? Well, whatever the hell it was, they'd have to end it rather abruptly now, halfway down the parking lot—forced to stand there, awkwardly, somewhere between his vehicle and hers.

There'd be no natural transition to the end of the night—at least not the way an open car door neatly severed one, anyway. No, instead they'd be forced to wait for the other person to make the first move, a protracted step backward, a well-placed check at their watch, the carefully enunciated "Well..."

The parking lot linger.

The most uncomfortable few moments, spent in a frantic kind of small talk, anything to beat back the dread of silence. It was then that Cassie admitted, if only to herself, that she should have let Brannt pick her up like he'd originally intended.

On the thought, she'd felt her feet slowing to a stop. It was probably best not to overthink it. Just say: "Thank you for the pleasant evening. Goodnight Brannt," and walk away.

Only she hadn't been given the chance. When she'd gone to break away from the hold Brannt still had on her, his hand had only pressed more firmly against the curve of her hip, forestalling the movement. She'd felt her feet being steered in the opposite direction.

"But...I'm over there," Cassie had said, her head bobbing toward Dr. Sam's beat-up work truck.

"To hell with your car," Brannt had bit out. Turning toward her, his hand had moved from her back to encircle her waist.

"Brannt?" she asked a touch breathlessly. She knew that look in his eyes.

"You said no misunderstandings?" he reminded her unnecessarily. Oh, she remembered all right.

"Then let me make myself very clear," he expressed, before quickly tugging her nearer. "This is what I want," he told her seconds before his mouth swooped down against hers.

Moaning at the unexpectedness of it, or had it really been unexpected? Hadn't she secretly been hoping he'd do something like this all night? Cassie's fingers had curled around his forearms as her mouth pushed roughly upward. His breath was hot, sweetly scented with the delicious cabernet they'd consumed... twisting her neck frantically to the side, this time it was Cassie who'd deepened the kiss.

Her aggressive response had momentarily knocked Brannt for a shock, but he'd recovered quickly, his teeth nipping gently, and then not-so-gently, a low growl gaining momentum from deep within his throat as his tongue swirled tantalizing patterns against the thrust of her own.

Cassie hadn't heard the door to the restaurant open, hadn't noticed the stares of passing patrons. She'd only vaguely recognized the sound of an engine turning over, of the fluorescent streetlight buzzing down over her mussed hair—her butterfly clip had long since lost its hold, the clasp hanging limply against her curls. Her eyes had been closed too tightly for any of that, her ears drumming heavily with the beat of her rapidly thumping heart.

"It was the most amazing kiss ever," Cassie told Ruger, who'd been sound asleep for some minutes now. She sighed.

If she closed her eyes, she could almost—the quiet, insistent beep from her watch, however, stopped her short. That was the five-minute alarm. Ruger's surgery was set to begin soon.

"Better go get Sam," Cassie murmured, with a last look at the peacefully snoring dog. Walking toward the surgery door, she stepped out into the hallway. She was halfway down the corridor when she heard it.

"It was a low thing to do...he couldn't have made his intentions any clearer if he'd just taken her to Betsy's Diner," a woman said sharply, the sound echoing from the front lobby.

Walking closer, Cassie just had time to make out BJ's response: "Guess he reached the end of his patience."

The other woman sighed disgustedly.

A tingling sensation of alarm stole through Cassie. Freezing behind the bulk of wall hiding her from sight, she pressed her ears closer, waiting...

"You know as well as I do that he's tried to rebuke her attractions before now, and she just wouldn't listen."

The woman scoffed. "But to rub it in her face like that? The whole town watched them canoodling all night. He even stooped so far as to shove her in Jon's face…Jon! Rachel may be tireless in her pursuit of getting Brannt's attention, but to go to such lengths—to openly reject her like that, and to the girl's own father?! The shame!"

Cassie felt dizzy.

Jon. Jonathon DuWald. He was Rachel's father?

BJ's voice was low and sympathetic. "We all warned her that something like this might happen, that at some point Brannt would finally lose his patience with her persistent chase. He's tried to be nice, to let her down easy, but she just wouldn't take the hint. Every time, she took it like another challenge, like she'd wear him down eventually. Looks like she did, just not in the way she'd imagined."

The woman snorted.

"How is she?" BJ asked quietly.

"How do you think? You should have seen her this morning down at the restaurant, just bawling her eyes out. And there's Bev smacking her jaw all over town about Brannt's new girl."

BJ made a tisking sound. "I'll drop by this afternoon, bring her some of my homemade chicken noodle soup."

The other woman didn't seem to have even heard her. "What I really don't understand, however, is why Cassie agreed to go along with this charade? She seems like such a nice person. It's pretty hard and underhanded, parading around with Brannt like that for the sole purpose of breaking another girl's heart…."

Cassie felt her stomach drop.

Charade? Breaking another girl's heart? This was all about Brannt rejecting Rachel?

No, it couldn't have been. It couldn't have…

"Maybe it wasn't just done for Rachel's benefit," BJ inquired, and Cassie loved the woman a little more for it. "Everyone's been wondering about the two of them. Who knows, maybe they finally—"

"Please, BJ," the loud-mouth went on, "from everything I've heard, they couldn't keep their hands, or their mouths for that matter, off one another the entire evening. It was a public scene. You know as well as I do that Brannt doesn't behave that way with the women he dates. He's a private man who conducts his affairs in just such a manner."

"Yeah." Now even BJ sounded hesitant.

"Can you honestly picture him taking a woman out and, and practically seducing her right there on the table for everyone to see?"

There was a long pause and then: "No. I don't guess I can."

Cassie thought she might be sick.

"Exactly." The woman sounded oddly proud of gaining BJ's capitulation. "This was all for show, to prove to Rachel in a cruel sort of way that he's done being her pet project."

"Be that as it may, I'm sure Cassie had her reasons for going along with it and it had nothing to do with being cruel," BJ defended. "She's a good person. You don't know her very well, but I do. She must have thought it would help in the end."

"They wanted to give the town something to talk about? Well, they did."

Whatever BJ said to that, Cassie never heard. Stumbling against the wall, her mind flashed back to the prior evening, her eyes seeing everything a little differently this time....

## CHAPTER FIFTEEN

Brannt's thumb circling across her knuckles—

Cassie closed her eyes. Someone had walked by their table when he'd done that. She remembered that vaguely now. Just as his thumb had arched across her skin...who was that? Ah, yes, Cole Bergen.

The superintendent of the local grocery store had come into view at the exact moment that Brannt made that move. Focusing hard, she could just make out the man's outline from her peripheral vision. Famous for his volunteer outreach efforts, Mr. Bergen was in almost constant contact with the entire town of Pantula, in one capacity or another.

It had been Brannt's left hand, the one closest to the end of the table, the one most readily on display, which had held Cassie's so snugly. Coincidence?

At the time, she'd thought it a spontaneous gesture, something which spoke of intent. Oh, it had definitely been intentional, just not of the sort she'd been led to believe.

Oh God.

"If I haven't told you yet, Cassie, you look beautiful tonight."

Brannt had whispered that seductively in her ear as they'd prepared to leave. But when she'd looked up at him, smiling like a foolish girl, there had been this look on his face. Cassie hadn't been able to define it at first but now she knew. It had been cutting calculation.

Because behind the hostess stand, barely a foot away, had stood none other than Bev Hickley, the proprietor of the restaurant. Bev, the town's biggest, juiciest gossip.

Cassie swallowed hard.

Brannt had been seen whispering sweet nothings in Cassie's ear to the only woman in the joint who'd happily spread that news as surely as if she owned a broadcasting station. And Cassie had fallen for it, hook-line-and-sinker.

It was all starting to make a sickening sort of sense. Everything that had been done had been done with purpose, under precise timing. Putting a shaking hand up against her mouth, Cassie kept replaying the night over again, putting the fragmented pieces together:

They hadn't rushed out after finishing their meal. Brannt had seemed only too content to remain right where he was, even stooping to order a second bottle of wine. Cassie hadn't offered up a token protest, either. Lulled into a false sense of security, she'd happily let the conversation flow gently between them, her hands playing with the stem of her wineglass. She'd been consumed by him. But he'd only been letting everyone get their eye-full. No one would be left unaware that Brannt and Cassie were out on a date. A three-hour date.

And then, when they *had* stood up to leave…Cassie felt bile rise up in her throat. It had been so sudden, his quick signal to the hovering waiter for the bill. Closing her eyes tightly, Cassie saw it all again. One moment Brannt had been smiling across the expanse of table at her and in the next, his eyes had shifted, interrupted by the presence of someone walking past them. She hadn't thought anything of it at the time, but with the clarity of hindsight…

Focusing hard, Cassie tried to remember who it was that Brannt had seen, but then, it didn't much matter if she could properly identify them in that moment or not. She knew who it was. Only one other person had met them at coat check. It was rather a dead giveaway, wasn't it?

Twenty seconds had separated Brannt and Cassie's exit from that of the other individual.

Jonathon. That's who had walked by. Rachel's father.

Brannt had done a good job, acting surprised when they'd joined him in the foyer. Because he hadn't been surprised at all, had he?

It had been a deliberate move.

Tears crowded Cassie's throat.

Oh. And the kiss.

Biting back a sob, Cassie pressed a hand to her mouth.

She'd been about to walk away in that parking lot, on the verge of saying goodnight when Brannt had stopped her. Only, he hadn't just stopped her, had he? He'd moved her too. Just a little to the left.

Right under the parking lot lamp, where they would be most noticed.

Curling her fingers into tight, impotent fists, Cassie clenched her teeth together, anything to keep the sound of her feelings at bay. She was still at Tiamango. She needed to find Dr. Sam. They had a surgery to attend to.

Brannt had used her. Viciously.

She was so lost in her thoughts she didn't see the door opening farther down the hallway, didn't notice Dr. Sam emerging out of the shadows from within. But he saw her. In that moment, she couldn't have known how badly her face looked.

"Cassie?" Dr. Sam asked, his steps taking him quickly to her side. "What's wrong?" His voice was soft with concern, the way it was when he spoke to skittish animals.

Jerking at the sound of her name, Cassie pushed herself off the wall. Wiping circumspectly at the tears crowding her eyes, she shook her head. "Nothing. Sinuses, that's all." She would rather die than admit to the truth. "Are you ready for the surgery?"

There was no mistaking the snubbed change of conversation.

Dr. Sam looked like he wanted to say something more, but then he changed his mind. "Yes. Ruger's all set to go?"

Cassie straightened her shoulders. Nothing would compromise her professionalism. Nothing. "Yes."

"All right. Let's begin."

\* \* \*

Cassie wasn't sure how she made it through the rest of that day. Her stomach twisted with a dull sort of ache. Her chest felt too tight. Both of which were made worse by the questioning looks she'd fielded from BJ all afternoon. The woman hadn't said anything to Cassie about her so-called date with Brannt, hadn't so much as breathed in suggestion of it, but her eyes had been searching, nervous, filled with doubts.... Dr. Sam had been almost as bad, walking wide circles around Cassie.

Later that evening, aimlessly prowling the length of her small upstairs loft, Cassie tried to calm down. Now that she was finally allowed to give full vent to her feelings, she found herself buoyed up with an energy she didn't know how to extinguish. It seemed to be eating her alive.

She wanted some answers for last night.

She was terrified to learn the truth, to have her fears recognized.

She paced some more.

It couldn't have *all* been fabricated. She'd felt his attraction. It had been right there between them—an almost tangible thing, hadn't it? Or was this just her ego talking, pride refusing to believe she'd been so thoroughly duped. Not just duped but hurt, ravaged.

She wanted answers for last night.

She'd know no peace until she had them.

Reaching for her purse, Cassie grabbed the truck keys off the kitchen counter.

Nothing could be worse than the torture of not knowing.

She wanted answers and she wanted them tonight.

\* \* \*

That thought took Cassie all the way through town and down the country road that would eventually lead her up the long drive to the McDowell Estate. Parking crookedly before the front sweep, she killed the engine. Without giving herself time to change her mind, she climbed out of the vehicle.

Brannt had used her to hurt another woman. He'd made a first-rate idiot out of Cassie. Gaining the front steps, Cassie marched herself up to the door. He'd made a bully out of her. Pressing her finger against the buzzer, Cassie waited for the fall of footsteps she knew belonged to Brannt.

She didn't have to wait long.

Brannt's face was a picture of incredulity when he swung the heavy door open and saw her standing on the other side.

"Cassie?" he asked, and to her ears, he sounded uneasy, edgy. Probably he thought she'd taken him so seriously last night that she'd come to literally throw herself at him. It would have served him right if she had!

Nerves momentarily seized Cassie's speech, her thoughts melding at the forthcoming confrontation. Drawing herself up to her full height, she repeated the words that had brought her here. Plain and simple: "I want some answers. Right now."

Brannt cocked his head a little to one side, a small smile playing at the corners of his mouth. "Excuse me?"

"Last night. Was it,"—Cassie licked her lips, unsure how to proceed. "Was it just a ploy, some twisted means to an end? What's that line, you must be cruel to be kind?" She laughed roughly, the sound ugly. "Was I some demented kind of bait?"

Brannt's eyebrows furrowed. "What the hell are you talking about?"

Cassie curled her lips. "Rachel. I'm talking about Rachel."

And then his expression cleared. And the look on his face told Cassie everything she needed to know.

"You son of a bitch!"

"Cassie, wait!" Reaching out, his hand made contact with her fingers. Flinching, Cassie yanked her arm back.

"Let me explain…"

"Go to hell." She took a stumbling step backward.

"Cassie. Stop."

"Why bother?" She cried. "You're too late. I heard it all. The whole grisly story. Everyone's talking about it, about how you used me to get to her."

He shook his head. "No, that's not—"

"Was that why?" Cassie felt tears crowding her throat. "Just be honest. Was that why you asked me out to dinner?"

He hesitated. "There were many reasons why I asked you out to dinner. "

"But Rachel was one of them, right?"

Brannt made a low sound in his throat. "No, but…"

Cassie wasn't listening to him, didn't believe him anyway. "Why didn't you just tell me the truth about what we were doing there? I mean why lie, why try to cover it up?"

"I wasn't—"

"Because you knew I'd never go for it if you did?" Cassie interrupted him, her head nodding alongside the words. "Yeah, that makes sense."

Brannt's jaw clenched, his face tautening over his cheekbones. "If you would let me get more than two words out at a time…" The threat in his voice was unavoidable.

Cassie snapped her mouth shut, hands planted firmly on her hips. The overhead porch light cast ghostly shadows over her expression. With a wave of her hand, she invited him to speak. "Go ahead."

Brannt sighed. "I asked you out because I wanted to spend the evening with you."

"Sure, and that's why you made such a point of introducing me to Rachel's father."

Brannt's hand tightened its hold against the side of the door he was still holding. "That wasn't..." He shook his head. "Yes, I wanted him to see me with you, but that was only after—"

"So you admit it was premeditated?" She could hardly spit out the words.

"No," Brannt insisted. "But when I realized all the attention we were gaining..."

"You decided to play up to it?"

"The whole town was watching us, getting their fill of what they'd already stamped as a romantic encounter, regardless of anything I could have said or done to stifle that theory."

"So you used it to your benefit."

Brannt's eyes shifted. "When I saw Jonathon enter the restaurant," he blew out a tired breath. "Yeah, okay, I thought...I wanted him to see me with you."

Cassie braced herself.

His chin jutted out arrogantly. "I figured I'd let local gossip work in my favor for once. I thought maybe if he were the one to tell her, I don't know, that it might finally get through."

"So you were doing Rachel a kindness?" Cassie bit out the words.

Brannt sighed. "Rachel's a nice kid, but she won't take no for an answer. Uses any excuse she can find to tag along after me, to pester me. She's a nuisance. I've tried to politely brush off her advances but that only made her try harder." He shrugged with cruel finality.

"But public humiliation, that would be her cure?" Cassie laughed harshly. "How heroic of you."

He gritted his teeth. "I thought public testimony would make her see sense."

"So Jonathon's being there was just some big coincidence?" Cassie asked. It was really too much.

Brannt seemed to understand the incredulity. "I didn't know he'd be there if that's what you're asking."

"I'm so sure."

"I didn't," he insisted roughly.

"And what about me?" Cassie asked, her voice getting a little higher. "What about my feelings? I thought—" biting back the words, Cassie couldn't bring herself to admit how seriously she'd taken him that night.

"So you made this big production of taking me out to dinner, of parading me throughout town, all so you could safely get Rachel's attentions averted elsewhere, and it never entered your head to tell me about it? To give me notice of the sham of a date we were on?"

"For the last time," Brannt bit out, "It wasn't—!"

"How foolish I must look to you now," Cassie went on brokenly. "Standing here, so upset because I was too blind to realize the truth. That I was merely a prop in your little game."

"Stop it," Brannt demanded. Inhaling roughly, he tried again. "It wasn't a sham."

"It just wasn't exactly what it appeared to be, either," Cassie finished for him, monotone.

"Dammit Cassie, what do you want me to say?" Brannt asked, exasperated. "Yes, I wanted our date to prove to Rachel, once and for all, that I'm not available. But that wasn't—look, it was nothing more than a convenient opportunity, an after-thought to an evening we were *already* enjoying. So I decided to put it to good use. But it wasn't a lie, Cassie. I asked you out for myself, not for her."

"Maybe so," Cassie conceded, "but she certainly had an effect on the way you treated me that night. Caressing my hands, whispering suggestively in my ear, kissing me…! Can you honestly say that had nothing to do with *Rachel*?"

Brannt's hesitation cut Cassie to the quick.

"I didn't think so," she whispered. "All of that was false, disgusting now."

Brannt looked like he was at the end of his rope, his brows crashing against one another, his lips pulling down dangerously. "Dammit Cassie, you're not listening to me."

"Oh, I've heard enough. I just don't believe what you're saying," she clarified. Backing up toward the stairs, she shook her head savagely, her hand reaching out for the railing.

"If you would just stop—"

But she was already at the head of the front steps. "What's the point? We have nothing left to say to one another." Pivoting on her heel, she walked away. Ignoring the sound of her name on Brannt's lips, Cassie opened the truck door, her legs shaking as she clamored onto the seat. Her fingers cranked hard on the ignition.

Rachel wasn't the only person who'd been humiliated.

Holding back tears she was too proud to shed, Cassie drove herself back into town. She would not cry over Brannt McDowell. It had been one date. Nothing to get worked up about. It's not like it had been anything serious.

Pulling up outside her small apartment, she put the truck in park before bringing her hands up to her face, just in time to absorb the sobs retching up her throat.

## CHAPTER SIXTEEN

Thirty minutes later, safely inside her small loft, wearing a pair of cutoffs and a loose-fitting tank top, Cassie stared numbly at the television screen in the corner of her living room. She hadn't actually turned the set on, but then she probably wouldn't have had the attention span to watch anything anyway. Her thoughts were echoing too loudly for that.

She'd never felt so alone.

So confused.

So lost in her own surroundings.

And she just wanted to go home.

The sudden, quiet knock outside her apartment door had Cassie jerking upright. Rubbing away the tracks of tears still visible on her cheeks, she took a deep breath. Then another. There was only one person who that could be. Moving with a speed she hadn't known she possessed, though she didn't dare admit it, Cassie felt something flutter in her stomach.

Grabbing the doorknob in her hand, she twisted it open with unceremonious anger. "I meant what I said, there's nothing ..."

Only, it wasn't Brannt standing on the other side of the threshold.

"Andrea?" Cassie asked, her voice coming out in a surprised croak.

"I heard you and Brannt went out on a date?" her friend asked uncertainly.

Cassie snorted. "It was more like we put on a community show. Great acting!" She mockingly clapped her hands together.

Andrea nodded meaningfully. "Yeah, I know," and at Cassie's quick look, she shrugged: "Ben called me."

At the words, at their knowing implication, Cassie's face crinkled. "I hate him," she whispered.

"Oh baby," Andrea cooed, her arms reaching forward to envelop Cassie in a tight hug. "I know. I know."

\* \* \*

After an incredibly therapeutic night spent intermittently crying, cursing, and all-around Brannt-bashing with Andrea, Cassie woke up the next morning with a mild headache, a blotchy expression, and a clear agenda in mind.

There was something she needed to do.

And it all came back to Rachel.

She owed the girl an apology. At the very least, an explanation for her actions. She needed to wipe the slate clean, to confess her innocence, absolve herself of any wrongdoing she had committed, whether knowingly or not.

Zipping up a pair of thin cargo pants and buttoning up a red shirt, Cassie stalked out the front door. The girl may have been a pest, Cassie knew, but she hadn't deserved that. No one deserved to have their feelings thrown in their face.

Locking the door behind her, Cassie caught sight of her wristwatch. It was 8:10 a.m. According to her calculations, the breakfast rush at the diner would be just about wrapping up and, since Cassie had it on good authority Rachel would be there that morning (thank God for Andrea!), she figured it was as good a time as any to pop over and offer up her sincerest defense.

She would have rather done this in private but then, if Rachel had to be rejected in public than it was only fair she receive Cassie's apology in kind. (Plus, it would have been plain weird to just show up unannounced to Rachel's place of residence.)

So, with that in mind, tripping hastily down the stairs, Cassie made a beeline for the truck. Crossing her fingers as she slowly backed out of the parking spot, headed toward for town, she only hoped Rachel had a forgiving nature.

Pulling up to Betsy's Diner, Cassie was relieved to see the parking lot less than half full. Getting out of the truck, she took a deep breath. She stared up at the front of the building. Her stomach felt like it was about to revolt.

"Do it anyway." With that, she took herself inside. A nice-looking middle-aged woman met her at the door. "Good morning, how many today?" she asked mechanically, reaching for menus even as she spoke.

"Just me," Cassie muttered uncomfortably. "Can you please seat me in Rachel's section?"

Glancing up, the woman stopped. Her eyes narrowed, lingering on Cassie's face. There was a telling look in her eyes. "I won't have my staff upset, you understand?"

Cassie's fears had proven true—everyone in Pantula knew what she'd done. Without meaning to, she'd made herself enemies in this small, close-knit community. The very last thing she'd ever wanted to do.

Closing her eyes, Cassie nodded unsteadily. "Of course," she agreed with the woman, whose nametag read, Susie. "I would never..." Cassie paused because she doubted the older lady would believe her assurance that she would never deliberately upset Rachel. Changing tactics, she promised: "I just want to talk to her, that's all. I owe her that much."

Susie gave her a hard look but besides a muttered 'humph,' said no more on the subject, merely leading Cassie down the aisle toward where Rachel could be seen, taking orders from nearby customers.

Slapping the menu down hard on the table, Susie gestured for Cassie to take a seat. "She'll be with you in a moment," she huffed. Circling back, she imparted this final threat: "One hint of impropriety, and I'll be back."

Sliding unsteadily into the booth, Cassie reached tentatively for the menu. She wasn't hungry. Still, it was something to do. Opening it up, she was halfway down the sandwiches when a thin shadow settled over her shoulder. "Hello! How are you do—?" the last of Rachel's greeting died in the air when she looked up from her notepad, startled eyes staring dead into Cassie's face.

Cassie looked up hopefully. Rachel's mouth twisted into a mutinous shape. "Please," Cassie pleaded. "I just want to apolo—"

"Can I get you anything to drink?" Rachel asked, cutting her off ruthlessly, her pen poised over the pad. Her knuckles were white around the writing utensil.

Cassie wanted to crawl underneath the table. She could almost feel the hurt radiating off the waitress. "I didn't know, Rachel," she tried to say, but again she was interrupted.

"Didn't know what?" Rachel hissed. "That it was my father whose face you threw your newfound relationship into?" Cassie winced at the guttural tone. "That he had to walk right past the two of you making out in the parking lot, right there for half the town to see?"

Cassie's eyes closed on this new realization. Would her humiliation never be complete? Surely, Brannt had been aware of the man's location. It made sense. She felt sick all over again.

Focusing, she tried to pay attention to Rachel, who was still going on: "That everyone would be talking about it for days and days on end? That I wouldn't be able to get away from hearing about the two of you? What, Cassie? What didn't you know?"

"Any of it. I didn't know any of it," Cassie confessed.

"But you're here, aren't you?" she asked quietly. "So clearly you knew how much it would hurt me."

Cassie's eyes fell. That she couldn't deny. Dr. Sam had told her, hadn't he, how deeply Rachel's feelings for Brannt ran. She'd seen it for herself.

"I asked you if there was anything going on between the two of you," Rachel remaindered her ruthlessly.

Cassie nodded weakly, despondently. "I know."

"You could have just told me then. You didn't have to do this."

Cassie's head shot up. "Rachel, no! It's not what you thin—"

"Coffee? Milk? Water?" Rachel asked. Her eyes had returned once more to her serving pad. Her voice was cutting, hard...

Cassie blinked at the sudden change in topic.

"Uh, coffee," she supplied randomly. "Rachel if you'll just let me—"

"Coming right up," the younger girl snapped before turning to walk away, just as though Cassie hadn't still been speaking to her.

Marshaling her thoughts, Cassie tried to figure out just what it was she wanted to say. If the past two minutes were anything to go by, she had about ten words or less in which to do it.

A steaming cup of coffee was set none-too-gently on the table, its sudden, loud appearance startling Cassie out of her thoughts. "Are you ready to order?" Rachel asked.

Cassie refused to play along. "Brannt played me...he made me out to be someone that I'm not. I swear it. I thought—" Cassie shrugged. "Well, it doesn't matter what I thought. He lied. To me, to your father, to everyone. It meant nothing. All of it meant...nothing," Cassie insisted, staring down at the cup of coffee in her hands.

"Are you going to order anything?" Rachel asked sharply. "If not, I have other customers to attend to...?" Her left shoulder hitched aggressively over the words.

"I'll have a cinnamon bun," Cassie managed. Anything to prolong her stay at the diner, anything to keep her within talking distance of Rachel.

"Would you like that warmed?"

"Uh...sure?"

"Fine."

Cassie took a deep breath. "It if makes you feel better, you aren't the only person he was cruel to that night," she blurted out in a last ditch effort to explain herself. Rachel stopped just short of walking away. "You aren't the only person he rejected. I'm sorry, so sorry for what you think I did that night. Please know, I was just as blindsided as everyone else. I had no idea."

Cassie closed her eyes. It was going to take a lot of courage to say what she needed to say next. "He made a mockery of your feelings that night, and I was cast to play the unsuspecting accomplice. Please believe me when I say I didn't know. But I am truly, deeply, forever sorry for my part in all of it. No one should be made to feel that way.

"If it helps, he led me to believe he had feelings for me, but he didn't. He doesn't." Cassie bit down on her lower lip. "I got hurt, too."

Slowly, Rachel turned to face Cassie, her expression grim. "No," she finally said. "It doesn't help, knowing how he treated you." Her face looked tired. "I'm sorry."

Cassie's eyelids flinched. "Thank you, but I don't deserve your compassion, Rachel. I'm the one who's sorry."

Rachel nodded slowly. "I know."

"I just—I don't want you to hate me."

Rachel looked down at the faded carpet. "I don't hate you."

Cassie bit her lip.

"I'm embarrassed and I'm angry." Rachel shook her head. "But mostly I'm just hurt."

"I know, and—"

Rachel held up a hand. "He made a town spectacle of me."

"Only if you let him."

Rachel laughed knowingly. "Get over Brannt, you mean?"

Cassie shrugged uncomfortably. She may have overstepped.

"Oh, I intend to," Rachel promised her. "And if you don't want to end up like me, you may want to do the same." With those parting words, Rachel turned and walked away.

The faux-wooden veneer of the table blurred in Cassie's vision.

Get over Brannt.

It wasn't likely.

# CHAPTER SEVENTEEN

"I'm just about to head out to the McDowell Estate for a last check on those pregnant mares..." Dr. Sam's voice hit Cassie hard as he popped his head inside the exam room she was readying for Dr. Stevens.

Steadying her breath, she looked up at him impassively. Her face looked pinched, despite her best efforts. "Okay. I'll just finish up here...." Her fingers trembled against the x-ray film she held in her hands.

Dr. Sam coughed. "Well, but I was going to say... we do have that surgery this afternoon and, if you wanted, you could stay back to sterilize the equipment, make sure we have everything we need?"

Her heart jumped. "Yeah?"

He inclined his head. "Save us some time."

"Okay." She nodded eagerly. "Yeah, I could do that."

He smiled nicely. "Good. I shouldn't be gone long."

Walking out of the examination room a few minutes later, Cassie took herself promptly to the surgical suite. Opening up one of the cupboards in there, she took stock of the inventory.

"Cassie! There you are."

Glancing around her, Cassie looked over to see Andrea breeze through the swing door.

"Looking for me?"

Andrea didn't answer her directly. "What are you doing right now?" she asked instead.

"Just about to prep for the surgery Sam and I have scheduled at noon."

"The Bloom's cat, right?"

"Yup."

Andrea looked down at her watch. "Plenty of time for that."

"Huh?" Cassie asked. Andrea was acting strangely.

"Get a cup of coffee with me?" she asked, but it didn't really sound like a question.

Cassie gestured to the surgical cart. "I've got—"

"An hour to kill before you need to start in on that," Andrea informed her. She was right, of course. "My treat?"

"All right." What else could she say?

\* \* \*

Making his slow way inside the dimly lit barn located on the McDowell Estate, Dr. Sam spotted Brannt coming out of one of the stall doors, inside of which stood Berma, a grain bucket held in his hand. The crunch of Sam's booted feet against the dirt-littered cement flooring had the younger man turning expectantly.

"'Morning Brannt," Dr. Sam called. Pulling up beside him, Sam reached across the stall door to pet Berma behind the ears. "You too, darling." She whinnied softly.

Brannt's eyes looked meaningfully over Dr. Sam's shoulder, but they didn't encounter the slim, feminine shadow which was usually close in attendance. "Missing someone?" he asked cuttingly. His eyes were hard, his body defensive.

Dr. Sam pretended not to notice. "Cassie, you mean?" His tone was innocent in the extreme. "She won't be joining us today. I had her stay back at the office. Heavy workload this afternoon." He grinned boyishly.

Brannt scoffed. "What's the point of having a student if they don't show up to do the actual job? I thought that was the point, that she was supposed to work *alongside* you?"

Dr. Sam shrugged good-naturedly, his eyes refusing to meet Brannt's. "That's true," he conceded. "However, I thought it best that she not work alongside *you*." The words were said quietly but powerfully nonetheless.

Brannt's head snapped backward, his shoulders pulling back at the mild attack. "And what's that supposed to mean?" There was a lot of fight in that short question.

Sam chuckled, his hand brushing absent circles against Berma's neck. "I try not to know," he confessed. "But, it's my job to see that she can do hers and she can't when you're around." Taking his hand off the horse now, Sam turned to fully address Brannt. "That's enough for me."

Brannt blustered. "She's acting like a child—!"

"Well, then consider yourself lucky that you won't have to deal with it. And anyway, you never seemed to approve of her work here, did you?" Dr. Sam asked conversationally.

Brannt sighed. "I asked her out. On a date, I mean."

A pause settled over the dusty barn. "I know."

"But now she's got it in her head that I had purely ulterior motives for doing it." Brannt shook his head.

"Did you?"

"So, you *do* know," he accused. "About Rachel?"

"It's hard not to," Sam quipped. He smiled at Brannt's quick frown. "It's a small town, people talk. And you put Cassie right in the middle of it."

"I know," Brannt admitted quietly. "I didn't—I wasn't thinking."

"That's not like you."

Brannt had a self-deprecating look on his face. "Cassie seems to bring it out in me."

Sam laughed. "Yeah, I've noticed."

"She thinks I played into our date to prove to Rachel once and for all that I'm not interested. But—" Brannt stopped.

"But?" Sam prompted.

A long, slow exhalation of breath preempted Brannt's words: "I don't know."

"But perhaps you used Rachel as an excuse to allow yourself to have feelings for Cassie?" Sam queried wisely. His tone was casually nonchalant.

His jaw flexing, Brannt cursed. "I've got a busy day ahead of me," he said instead, gesturing toward Berma. "Shall we get on with it?"

"Of course," Sam agreed immediately. Sliding the stall door open, however, he couldn't deny himself the pleasure of a small, self-satisfied smile.

Maybe, just maybe.

\* \* \*

Across town, slinking back against her chair, Cassie stared across the small bistro table separating her from Dr. Andrea Coleman. Two steaming cups of black coffee sat between them. It was almost ninety degrees outside, but when Andrea had placed the order with the young barista working at the café, Cassie hadn't had the heart to contradict her half of this instruction.

She wanted coffee right now like she wanted a sunburn.

"I thought Dr. Sam had an appointment at Brannt's this morning?" Andrea mused, her eyes flicking down to the watch clasped around her thin wrist. "Right about now, as a matter of fact?"

Cassie eyed her friend warily. "Yeah."

"You didn't go with." It wasn't a question.

Cassie snorted. "Not likely."

Andrea sighed. It was tinged with disappointment. Cassie took a quick drink of her unwanted coffee—there was something unnerving in the look Andrea was giving her.

"Actually, I'm surprised at you," Andrea finally said.

"You're surprised at me?" Cassie stuttered. Her eyes skipped nervously to take in the sundry wind chimes decorating the outside of the coffee shop. They were blowing a musical frenzy.

Out of her peripherals, she saw the tip of Andrea's finger just lightly skim the top of her ceramic mug. "I know Brannt hurt you. What he did was low, but…"

"But what?" Cassie asked, affronted, her gaze shifting back to Andrea's.

Andrea shifted, looking uncomfortable. "But I would've thought a big city girl like you wouldn't be so easily swayed by small town gossip."

Cassie put her cup down hard on the wrought-iron table, her fingers shaking. As if it wasn't bad enough, being the butt of the entire community's criticism, now she was being labeled a baby about the whole thing?

Enough was enough. Pushing her chair back, she made to stand up.

"No, don't go," Andrea pleaded, reading Cassie's cues correctly. "I'm just saying—where's that fighting spirit we've all come to know and love?"

Cassie snorted rudely. "It was thrown in my face." The chimes were ringing a more ominous tone suddenly.

Andrea's lips thinned. "I know that, but you're missing something in all this talk. Look, I'm not saying—Brannt may have seized an unfortunate time to make a point to Rachel, but believe me, I know him, and if his only purpose that night had been in getting her off his back, he could have done that easily enough, and without any involvement on your part." Andrea searched Cassie's face. "Do you really think he'd have gone to such lengths, creating a buzz throughout the whole town that, instead of Rachel, the woman he actually wanted was you, if that wasn't at least partially true?"

Cassie's face looked to be carved from stone.

Andrea tried again: "Only a stupid man fixes a problem with a problem. And Brannt is not a stupid man. So why then would he choose to fight off the advances of one woman only to encourage them in someone else, if it wasn't what he wanted? What would have been the point in finally getting it through to Rachel that he wasn't interested, only to have you replace her in his life?" Andrea asked rhetorically.

Cassie shook her head vehemently from side to side. "You're right, Brannt isn't stupid. I am." Holding her hand up, she firmly denied Andrea's attempt to interrupt. "You weren't there that night Andrea. He, he was so present, you know. Attentive and open, expressive, the way a man acts when he's around a woman he likes. There was this look in his eyes whenever he touched me and I thought..." Cassie choked back the words. "And the whole time he was thinking about her."

"Cassie..."

The multi-colored paint splattered on the walls of the small coffee shop dimmed as Cassie's mind recreated the pictures of that night: "And I'm so embarrassed when I remember how I felt. Special. I felt special. But it was make-believe, Andrea. No, if it had really meant something to him, if *I* had really meant something to him, Rachel wouldn't have been there."

Cassie couldn't hear the wind chimes blowing anymore.

"Maybe so," Andrea conceded. "But you can hardly argue that she was there when he kissed you out at his barn a few weeks ago, after that fateful trail ride?"

Cassie's mouth dropped. "What? How did you—?"

Andrea waved her words away. "I'm not an idiot, either. I recognized the signs when you called me in such a frenzied panic to come pick you up that afternoon."

Cassie sputtered, taken aback: "That has nothing to do with—"

"It has everything to do with it, Cassie," Andrea argued doggedly. "That's my point. That time you were all alone together. No one saw you. Brannt never told anyone about it. Not even Ben, who's his best friend. You sure didn't say a word." Andrea leaned back smugly in her chair. "So, if it all meant nothing to him, then why...?"

Cassie's skin felt cool. Crossing her arms defensively, she smiled. "Because I'm a novelty? Something new and shiny to play with? Because he knew he could?" She sighed hard. "I don't know, Andrea; and honestly, I'm not sure I'm willing to find out. Fool me once and all that jazz..." She shook her head. "No. As far as I'm concerned, Brannt McDowell is nothing more than one of Tiamango's best clients."

"Maybe I was wrong," Andrea said after a brief passing of silence. "Hearing you say it, Brannt certainly cut off his nose to spite his face. Maybe he is a damn stupid cuss."

Cassie smiled sadly. "I know you and Brannt are close. I probably shouldn't have involved you—"

Reaching across the small table, Andrea's hand cupped Cassie's elbow, the action effectively cutting the younger woman off. "I'm your friend, too. You can always talk to me."

Cassie nodded jerkily. "Thank you."

"And hey, I probably owe you an apology," Andrea started to say. "About what I said earlier, I understand why you might want to keep away from Brannt, even during office calls—"

"No, in that you were right," Cassie admitted, though she hated doing so. "If he's just a client then I need to treat him like one." She looked down. "I'm not proud of my behavior today."

Andrea gave her arm one last squeeze before taking her hand back. "Stand your ground, girl. That's the only way it works with a man like Brannt."

"I'm slowly getting that impression."

# CHAPTER EIGHTEEN

Sitting alone in her makeshift apartment later that evening, Cassie felt restless. It was Friday night and through her open living-room window she could hear the faint sounds of the city opening up for the weekend, of tequila splashing into shot glasses... And there she sat, wearing sweats and a baggy t-shirt, with nothing to show for her night.

Andrea and Ben were taking in a show at the downtown cinema; they'd invited Cassie to join them but she'd declined. Third wheels were notoriously unpleasant company. BJ was spending the weekend down at her parent's house, a few hundred miles south of Pantula. Dr. Sam...well, Cassie had no idea what Sam did outside of work.

Screw it.

Springing up from her couch, Cassie marched determinedly toward her bedroom, whipping her shirt off over her head as she went. She was done moping about. She was done with not having fun.

She was going out.

She was going drinking.

And damn anyone who got in her way.

Sidling up to her closet, she reached in the far back for a slim-fit black tank-top and a pair of equally tight jeans. With these possessions in hand, she turned toward the bedroom bureau where, sitting atop the antique furniture, laid her limited supply of jewelry. Grabbing up a large gold locket and a pair of stud earrings, she took herself off to the bathroom.

She wasn't just going out. She was going out with style.

And, just for the record, she wasn't above flirting with any of the men she happened upon. And she could only hope she happened upon quite a few.

So take that, Brannt McDowell!

\* \* \*

Cassie's face felt numb. Patting the palm of her hand against one cheek, she giggled. She couldn't feel anything. Slumping unsteadily into her bar stool, she waved for the bartender's attention.

"Yes?" he inquired politely. He was young, with slicked back black hair, his face sporting a slight stubble. His work attire was a little less than tidy, but the boy made a mean martini.

"I'll take another one of these, please," she said, her finger tapping the side of her empty drink glass.

He looked uncertain for a second, but then he nodded his head, reaching under his rail for the bottle of vodka. As she waited for her drink—how many was that now, four, five?—Cassie spied the dance floor. There was a local band playing live music for the packed house. Her foot tapped rhythmically to the sound of the bass guitar. They weren't half-bad.

"Thanks," she mumbled to the barkeep when he set the new pink concoction in front of her. Glass in hand, she stumbled to her feet, making her way towards where a group of girls stood on the makeshift dance floor, swaying to the music.

"Girl, we were wondering where you'd gone!" One of them yelled as Cassie joined the circle they'd made, her feet slip-sliding across the floor, her body quickly finding the beat.

"Drink!" She hollered back, indicating the glass in her hand, its contents spilling over the edges as she shimmied to the music.

This was, by far, one of the best decisions she'd made in weeks.

At first, it had been difficult. She'd felt undeniably awkward walking into the place. Couples and groups had been lined up in packs, laughing merrily with one another, sure of their company, completely without self-conscious awareness. It wasn't an ideal locale for singles.

Cassie, on the other hand, who had no one to talk to, had stuck out like a sore thumb. It had taken two stiff cocktails before she'd had the courage to properly check out the people partying around her, before she'd stopped feeling so uneasily conspicuous. It had taken one more before she'd found the confidence to walk up to these yet-unknown faces and make some friends...

And make friends she had. She couldn't remember any of their names, but that was a moot point. It seemed the only requirement was ordering the first round of drinks. After that, it was just a matter of keeping up with everyone else.

"Cass!" One such comrade called out to her now, grabbing for her arm.

Turning, Cassie found a young girl, probably no older than twenty-two, standing beside her. In her hands were two shot glasses filled with some mysterious green-colored liquid.

"Hey!" Cassie shouted above the roar of an electric guitar.

"Here," the girl—Mara, Cassie thought her name was—shouted, shoving the alcohol firmly in Cassie's uncoordinated fingers. "Take this."

Cassie didn't have to be told twice. "Down the hatch," she cried. Dumping the empty flute down on a nearby table, Cassie cringed as the slimy substance crawled down to her stomach. "God, that's awful," she said, but there was no mistaking the game smile on her face; if they asked her to she'd have another.

"Damn girl, you can really throw 'em back."

She smiled hugely. Swap the location and the name of the bar, give them different faces and identities, and these people could have passed for any of her friends back home.

"Dancing!" she yelled, uncaring if anyone followed after her or not. Stepping out back onto the dance floor, she soon found herself swallowed up with another party.

More friends.

\* \* \*

"Can I have another?" Cassie asked, her words hardly intelligible now. Leaning heavily against the ornate wooden bar, she blinked woozily at the bartender standing face-to-face with her.

Was that the same guy as earlier in the night?

Squinting, she looked harder.

He frowned at her request. No, it couldn't be the same guy. The other bartender was much friendlier. "I think you've probably had enough."

"No way! Me and my friends want more—!" As if to prove her point, Cassie turned to point them out to this curmudgeonly server. Only, the dance floor was pretty much empty by now. The band had gone. A digital jukebox played over the loudspeakers. The tables dotting the floor were littered with empty bottles and half-consumed appetizer plates. Even the pool table, which had seen scores of players that evening, was barren now, unattended.

"I think your friends all went home," the bartender informed her nicely.

Shifting her gaze back to his concerned face, she waved this statement away. "Well, who needs them anyway? I don't."

"Ms. Hastings—"

"Please?" Cassie asked, pouting cutely now. "Just one more?"

He sighed. It was a lofty, unappealing sound. "Fine. On one condition."

"Anything!" For the first time in weeks, she felt good. Great. Even better, she didn't really feel anything at all.

"Hand over your car keys."

Cassie wasn't an idiot. She'd had no intention of driving home in her condition. Without a second thought, she tossed them on the bar. "Is that all? No problem!" she consented, giggling as she waited for him to replenish her nightcap.

She'd call for a taxi soon.

\* \* \*

As it happened, a cab ride wouldn't be necessary. Thirty minutes later, as Cassie was struggling to keep her head off the hard slab of the bar counter, over the din of loud conversation she vaguely made out the sound of the front door to the establishment banging open. She smiled vacantly, her fingers playing with the short stem of her glassware. She had to keep one eye closed to do this though. She'd discovered a rather unfortunate side effect to her particular drink of choice: too much brought on a terrible case of double vision.

A long shadow fell over her hunched position.

"Cassie? Jesus—!" The last word was bit off ruthlessly.

Body slumping dejectedly at the sound of this angry exclamative, Cassie groaned, her forehead falling effortlessly against the lacquered finish of the bar. "Oh bother. Not you again," she cried wretchedly. "Go away, Brannt."

"What the hell...?" he asked, but he wasn't looking at Cassie's pitiful shape, his eyes zeroing in on the poor bartender standing sheepishly just off to the side.

"Don't be such a fun-sucker," Cassie breathed, talking into the wooden grains beneath her mouth. "So I had a few cocktails, no big deal."

"You're drunk, Cassie," Brannt decided harshly.

"Yeah, it's a bar, people tend to do that in them," she returned edgily.

Brannt's lips thinned.

"What are you even doing here?" she asked, turning her head to stare at him accusingly from its cradled position against the hard countertop.

"Taking you home." His voice was clipped, hard. "Now get up, we're leaving."

"No, I don't think I can do that." Cassie burped.

Brannt took one menacing step closer. "Don't be juvenile Cassie. Liking me has nothing to do with getting home safely. Don't be so stupid—"

"No, I mean—" Cassie swallowed back a sudden urge to vomit "—I don't think I can get up."

Brannt stared at her incredulously before transferring his glare back to the bartender again, whose expression had only worsened in the ensuing exchange. Poor kid, he didn't stand a chance against Brannt's anger. "What the hell kind of business are you running here?" Brannt spat, his body vibrating as he watched Cassie struggle to lift her head.

"Don't you dare yell at him, Brannt," Cassie demanded. This reproach would have come off stronger if she'd been able to pronounce half these words correctly. "If you want to be mad at someone, go shout in front of the mirror!"

"You're awfully brave all of a sudden, aren't you?" Brannt accused, though there was no real malice in his voice.

"Yup. And that's all thanks to my good friend over here," she said, pointing erratically at the young man behind the bar. He swallowed thickly. "What's your name again?"

"Never mind his name," Brannt interrupted, his patience long since passed. "We're leaving. Now."

"I'm not ready yet."

"Oh yes, you are," Brannt returned, more forcefully this time. "The choice is yours: either you walk out of here on your own two feet or I'll carry you out. One way or another, we're going. And I mean this very minute."

Cassie looked down at her ungainly feet then back up at Brannt.

He pursed his lips at her sullen expression. "How do you want to play this Cassie? Up to you…."

# CHAPTER NINETEEN

It had been a hard, rough day. Walking into his home earlier that evening, sweat dripping down his back, dirt and mud stuck to his clothing, Brannt had envisioned nothing more than a quiet, early night ahead of him. And a long, hot shower.

How'd that old saying go: one out of two ain't bad...?

It had been twenty minutes after midnight when he'd gotten the call. Sitting in the comfort of his semi-dark den, the news droning out of the television set, a half-full glass of scotch resting on the side-table, he'd been on the verge of sleep when the phone had rung out so chillingly.

Who the hell...?

"Hello?" Brannt's voice had been groggy, unused. He'd worked more than twelve hours that day, hauling cattle from one pen to another, fixing fence in the south pasture, pitching winter hay bales... He'd been far from his usual, authoritative self. This time of year was always busy, hectic at his ranch. By now, the entire town of Pantula, Texas should have known that. They also should have known better than to rouse him frivolously from the breakneck pace of culling, breeding, and branding—especially in the middle of the damned night!

A nervous voice broke out of the speaker: "Uh, Mr. McDowell? Brannt?"

"Speaking."

The other end of the line paused uncertainly. "Sir, this is Mark. From down at Lucky Lucy's Bar..."

Brannt frowned. What was the bar manager at Lucky Lucy's calling him for? Brannt bit back a curse. If this was about one of his ranch hand's getting fresh—! Brannt did not abide by indecent drunkenness, not on his operation.

Mark hastened at Brannt's ominous: "What can I do for you, Mark?"

"I think you may want to come down here, sir. Ms. Hastings has had a little too much to drink, and I, uh—" Mark struggled for words.

Brannt sat upright at the mention of Cassie's surname. Shaking his head, he asked: "Excuse me?"

"Ms. Hastings, sir..."

Brannt's wits felt addled. "She's drunk?"

"Oh yeah." In the background, Brannt could just make out the sounds of loud, loose voices yelling over the unnecessary volume of music belting out of the speakers.

"And she asked you to call *me*?" Brannt asked incredulously. That hardly seemed likely. Cassie hated him. And he could only assume those feelings would intensify with the addition of liquor, not diminish.

The disembodied voice coughed uncomfortably, his voice low. "Well, no, not exactly. I heard you two were dating, and I thought…"

Brannt sucked in a hard, forceful breath. A deathly, stiff sort of silence descended.

"Oh," Mark realized with unerring perception. "Is that not quite…? I didn't mean to… Should I, that is, I can ask somebody else if you'd rather?" Mark's voice sounded small, as though the man were physically shrinking in his unease.

Brannt muscles tightened, jumped. Ask someone else? And just who the hell was Mark thinking of enlisting? Brannt could only imagine the line-up of drunk losers hanging over Cassie's every word, just waiting to pick her up—

Brannt's teeth snapped together.

"Yeah," Mark decided, still talking nervously. "I'll get someone else. Sorry to bother you."

"I'll be there in five minutes." Brannt's voice was clipped. Punching the call short, he quickly gained his feet.

Cassie was going to raise sweet hell when he walked into that place. He could only imagine that the appearance of a rattler would be better received than the sight of himself, but still, if Brannt didn't rescue Cassie from herself, she'd be left to the devices of some ill-intentioned good ol' boy… That thought had taken him all the way to Lucy's.

It hadn't been easy, persuading Cassie to get in his truck, but when he'd threatened to carry her out over his shoulder she'd seemingly read the promise in his eyes and, though she'd made a point to defy him every step of the way, had consented.

She'd been adamant. She'd managed to get herself into Lucky Lucy's, and she would take herself out, and all by herself, thank you very much. She'd shucked off Brannt's assistance when his hand had instinctively reached for her elbow as she'd started to veer sideways, batting at his hold insistently.

"I can walk," she'd informed him sourly. "Been doing it since I was one year old."

"And by the looks of it, you haven't gotten much better since those first steps," Brannt hadn't been able to help replying as she'd stumbled against one of the tables impeding her journey.

"Just shut up, Brannt. No one asked you to come anyway."

Brannt, at Cassie's bidding, had kept his mouth shut. The less she knew about all that, the better. Her pride probably wouldn't take the abuse of knowing he had, indeed, been wrangled into this little babysitting assignment.

But finally, finally...she got herself up and inside his waiting truck. Unfortunately, she hadn't lasted five miles down the road when she passed out, her head pressed up against the window, one-half of her face smashed up to the glass, fogging up the place. She snored quietly.

Brannt couldn't fight back a small smile at the sight of her disheveled position.

Slowing down, ready to turn into the parking lot at the vet clinic, at the last minute, he changed his mind. Righting the vehicle, Brannt drove on, straight down the road.

He didn't feel comfortable leaving her in that small apartment all by herself—not in her current, unconscious condition anyway. He had no idea how much booze she'd consumed, but he knew she shouldn't be left on her own. Drinking 101: when someone performs a blackout, extra recruitment is required. What if she had alcohol poisoning? What if she puked in her sleep? What if she fell down? No one would find her until it was quite possibly too late.

These were all rational, solid, even logical explanations; however, none of them were the real reason why Brannt bypassed her small residence.

It never once occurred to him to bring Cassie anywhere else but his home. He'd be able to keep a close watch on her and when Mary, his housekeeper, came in the morning, he'd be able to elicit her mothering help, as well. Nodding in satisfaction to all this high-handedness, he took himself, and his newfound guest, back to the McDowell Estate.

"Cassie?" Brannt called softly. Standing in front of the open passenger door, he shook her arm gently. The big vehicle was parked neatly on the front sweep leading up to his house. "Cassie?" he tried again.

"Hmm?" she breathed gently, her eyes still closed.

"We're here, Cassie. Can you walk?"

Cassie pried one heavy eyelid open. It looked like it had taken all her concentration to do it. "This isn't my home," she informed Brannt before dropping the lid once more.

"I know. You're staying at my place tonight," Brannt informed her factually. And then, just in case she got the wrong idea: "You're sleeping in one of the spare bedrooms."

"Oh. Okay." Cassie yawned, and then, without notice, dropped off once more.

Brannt sighed, looking down at her soft features, illuminated by the glow of the single yard lamp outside. She really was beautiful, with her long lashes sweeping down against her pink cheekbones, her sweet mouth puckered softly in slumber.

"Cassie?" Brannt tried again, but it was useless. She was out. Reaching forward, he quickly scooped her up in his arms, her body resting easily in his sure embrace. "If you wake up, don't, for the love of God, freak out on me," he pleaded quietly as he made his way slowly towards the front door.

Once inside, Brannt didn't bother trying to kick off his boots. Instead, his stride took him steadily toward the grand staircase facing straight ahead. Cassie may have been a small, slim woman, but dead weight was dead weight. Breathing hard, he mounted the first landing where the stairs split into two separate wings. Treading up the left-hand side, he soon found himself atop the wraparound gallery above, his feet hurriedly swallowing up the distance to the third door on the right-hand side. Propping Cassie against his chest, he pulled the brass latch open....

A four-poster bed, covered with a floral quilt, sat squarely in the middle of the large room. At one end, three large windows stood, facing out eastward. Placing Cassie on the heavy blanket, Brannt carefully pulled off her boots. The rest of her clothing, however, he didn't dare touch. He debated whether or not to actually tuck her under the blankets, but somehow that didn't feel right either. If she got cold enough in the middle of the night, she'd find her way underneath them.

Moving back, he couldn't help throwing her sleeping form one last, lingering glance before heading out into the hallway once more.

Setting an alarm on his clock, he took himself to his bedroom. He'd check on her in a couple of hours, just to make sure she was all right. It never occurred to him to mind the more-or-less sleepless night he was in for.

Cassie was in his home. Safe. That was all that mattered.

# CHAPTER TWENTY

Sunlight streamed through the open curtains, blinding Cassie's closed eyes. Groaning painfully, she flicked them open. Shielding her face with one hand, she squinted toward the offending radiance dancing off her heated skin.

Wait. Those windows looked strange.

Glancing down at her bed, she gasped. That looked strange, too.

Jerking upright, through the heavy protestation of her head, Cassie looked around her: where the hell was she?

White painted panel walls. A painting depicting a mossy landscape. A triple-sided mirror over a dainty vanity. These sights offered her no real clues.

Panic climbing up her throat, Cassie clambered to her feet. Shuffling unsteadily toward the door, small snatches of the night before floated across her consciousness. She'd been at Lucky Lucy's drinking. The pounding ache in her head reassured her of this as she reached for the door handle. Oh God. She felt her body go limp. Brannt had been there. She remembered him walking into the bar, walking her to his truck...

He'd taken her home, hadn't he? Only, this wasn't her home.

Walking out into the hallway, her eyes met more foreign sights: a long, square gallery overlooking a grand staircase below. Polished wooden rails curved all the way around this massive structure, with copious doors posted against the four walls surrounding it.

This most certainly was *not* her home.

For a moment, Cassie froze. Then she heard it, the sound of running water, a frying pan clanging quietly against a stove. Oh, and what was that smell? Wrinkling her nose, Cassie took a gentle sniff of the air wafting upwards: was that bacon?

A sensation of nausea smacked her in the face.

It was coming from downstairs.

Scurrying quickly to the head of the stairs, Cassie tripped down the carpeted treads until her feet hit the bottom landing of the big house, her nose still twitching with the heady aroma of—was that pancake batter? She wasn't sure if she was hungry or going to be sick. Following the scent, she turned down a narrow hallway at the back of the stairwell, her feet shuffling along unsurely.

Pushing through the swing-door located at the back, Cassie found herself standing on the flagged stone steps of a kitchen she remembered all too well.

She was in Brannt McDowell's house.

Cassie wasn't really all that surprised. Where else could she have been? Still, the reality of this newsflash had her stomach somersaulting furiously (as if it needed any motivation on that front)...

"Good morning," a woman said, turning with a wide grin, her dark black eyes taking in Cassie's disheveled appearance and shocked gaze as naturally as though this were a daily happening.

"Ah, good morning," Cassie muttered, her feet rooted to the cold flooring.

"Have some breakfast, love. I made all the best foods for a hangover. Greasy eggs, fried hash browns, toast loaded with butter. I'll have you all fixed up before long."

Cassie smiled nervously. Where the hell was Brannt?

As if she'd asked the question out loud, the lady answered: "Mr. McDowell is out in the barn, helping the boys cull the herd."

"Oh."

The woman bustled quickly around the room, throwing dishes into the soapy sink and humming merrily to herself. "Eat," she said over her shoulder when Cassie hadn't yet moved from the doorway. With a pointed look, the woman directed Cassie toward the butcher block topped island, where a plate was already set, piled high with food.

Cassie's stomach growled.

"I'm not sure I can," she admitted.

The woman only laughed. "Eat," she insisted again. "You'll feel better when you do. I promise."

"Thank you," Cassie murmured and, seeing no other options for it, walked daintily forward. Pulling back one of the heavy, ladder-back chairs pushed beside it, she sank gratefully off her feet.

"I'm Mary, by the way," the woman supplied then, grabbing for more dishes, her hands submerged in the sink as she scrubbed various pots and pans.

"I'm Cassie."

"Oh, I know that all right," the woman said on a laugh. She had a nice laugh. Infectious—the kind that seemed to stem right out from her belly.

Cassie didn't know how to respond to that so she didn't, instead placing a strip of bacon in her mouth. Chewing carefully, she waited for her stomach to revolt. When it didn't, she swallowed. Questions buzzed through her muddled brain: was she expected to just quietly leave after her breakfast? And how did she manage that, without a vehicle? She supposed she could call a cab, but then again, the last time she'd left without saying a proper goodbye Brannt had been ready to blow a proverbial fuse.

Her thoughts were happily cut short.

"I run this home—and make no mistake about it." Mary was murmuring to the spatula in her hand. "So of course I know who you are. Knew about you long before this morning, I did. Though I must admit, *that* was a rather interesting entrance."

Cassie blushed, stuffing eggs into her mouth greedily. Now that she knew she wasn't about to throw-up all over Mary's spotless kitchen, she realized she was rather famished.

Mary turned to give her a wink. "And I like the stories I've heard about you, Cassie. Yes, I do." There went that sweet, hearty chuckle again.

Cassie coughed, her hand fumbling for the glass of orange juice beside her plate.

"Lay off, Mary. You're giving Cassie panic attacks over there. Just look at her face."

Spinning dizzily in her chair, Cassie turned to see that the back door was open, and Brannt was leaning nonchalantly against it. She hadn't heard it open. Mary, however, turning at the same time, didn't seem the least surprised at Brannt's silent arrival.

She cracked her spatula against the side of the porcelain sink. "If anyone should be apologizing for that, it's you! She looked white as a sheet when she came down here this morning...and you, nowhere in sight!"

"Hell, I waited as long as I could," Brannt insisted, talking as though Cassie wasn't sitting there right in front of him. With a deliberate flick of his wrist, he caught sight of his wristwatch. "You can hardly call it breakfast when you eat at eleven o'clock."

"Eleven?" Cassie squealed. "Like, eleven in the morning?"

"More like afternoon if you ask me," Mary tut-tutted quietly to herself.

Brannt fixed his eyes on Cassie. "Don't look so shocked. You went to bed at three, after all."

"Oh God," she groaned softly. Dropping her head in her hands, she mumbled: "I am so, so sorry, Brannt."

Sharing a circumspect look with his housekeeper that Cassie didn't see, Brannt advanced a little farther in the room, Mary coughing out some excuse about needing to start on the day's vacuuming, before letting herself quietly out of the room.

Cassie could feel, she could actually *feel*, a change in the air at the woman's exit.

"How're you feeling this morning?" Brannt asked coolly, coming to stand in front of her.

Lifting her face once more, Cassie shrugged as nonchalantly as she could. How did she feel? Like a world-class ass. "My head's a little achy, and my memory's a little sketchy...but other than that, pretty good."

Brannt smiled. "You were definitely on a mission." He didn't sound accusing, or even upset.

Somehow, though, that made Cassie feel even worse.

"Yeah, I guess." Hunching her shoulders defensively, she finally spoke aloud the thought which had been consuming her ever since she'd found herself in his home: "Why am I here? I mean, how did you? That is, where did, ah," she paused, gathering herself: "Did I, did I call you or something?"

God, could it get any worse?

"No..."

What a relief! Now that her hunger pains had subsided, Cassie was filled with questions about the preceding night. "Then how—? What happened?"

Brannt pursed his lips amusedly. "You don't remember?" His eyes narrowed.

Cassie felt her face flame. Shrugging uncomfortably, she confessed. "Not really. It's all kind of a blur." And when Brannt didn't immediately respond, she wailed: "Please tell me I didn't say or do anything stupid."

"You don't remember anything?" Brannt repeated. When Cassie shook her head weakly, he smiled. The sudden upturn of his lips should have warned her. "Not even what happened after I brought you back here?" The new, suggestive note in his voice was heavy, not to be ignored. If Cassie had looked closely, she might have been alerted at the devilish gleam in his eyes. But she was too mortified to lift her eyes higher than his chin...

She blanched at the insinuation.

Brannt whistled tellingly. "You were, you were really something, Cassie."

"I, uh..."

He shook his head in disbelief. "Not even when I carried you up to bed? God, you were all over me..."

Then she saw it, that glint of mockery marking the corners of his mouth.

Cassie laughed shakily. "All right, all right, you've had your bit of fun—!"

Brannt only smiled wider.

That grin unnerved her. "Because you *are* only teasing...right?" she asked, her confidence fledging once more.

Pressing the palm of one hand flat against the island countertop, Brannt leaned in close, his face mere inches from Cassie's now. She couldn't get enough breath suddenly. "I don't know, am I?" The question hung seductively between them.

"That's not fair..."

"Guess there's only one way to find out," he whispered, his breath tickling her senses.

"Yeah?" Cassie managed weakly, refusing to back down even though they both knew he'd won. "How's that?"

"Stay."

The single word hit Cassie hard.

"Stay?"

Brannt smirked. "I've got to get back outside, help get cows arranged for auction, but I should be back in an hour or two. Wait for me?" There was no mistaking the challenge in his voice.

"Brannt, I don't think that's a good idea," Cassie stalled.

"Maybe not," he agreed quietly. "But then, neither is this." Without warning, he bent his head the rest of the way, brushing his lips softly, slowly against hers. Clutching hard against the edge of the counter, Cassie let her eyes flutter closed at the gentle, barely-there contact.

And then it was gone, and Brannt was shifting back, looking down at her.

Tapping one long finger against her nose, he stared across at her thoughtfully. "No running away this time."

\* \* \*

Cassie stared bemusedly out the back door of the kitchen, watching Brannt's long-legged strides take him quickly to the barn at the edge of the massive yard. Her stomach was still flipping uneasily at his words.

*Stay.*

Looking down at her half-eaten breakfast, Cassie pushed the plate away. She couldn't eat another thing. If nothing else, Brannt had managed to distract Cassie from her raging headache. She was too consumed with his whispered promise.

*There's only one way to find out.*

Taking herself back into the hallway, she listened for the soft sound of Mary's footsteps. Guided by the gentle hum of the vacuum cleaner, Cassie soon found herself in an open entryway leading to a large, lofty living room. The oak flooring was nicely polished, though half of it was concealed underneath faded, but nonetheless beautiful floor rugs—which were currently being cleaned by Mary, her peppery hair swept untidily atop her head, the industrial vacuum in one deft hand.

Spying Cassie standing uncertainly just inside the room, she quickly powered the machine off, smiling in greeting.

"Sorry to bother you," Cassie said softly, unsure of herself.

"Any excuse—" Mary offered with a smile, shooting the vacuum a loathing look.

Pushing her unruly hair back, Cassie wasn't sure how to begin. Brannt wanted her to stay; he wanted her to wait for him. The words had held untold promise, shooting funny feelings up and down Cassie's tense body.

But, well, her hair was a mess, smudges of dried mascara sat stiffly against the skin underneath her eyes, and her clothes—? They reeked of alcohol. And, for that matter, so did her skin. It was secreting out of her with nasty repercussions.

None of this would have mattered. Hell, none of it should have mattered. Except... He'd asked her to stay. And despite it all, she wanted to. Desperately. Indeed, she couldn't think beyond it. The anticipation was like a live thing. But she needed a shower first, and a change of clothes.

Cassie shifted uncomfortably. "Brannt asked me to, um…" Trailing off, she felt her face heat up at Mary's expectant look. On second thought, the less she said the better. "I have to run home quickly, but I'll be back. You'll tell Brannt that, if he comes in while I'm still gone?"

Mary nodded at Cassie's imploring look, but there was no denying the smile perking up her craggy features. "So it's like that, is it?" she asked.

Cassie stared back at her stupidly.

Mary shot her a wicked wink. "I thought as much."

Cassie figured it was better not to answer the woman.

"Now, as to leaving," Mary went on, ignoring Cassie's silent reticence on the subject. "How are you planning on doing that? As I recall, your vehicle was not parked out in front of the house when I pulled up for work this morning." Mary offered Cassie a speaking look.

"Cab," Cassie just managed through her mounting embarrassment. "I thought I'd call a cab. That is, if that's okay?" Cassie wasn't sure why she was asking for permission.

"Nonsense," Mary told her. Moving away from the vacuum, she quickly scuttled past Cassie to the front entryway where, hanging up on an open cupboard stationed beside the door, she grabbed for a pair of keys. "Take one of the ranch trucks. It won't be missed," she assured Cassie when that woman looked doubtful.

"I'm not sure if Brannt would like that…"

"Consider it insurance," Mary said. "This way, you're guaranteed to return. You'll have to bring it back," she explained in a co-conspiratorial fashion. "And I'll get to keep my job for another day."

Cassie croaked out a weak laugh, but then, against her better judgment, she saw her hand reaching out and snagging the key-ring out of the woman's fingers. "Thanks."

# CHAPTER TWENTY-ONE

Back at her apartment, Cassie lost no time jumping into the shower. Letting the water spray away the remnants of the previous evening's drunken sprawl, she couldn't stop wondering what the next few hours would hold in store. An entire afternoon spent with Brannt. Alone. At his home. Her body all but buzzed at the notion, at the daydreams flittering persistently through her mind.

Smiling as she stepped out of the shower and started toweling off, Cassie grinned at her reflection. She should be calling herself a fool. She should have outright refused his arrogant invitation…

Her grin slipping at the thought, Cassie pulled a brush through her hair. *After all, Brannt was dangerous.* Shucking the thought to the back of her mind, Cassie moved into her bedroom. Grabbing a pair of loose floral pants and blue silk top, however, her fingers slowed. *He made her feel things, too many things.*

But he'd been different this morning, she assured herself as she reached for a tube of lipstick. *Then again, he'd seemed different at Bev's Steakhouse, hadn't he?* Leaning over her vanity, she stilled. *He'd hurt her once and he could do it again. Very easily.*

Staring back at her reflection, the reality of what Cassie was doing, what she was preparing to do, hit home. The bubble snapped. Outside of his home, away from those eyes, Cassie fought back a return of reality. He'd hurt her. And he could do it again. And there was still the knotty problem of his feelings. Cassie wasn't altogether sure he had any for her. At least, not in any real sense.

And what was she doing about it? Running right back into the fire. She probably needed her head examined.

The pallor of her skin whitening, even under the effects of her make-up, Cassie saw her head shake itself roughly in denial. This was a bad idea. Brannt was a bad idea.

She set the tube of lipstick back down.

She couldn't do this. She should not do this. And then she remembered Mary's words:

*Consider it insurance.*

Cassie had Brannt's truck parked outside.

Dammit. When Mary had first tempted Cassie with the idea of borrowing Brannt's truck, Cassie had supposed the fiery housekeeper had done it for Brannt's benefit. A way to reassure him that Cassie wasn't, as he so frequently put it, running away.

Now, she wasn't so sure Mary hadn't done it in expectation for this very moment, when Cassie's nerve would run its course.

She had to go back. Staunchly ignoring the little voice in the back of her head cheering victoriously at this flimsy excuse, Cassie frowned all the more fiercely. She had to go back.

Blowing out her breath, she made a deal with herself. Yes, fine, she would bring the truck back, but then, immediately after dropping the keys in Mary's cunning hands, she would leave. She wouldn't be sucked in by Brannt's magnetism. She would call a cab. She would hitch a ride. She would walk home. Whatever. Either way, she was gone.

The sudden brightness gleaming in her eyes, the jittery shake of her fingers, however, didn't seem to have heard this strong resolve as Cassie headed back down the stairs of her second-story apartment to the waiting, damned truck parked before it.

But, like so many things that had happened to her in Pantula, her best-laid prayers went unheeded. Braking hard before the long sweep to Brannt's home, she'd barely had time to unbuckle her seatbelt when the front door opened, Brannt's tall silhouette appearing before her. Stalling, Cassie watched as he advanced onto the long veranda skirting the length of the mammoth structure. His eyes stared straight into hers as he moved slowly forward.

Hands clenched on the steering wheel, for one wild second she considered throwing the truck in reverse and backing out as quickly as she'd come in. But, as she gazed across the distance that separated them she knew she wouldn't do that.

Shutting the engine off, she unlocked her door, her feet touching the ground at the same moment Brannt reached the bottom step leading down from the front entrance.

No more than ten feet stood between them.

"Sorry," Cassie said nervously, indicating the truck. "I-uh, I wanted to run home quick. Mary said it would be okay." She was rambling, nervously tucking and untucking a stray piece of hair behind her ear.

Brannt closed the remaining small gap which still separated them, his hands reaching down to take the keys out of her now numb fingers. "Don't," he told her firmly.

"Don't?" Cassie parroted. She had a terrible habit of doing that around him.

"Don't back away from me. Not now."

Cassie felt her chin lift at the accusation. "I'm not."

"You are," he returned calmly. "Come on." He held out his hand.

Cassie stared down at it before carefully taking hold. "Where are we going?" she asked when he turned her away from the house, toward a small path winding around the far side of it.

Brannt looked down at her, his grey eyes soft under the brim of his ever-present cowboy hat. He looked so at home in dark blue jeans and that long-sleeve button down shirt. "Somewhere private."

"Private?" There she went again, just repeating everything he said. She'd never met a man who spoke so outrageously with so little regard to its shock-and-awe factor.

Brannt stopped and, with a quick whip of his hand, brought Cassie up close. "Don't panic," he urged softly. "Nothing's going to happen...unless, that is, you want it to."

Cassie couldn't quite meet those penetrating eyes.

"You have a way of confusing what I want," she admitted.

Brannt laughed but without any real mirth. "I could say the same to you."

The faint sound of men cursing out unruly cows, coming some hundred yards away, just barely reached Cassie's ears. Momentarily distracted, she turned her head, only to find she couldn't see anyone—that she couldn't be seen. Obscured behind the house, there was only Brannt. She was glad for that. Glad to be away from prying eyes...

"I'm sorry."

The words, rippling against the slight breeze, had the effect of whipping Cassie's head back around. This time, she couldn't help staring up at those dangerous grey eyes, at the ridged jaw, clamped shut now after that soft confession, that mouth, pulled taut as it waited for a response.

"It wasn't what you thought," he uttered when she just stood there, staring up at him.

She was silent for a moment. "How many times have you apologized in your life? I mean, out loud and in person?"

Tilting his head a little to one side, Brannt smiled ruefully. "Not many."

"Then thank you," Cassie said softly, speaking so quietly he almost didn't hear it.

"I never meant for—"

Cassie put her finger against his mouth. "No, I know. I believe you." She wasn't sure where the words came from, but she felt the truth in them all the same. The fears that had gripped her only minutes ago might not have ever been. Yes, he'd hurt her, but it hadn't been deliberate. And though she was terrified to believe him, after everything they'd been through, she found herself doing so anyway.

Still, if Brannt looked nonplussed by the soft admission, Cassie felt equally mystified by it herself.

He blinked. "Yesterday you hated me. You damn near said it to my face. What's changed?"

Cassie shrugged. "You." She glanced at the house. "Last night. This morning. You took care of me anyway. Even *if* I had hated you, you were there for me." Cassie nudged his shoulder teasingly then. It was getting a little heavy. "Of course, the regret I heard in your voice just now helped a little, too. To be one of the few honored with words of your repentance…"

Brannt laughed quietly.

"But mostly," she added then, "because I *want* to believe you…"

Brannt exhaled slowly. "Trust that instinct, Cassie."

"Better prove me right." As far as challenges went, hers was far from subtle.

Brannt pursed his lips at this. "As you say." Shifting, he turned his gaze to look pointedly around them. "There's no one here but us," he said.

Curious, unsure where he was going, Cassie nodded a silent agreement.

"No one to see me bend down and take your lips under mine…"

Cassie caught her breath.

"But I'm going to do it anyway. Believe *that*."

\* \* \*

But, as it happened, Brannt didn't kiss Cassie. Oh, he meant to. It was just, at the very moment his head curved in her direction, in the instant when Cassie's breath stuck in her throat, her neck inching upwards, Mary had come bustling out of the back door, her arms loaded down with rugs.

"Oops!" she called gaily, spying the two of them springing guiltily apart. "Didn't mean to interrupt. Carry on now. Don't mind me—"

"It's a little late for that," Brannt muttered.

Mary laughed, completely unfazed by the bark in his voice as she began to shake out the first of the mats. "Spoilt the moment, have I? May I suggest going somewhere a little more private then?"

Cassie blushed to the roots of her hair.

Brannt swore quietly under his breath. "So much for being alone."

Cassie couldn't help herself. She laughed. It felt good. Some of the nerves which had been pinching in her stomach loosened.

"Think it's funny, do you?" Brannt asked, a low menacing growl in his voice.

"A little," Cassie admitted.

Without warning, Brannt reached down to take hold of her hand. He didn't say anything, just turned and started walking, pulling her unheedingly behind him. His steps took him away from the house and the sound of Mary slapping the dust off the rugs in her hands.

"Where are we going?" Cassie panted. Brannt had a much longer stride than her. It was a struggle to keep up.

"I'm taking Mary's advice," Brannt threw over his shoulder. "We're going somewhere a little less public."

The pinchers around Cassie's stomach clenched down hard again.

"Oh," was the best comeback she could come up with as her feet were led toward a large outcropping of mesquite trees skirting the edges of the immaculate yard.

But it seemed they were destined for disappointment. They had hardly advanced more than half the length of the yard when a loud, agonized cry split out into the afternoon air, followed shortly by urgent, rushed movements down at the holding pens.

At the sound, Brannt stopped. Turning sharply, his eyes searched out the cause. Shifting uneasily, Cassie followed his gaze. A large billowing of dust was rising thickly toward the sky; it looked like it was coming from one of the riding arenas. Squinting, Cassie could just make out the form of a young man lying beneath the mushrooming cloud.

"Shit," Brannt cursed, and in an instant, he was gone, his booted feet sprinting toward the downed man.

Cassie's eyes grew large when the hazy form of a horned bull came into view next, his hoofs pawing ruthlessly against the loose dirt in the arena, his head lowered toward the cowboy sprawled out before him.

Without realizing she was even doing it, Cassie found herself racing after Brannt. If someone didn't get over to that cowboy and quick, he was going to get gored...The thought had no sooner entered her mind when she saw another of Brannt's men slip through the metal gates on the other end of the corral. Making a great ruckus, he succeeded in distracting the angered bull just long enough for three other cowboys to pull the injured man out of danger. Her heart in her throat, Cassie watched the brave man slip back between railings again, out into safety once more.

The bull remained in the arena alone now, his great snorts displaying his rage.

"What the hell happened?" she heard Brannt shouting as he reached the group of men.

"Carl got hooked—"

"What the hell was he doing in there?" Brannt yelled furiously. He was madder than Cassie had ever seen him, his face blanched, the skin taut against his high cheekbones.

"Don't know," the foreman admitted uncomfortably. "He wasn't supposed to be anywhere near here, to tell the truth."

"We were checking the weaned calves over in the south gate when we heard him."

"Hell, Carl was supposed to be helping sort out loading," Jacobs assured Brannt, sounding both disgusted and concerned for the semi-unconscious man stretched out between them. "Don't know what in world he was thinking, getting in the pen with *him*," he said, hooking his thumb toward the large animal in question.

Cassie, following the direction of his hand, blinked. Shit. "Ah, boys," she called out softly, edging closer to the big, beefy Hereford. "We've got another problem." Her voice was pitchy with nerves.

Brannt looked up at her blankly, almost as if he'd forgotten she was there, beside them.

"Look." She indicated toward the spotted animal. Brannt followed her directive. "Your bull is bleeding."

That caught Brannt's attention. He let out a spirited four-letter word. That bull was worth more than most of these cowboys yearly salaries combined. Looking helplessly between it and the wounded man down at his feet, Brannt seemed stuck in indecision.

"It's probably why Carl was in there in the first place," Cassie said quietly, talking more to herself than anyone else. "There's a cut, right there, above his back right hock. Probably kicked the fence or some dumb thing."

Then, without further disclosure, Cassie made up her mind. She knew what she had to do. The impulse was thrumming through her like a living thing. Wordless, she turned, heading straight for the tack compartment just inside the barn. Grabbing up a large cloth, some disinfectant and a bucket of water, she scurried back to the outside arena. Her steps were deliberate and decisive. Her eyes never once straying from the agitated animal.

"Cassie. No!" Brannt's voice bellowed thickly overhead. There was black terror in the tone as he watched her hand settle on the outside of the corral...

Cassie flinched at the fury in his voice, but she didn't stop. The bull was bleeding badly. She could see that clearly now. It needed attention, and quickly. Resolute, she continued forward, her body bending as she went to leverage herself through the panels. Only, she didn't make it that far.

Jerked backward with startling force, Cassie suddenly found herself held fast by the grip of Brannt's fingers, which had curled themselves around the collar of her shirt. He'd lost his hat somewhere in the middle of his mad-dash forward.

"Goddammit, Cassie stop—!" he bit off, swinging her around to face him. Cassie winced at the look in his eyes. "You want to end up like him?"

Cassie's eyes veered to the beat-up wrangler slouched so flat and still on the ground. "I won't."

"You sure as hell will, walking up there like that."

Cassie made an impatient gesture. "He needs attention, Brannt. He's bleeding profusely."

"Yeah, but you aren't going to help anybody this way. He'll kick you dead before he'll let you touch him," Brannt informed her heatedly.

Cassie felt her face heat up, her defenses rise at the patronizing quality of his tone. *He still thinks you're an idiot.* (Though perhaps she could have thought her plan through better.) "It's my job, Brannt," she told him stiffly. "Please, allow me to do it."

Brannt cursed roundly. "Kellar, Frank—grab your horses and come here," he yelled, waving two men, who'd been watching the ensuing confusion from the safety of an outbuilding nearby, forward with an impatient wave of his arm. "Help me get Big John"—Cassie presumed that to be the name of the bull— "stretched out on the ground. Ms. Hastings needs to address his wounds. Immediately, it would seem."

It took a couple of minutes, and a few colorful adjectives, but soon enough the two boys on horseback had Big John stretched nicely between their ropes, and, once settled safely and securely on the ground, Brannt went and sat on the animal's enormous head, using his body weight to keep it from trying to get back up again. Nicely restrained, they cautiously beckoned Cassie forward.

Now that she was being forced to act, Cassie wondered if she wasn't the world's biggest idiot. Beyond rudimentary knowledge, at this point, she didn't know what the hell she could do besides stopping the bleeding and cleaning the area. Her bravado of moments ago seemed to have deserted her.

The weight of what she'd been about to do seemed stifling now.

"Honey, we haven't got all day."

Brannt's insistent remark snapped her out of this temporary paralysis. Kneeling down before the subdued animal, towel in hand, she applied direct pressure to the gash, her fingers quickly lost in the red flow of blood oozing out its sides. Chancing a glance at Brannt, who was holding Big John steady, Cassie knew her eyes were frightened. The two-ton beast heaved, snorting at the contact.

Brannt smiled. It was encouraging.

Swallowing back her urge to throw up, Cassie tried to smile back. Her lips twitched unseemly though so she gave up the idea. She was so close right now, directly within the aim of fire, to those horns which had brooked so much damage for young Carl over there. Worse, she'd put herself in this predicament all on her own. She had no one to blame.

"Talk to me, Doc," Brannt said, and Cassie had the terrible impression he was doing it more for her benefit than his.

"Once the bleeding's stopped we'll need to flush the wound with disinfectant—" her voice was mechanical, cool, sterile even. Focus on what you know girl, she told herself, focus on what you know.

## CHAPTER TWENTY-TWO

Within minutes, the grounds were crowded with police cars, a firetruck, and an ambulance. Carl was being placed inside one of these wailing vehicles. The EMT's, however, seemed hopeful that he'd suffered little more than a concussion. Paying little heed to this, Cassie was only relieved from her pastime by the presence of Dr. Sam, his vehicle joining the parade of cars already strewn about the place.

"How's the patient, Cassie?" he asked, quickly sizing up the situation for himself.

Cassie glanced up at him, her face, had she but known it, marred with stains of blood and dirt and, beneath all that, paper-white. Her hands shook violently when Sam took the drenched towel out of her nerveless fingers.

"I can't stop the bleeding," she cried quietly.

"All right, all right, up girl," Sam said calmly, shooing her carelessly out of his way.

Cassie watched, petrified as he dug into his medicine bag. Unlike her, he seemed completely unfazed by the immediate danger directly beneath him, his hands moving deftly, surely over the quivering body of the mammoth bull.

She could feel her heartbeat pounding through her ears as the adrenaline she'd pushed to the back of her mind came flooding forward, full-blast. Her legs shook, and her breath wheezed uncomfortably past her lips. She was used to sterile, conventional environments, prescribed medicine, lab samples, appointments, and schedules...she was used to sedatives and anesthetics, operating tables.

What she wasn't used to, however, was this buzzing, hissing fear crawling through her system. It wasn't just the sheer weight and size of Big John, either. Cassie had been thrust into an unknown situation, and she'd been thrust there completely on her own, with no wizened teacher hovering overhead, making sure she didn't screw up, instructing her when she faltered, praising her when she succeeded. She hadn't realized how much she depended upon that until just now.

The fact that there'd already been one injury, and that half of Brannt's crew had been standing nearby, gawking unsurely, hadn't helped matters much, either. The wail of sirens and the rushed approach of peace officers and emergency responders had only added to the element of danger.

"It's her first on-site emergency..." she vaguely heard Dr. Sam saying to someone beside him.

Other words drifted through her consciousness as she slowly backed away from the crowds

A female voice: "...and all alone, poor thing."

"Kept her head on, though, didn't she? She even diluted the disinfectant, bless her!"

"—she doesn't look so good?"

"Oh, she'll be fine. Just needs a good strong shot of brandy."

"...no one under forty drinks brandy."

"No? Then perhaps whiskey. That trendy enough?"

"Whiskey I can do."

And then, she wasn't alone anymore. Brannt was beside her, his arm steering her delicately out of the arena, past the hordes of onlookers, and up towards the main house.

"I need to be down there—" Cassie tried to argue, looking helplessly backward as he thrust her into the kitchen. "Taking care..."

"The only thing you need to be taking care of right now is yourself," Brannt informed her, sitting her down in the same the ladder-back kitchen chair she'd used earlier that day.

Cassie sighed. "I failed."

Brannt laughed as he reached into the liquor cabinet for one particular brown bottle stationed there. "You were brilliant." He set a glass down in front of her. "And don't ever do it again."

"Brannt..."

"Drink that."

Cassie stared at it uncertainly.

"Drink it," Brannt insisted, pushing the glass toward her.

Pulling a face at his bossiness, Cassie downed the shot of whiskey. Looking up at him, however, she wondered if he didn't need the alcoholic depressant more than she did.

"You may want to pour another one of those," she muttered, wiping the back of her hand across her mouth. "You aren't looking so hot yourself."

"I wonder why?" Brannt growled with a meaningful glance.

Cassie shifted. "Brannt..."

"It was a reckless, stupid thing to do, Cassie."

"I was going more for brave," Cassie interrupted glibly. But now was probably not the time for flippancy.

"You could have—"

Cassie stopped him right there, placing the length of her index finger gently against his mouth. She knew he was having flashbacks to that horrible summer when his brother died, and she thought she understood his panic.

"But I wasn't. I'm fine."

Then Brannt did something unexpected. Grabbing her wrist, the one connected to the finger still over his mouth, Brannt brought her hand closer. Closing his eyes, he kissed her palm. Cassie felt tears prick against her eyelids. Then she felt her stomach give away at the hunger she felt against her skin there.

"Brannt..."

"You're right," he murmured, letting her hand go. Grabbing for another glass, he poured himself a generous amount of the heady alcohol. "Bottoms up." Tipping his head back, he swallowed the lot whole. Grimacing as the fiery liquid traveled down his throat, Brannt stared at her defiantly.

That's when he saw it. A large patch of red blood sticking wetly against the side of Cassie's shirt. His calm demeanor dropped in a flash. "Jesus Cassie—you're hurt!" His voice cracked over the confession.

"What?" Cassie asked and then, following Brannt's eyes, looked down at her shirtfront. But when he would have moved toward her, Cassie jerked out of his reach. Panic gripping her momentarily, her fingers pulled the fabric hurriedly aside as her terrified eyes gazed down at the gap in the opening at the top of her shirt.

But when she looked down the length of her stomach she saw nothing. Just skin. Unblemished.

"It's not me," she realized. "It's not my blood. It must have come from Big John."

By now, Brannt had taken in the whole of her appearance. Her shirt had a tear in one sleeve. Bits of dirt and blood were splattered everywhere.

"Oh baby," Brannt spoke quietly, unconsciously, his eyes soft now, sympathetic in the wake of her last confession.

"I'm fine," Cassie spoke sharply, not sure who she was trying to convince. "Just dirty. That's all. The shirt is probably done, but otherwise..."

"MARY!" Brannt's sudden bellow cut off whatever Cassie was going to say next.

Craning her neck instinctively, Cassie tracked the sound of approaching footsteps.

"You rang?" Mary muttered, poking her head just inside the door. Her eyes darted from Brannt to Cassie. "Oh, good Lord!" she breathed, taking in the ragged company. "What's happened to you?"

"Never mind that now," Brannt growled. "Take her upstairs. She needs to get cleaned up. You tell me if she's hurt."

Cassie rolled her eyes at his attitude.

And so, with Mary tut-tutting comfortably beside her, Cassie was led up the magnificent staircase at the front of the house, and taken into one of the largest bathrooms she'd ever seen.

"Leave your clothes with me," Mary ordered, having also made note of their tattered conditions. "I'm not sure what I can do with *this*," she admitted, giving the shirt a pitying glance, "but I'll give it a try."

"But—" Cassie squirmed uncomfortably. "I don't have anything else to wear."

"Just you let me worry about that," Mary informed Cassie, pushing her gently into the steaming, claw-foot tub. The smell of perfumed bath soap invaded Cassie's dulled senses. With a smile of gratitude, she allowed herself to be pampered.

Luckily her pants, while dirty, were easily cleaned and returned to Cassie by the time she'd finished her bath. The top, however, was still marinating in Mary's secret laundry elixir. So Cassie was presented with one of Brannt's shirts to change into instead.

Mary grinned as she passed the blue chambray shirt over. "It's the best I could come up with. No women's clothing in this house," she supplied tartly.

Cassie raised her eyebrows at the telling remark, though she couldn't deny the feeling of satisfaction it brought her to hear it. She looked down at the impossibly large shirt. "Well, I guess this'll have to do."

Mary pursed her lips. "I guess."

With nothing left for it, Cassie shut herself back into the privacy of the bathroom. Shucking on the offending article, she grimaced. The sleeves had to be rolled up past her elbows and the long tail tucked into the waistband of her pants. Ignoring the full-length mirror attached to the back of the door, Cassie felt more like a child playing dress-up than anything resembling a desirable woman. If she looked at herself now, she'd never leave the room.

Even Mary couldn't quite disguise her mirth as Cassie slowly emerged into the connected bedroom. "Well...it's decent, at least."

So, with no other clothing options available, Cassie made her way back downstairs and into the living room, where Mary had assured her Brannt was waiting. Walking on silent feet, she found him with his back to the entryway, his feet prowling restlessly across the length of the room. Knocking quietly against the arched doorway, she watched him spin on the heel of his boot, watched his head swing in her direction...

Those impossibly grey eyes narrowed as they skimmed over her appearance: wet hair curling down her back, against her shoulders, making patches of wet fabric where they touched against her shirt. Correction: *his* shirt. The wet fabric of *his* shirt, hugging *her* curves, touching *her* skin.

A heavy, uncomfortable silence thrummed as his eyes lingered on her person. "I—ah, there wasn't anything else to wear. I hope you don't mind...?" Cassie asked belatedly. Her feet shifted nervously, her hands motioning emptily.

"Oh, I mind all right," Brannt answered. His voice was husky, low. "Just not in the way you're thinking."

Cassie opened her mouth, but no words came out.

"That's a dangerous thing to wear in front of a man. His shirt."

Cassie's hands, which had been smoothing out the fine cloth material, stilled. Wide eyes glanced up, searching...

"Oh hell, never mind," Brannt decided, throwing a hand roughly through his hair. He was on the point of turning, ready to resume his pacing...

"Well, I don't see it," Cassie muttered, her voice stopping him. She gave a nervous, breathy laugh. Looking down, she watched her fingers pull at the fabric, stretching it off her body. "I mean, it hardly fits well." The words popped out of her mouth before she had time to fully consider them.

Brannt seemed to freeze for a second, his body half-turned away from her. His chest expanded on an uneven breath. He hadn't expected that. Cassie felt her heartbeat pick up. Truth be told, she wasn't entirely sure what she was doing, baiting him like that. Taunting him. Deliberately.

She smiled anyway.

Shifting his weight, Brannt moved to face her once again. Taking first one step, then another, he stalked toward her. "I *know*," he told her, his legs taking him ever closer, his smile predatory as he bridged the gap that separated them. "That's part of the problem. An outfit like that is just begging to be taken off..."

Cassie gasped softly.

He took another step, his body pressing up tight to hers. One hand reached forward, tilting her chin upward. "I'm doing my best here, but—"

Her eyes were large. "Brannt?"

"Come here."

And then Brannt's mouth was reaching for hers. This time, however, Cassie was ready for him. Her arms were already snaking up and around his neck, her body pressing tight against his when her lips felt the imprint of his own. This time, she was almost prepared for that pitch in her stomach that always predicated his kisses, the nerve endings slithering, ticking up-and-down, causing her to suck in sharply, making it difficult to breathe...ripples of sensation.

Pulling, biting, her teeth played with his lower lip, drawing it out, nibbling, then letting go. His fingers left the side of her jaw, twining themselves against the hair at the nape of her neck. With the slightest pressure there, he forced her head backward. Her neck arched. His lips traveled down her jaw.

That's when it hit her.

Brannt was experienced. Worldly. Not without notches.

He knew what he was about while she was only playing at it. Cassie was no femme fatale. She'd never seduced a man before.

She was guessing, fumbling. Faking.

"Cassie..." Brannt breathed, his lips settling against a spot just below her ear.

Shivering, Cassie bit her lip. He was too much man for her. Too much...everything.

Still, she wanted him. Wanted this. Just a few seconds more.

And then Brannt's mouth was back, pressing into the curve of her lips, and she stopped thinking altogether. Reaching blindly, hands splaying into the hair at the nape of his neck, she slid up on her tiptoes. Her throat swallowed the small sound he made at the contact.

Her heart was knocking against the walls of her chest. No. Wait. That wasn't her heart. Though the fog of adrenaline, the blood rushing, pumping between her ears, Cassie recognized that sound. It was a knock, all right, only it was coming from the front door.

Someone was knocking at the door.

In the second it took her to realize that, another sound invaded her ears. The click of the handle sliding over, the dull creak of its frame swinging open. "Hello?" A male voice called out.

Dr. Sam.

## CHAPTER TWENTY-THREE

Brannt's head lifted. His nostrils flared as he breathed roughly.

Cassie wasn't sure who broke free first—she only knew she was suddenly stumbling backward, her arms crossing tightly over her chest. Her eyes felt glued to the floor as she waited for Sam's feet to carry him forward.

"In here," Brannt called then. His voice sounded perfectly normal. Cassie's eyes peeked over at him. A good three feet away from her by now, his body was leaning casually against the back of the couch. Only his hair looked a little mussed.

Dr. Sam was dirty when he joined them, his jeans covered with mud, dirt, and something colored in an unfortunate green.

"How is he?" Brannt asked, sparing no greeting.

Dr. Sam grinned tiredly. Patting Brannt firmly on the arm, he didn't bother pretending to misunderstand the question. "He'll be fine. It was a nasty cut though. It'll need daily treatment for a while, but I've already talked to Jacobs and given him instructions about that. And I'll come by and inspect his progress in a couple days time."

Brannt's look of relief was almost palpable. Dr. Sam, who understood cattle prices, grinned broadly then. Replacing Big John would have been costly.

"How about Carl? Any news?" Dr. Sam asked. Cassie's head turned toward Brannt—in the midst of everything that had happened, she'd almost completely forgotten about the cowboy.

"Yeah, Pierce"—another hand, who'd gone to the hospital with Carl— "called a few minutes ago. Carl's going to be fine," Brannt informed him. "Two cracked ribs and a mild concussion."

"Not to mention a damaged ego, I'll be bound," Dr. Sam muttered.

Brannt laughed. "It happens to us all, every now and again. Bulls might not be smarter than us..."

"But they're a hell of a lot stronger."

Both men smiled.

Cassie nodded stupidly. "I'm so glad no one was seriously hurt."

At the sound of her voice, Dr. Sam's head turned, encompassing her person. "And how're you holding up?" If he noticed she was wearing

Brannt's shirt (she could only imagine what he'd make of that!) Dr. Sam didn't let on. His expression remained neutral.

"Me?" Cassie squeaked. "Oh, I'm fine. Just a couple scrapes and bruises. Nothing major," she muttered, feeling foolish under his eye. "I'm just glad you got there when you did....I- uh, I don't know what I would have done."

"Exactly what you were doing," Dr. Sam told her firmly. "Thought on your feet. That's the mark of it, girl."

Cassie glowed under the soft praise. Dr. Sam wasn't one to usually offer it for free. "Thank you," she said meekly.

"Speaking of that," Dr. Sam said, running a hand down the side of his face. "We'll need to get an incident report written up for our records."

"Oh. Yeah, I hadn't even thought of that..."

"I'm actually headed back to the office to get that done now." He scratched the side of his neck, clearing his throat eloquently. "So if you need a lift...?"

Cassie blinked. Oh God. He knew.

He shrugged perceptively. "I didn't see the work truck parked outside."

That's because it was still sitting, for all the town to see, outside Lucky Lucy's. What Sam must think!

"About that," Cassie tried to explain. "I just happened to be..."

"The truck ran out of gas," Brannt said, speaking at the same time as her. "When I saw her stranded—"

"...in the area..."

"No matter," Dr. Sam assured them doggedly, as though they hadn't both clearly lied to him. Probably, he didn't want to know why her truck appeared absent. "I'm sure I just didn't see it out there, what with all those emergency vehicles crammed together." Dr. Sam was giving them an out, sparing any further attempts at explanation.

"Yeah."

"Even so, I'm not sure if you should be operating heavy machinery right now, anyway," Dr. Sam argued.

Cassie felt her eyebrows slam together. "Excuse me?"

"The whiskey." He smiled at her consternation. "Who do you think suggested you take a nip or two?" His voice couldn't have been drier. "Besides, adrenaline of the sort you experienced out there with Big John can have unpredictable, prolonged side-effects." He shrugged. "All things considered, I think it's in everyone's best interest if you keep your hands off the wheel."

For half a second, Cassie considered being insulted. But then she remembered how poorly she'd reacted when Sam had arrived on the scene. She'd practically broken down in front of him. The man probably had a point.

"So, how about that lift?" He asked again.

"Oh..." Cassie stalled, her head swiveling toward Brannt, as she tried to gauge his response. "Well, ah—" What could she say?

"Don't worry about it, Sam."
Cassie felt her breath hitch at Brannt's quiet insistence.
"I can drive her home," he added.
"Are you sure?" Dr. Sam stressed. "I'm going straight there."
It was hard to argue against a statement like that.
"Big John…"
"Her shirt!"
In the second time in as many minutes, Cassie and Brannt spoke at the same time:
"…keep watch on him…"
"Mary's cleaning it right now…"
Dr. Sam lifted his eyebrows suggestively at the collision of their voices.
"It's only a matter of another half an hour in the rinse," Brannt continued, his voice overshadowing Cassie's now. That was probably a lie; her shirt was more than likely in the trash bin already. "Seems silly to have her go now, without all her clothes…."
Sam made a funny sound in his throat; it sounded like a smothered laugh.
Brannt grimaced. That hadn't come out the way he'd meant it to.
"I mean, obviously she's not—"
But Dr. Sam held up his hand, apparently having heard enough. "No, no, I'm sure you make a good point. After all, we don't need any more rumors when it comes to the two of you, now do we?"
It was as close as Cassie had ever heard Sam get to talk of a personal nature. She gaped at him, stupefied, but Sam only grinned. Tipping his hat genially in her direction, he told her he'd see her back at work, and Brannt later on in the week, and quietly let himself out.
"Cheer up, Cassie," Brannt said once they were alone again. He seemed to have read her expression only too easily. "At least he doesn't know you slept here last night."
"Oh, shut up." Folding her shirt more securely around her body, she glanced toward the open doorway uneasily.
"Looking for reinforcements?" Brannt mused, pushing himself off the back of the couch.
She raised her eyebrows. "Do I need them?" But still, she didn't look at him.
"That depends entirely on you."
Cassie shifted. Her eyes, when she finally raised them to his, were unknowingly vulnerable. "Please—"
"Please what?"
She shook her head. "I'm not up to sparring with you. Not today."
Brannt cocked his head to the side. "Not even if I surrender first?"
She didn't bother trying to disguise her confusion. "Why?"
He smiled. "Because I figure it's the only way I can convince you to have dinner with me tonight."
She caught her breath. Held it.

"Let me make up for the last time I asked you."

"Why?" Good. That parroting thing was back again.

"You know why," Brannt informed her.

And she did. Brannt may have been out of her league, and he may have been used to this sort of play, he may have been a lot of things but, at the end of the day, he wanted her. *Her.*

Cassie was in control. "Okay."

"Okay?" Brannt asked.

She moistened her lips. "Yeah. Okay."

He nodded abruptly. "All right." And then, just like that, he was moving, his steps taking him out into the large hallway toward the key rack beside the door. Grabbing up a set, he sent her a look. "You coming?" He gestured toward the door.

Cassie was still trying to get her breath. "Where?" She pulled at the too-large shirt swathing her person. "I can't go anywhere in this—"

Brannt whistled. "Certainly not inside Tiamango," he agreed. "People are bound to notice."

"Tiamango?" Cassie echoed, latching on to that one word.

Brannt gave her a look. "For that report Dr. Sam asked you about." His lips pulled up at the corners. "Or had you already forgotten about that?"

"Of course I hadn't forgotten." She had. "I just wasn't sure what you meant—"

She needn't have spoken. Brannt clearly didn't believe her anyway. "While I appreciate your enthusiasm for tonight, I'm afraid it'll have to keep. I've got work to do yet." He grinned wolfishly. Damn him anyway.

Cassie bit down hard on the inside of her cheeks.

"And we best get that truck back to Dr. Sam before he does start asking embarrassing questions."

"Could you be cruder?" Cassie spat.

"Sure. Want me to show you?"

Clamping her mouth shut, Cassie shouldered past him, her head held almost painfully high. Marching toward the door, she threw the thing open with the force of her annoyance. But before she made it onto the porch his hand shot out, the fingers caressing against her upper arm, pulling her back against the bulk of his frame.

Leaning down, his breath whispered against her ear. "Believe me, there is nothing I would enjoy more than starting our evening off right now. But I'm afraid if we did that we'd never make it to supper anyway."

Cassie shook her arm free of his grasp. "Oh, let me go."

Laughing delightedly, Brannt did as requested. "Fine, but I make no promises on that later on tonight." Setting her chin at a jaunty angle, Cassie didn't dignify that with a response.

* * *

Instead of taking Cassie to a restaurant that evening, Brannt asked her over to his house. He didn't say as much, but Cassie had the feeling he was trying to make a point. No curious onlookers. No gossip. No outside knowledge of their date. Just him and Cassie. A man and a woman spending time together with no agenda.

Cassie wasn't sure she'd ever enjoyed a meal more. Mary had simply outdone herself—tossed salads with homemade bleu cheese, salmon crepes, and thick porterhouse steaks. Sitting to one side of Brannt, the conversation between them had never lagged. It was only as Cassie took the last bite of her whipped mousse dessert that it occurred to her:

She was well and truly alone with Brannt. After sending out the last course, the housekeeper had taken herself home for the evening. There was no one to see them.

Suddenly, the thought brought an entirely new connotation to light.

"That was delicious," Cassie said demurely, placing her napkin carefully over her plate. Her fingers itched for something to do. In response, she gripped them tightly in her lap.

Brannt smiled, watching indulgently as her fingernails nervously picked against the denim of her jeans. Pushing back his chair, he gained his feet. "Care for a drink?" He held out his hand to her.

Scooting her chair back nervously, Cassie placed her hand in his open palm. Nerves ran up her arm at the touch. She rose gracefully to her feet.

"I have an excellent bottle of merlot."

"I'd love a glass of wine."

Placing his hand against the small of her back, Brannt led her out into the hallway and through the door to his den. A fairly impressive liquor cabinet was arranged against the back wall. As though he'd sensed her curiosity, Brannt smirked. "Business meetings, I've come to find, pair best with an aperitif."

"I can only imagine," Cassie murmured as Brannt went to pour them their drinks. It was while he was doing this that she saw it, tucked to one side of the couch: a small, padded tackle-box looking thing with many brightly-colored objects spilling forth from underneath its lid. Beads. Feathers. Yarn. Corks. Strings.

Cassie's head tilted amusedly to one side. What in the world. Could it be? Was big, burly Brannt a crafter? It was so...well feminine. Waiting patiently until he turned to hand her the glass of wine, Cassie nodded toward the source of her concentration. "Can I put in an order for a friendship necklace, please?"

Following her gaze, Brannt managed to convey his disgust rather well. "It's for fly-fishing."

Okay, that made sense, but Cassie wasn't quite yet ready to concede defeat. "Mmm, I'm so sure."

"It is."

"It's okay, you don't have to be embarrassed..."

Cut to five minutes later, and Cassie was quickly put in her place…and to her paces. Unable to convince her otherwise, Brannt had decided to prove to her his prowess at fly-tying. Without prompting, he'd quickly fashioned one such pattern together—something he'd called the Coachmen. It had looked so easy when he'd done it that Cassie had decided to give it a go.

Brannt had scoffed at this. "Cassie, it's not as easy as all that. You can't just slap something together, not without practice—"

"Is that a challenge?"

He pursed his lips. "How about a bet?"

"A bet?"

"Yeah."

"What's at stake here?"

"That's the best part. The winner gets to decide."

Cassie had pretended to think about it for a moment before sticking her hand out determinedly. "Deal."

And now, taking a generous sip of her wine, Cassie was willing to admit, if only silently, that mistakes had been made. And all of them on her part. Staring down at the distorted lump in her hands, she twisted her head a little to the left. The beads and hurl were lopsided, the feathers shooting out of the head at odd angles. It was official. Her first attempt at fly-tying had been a dismal failure.

Brannt seemed to agree. "Good God," he said, spying the sad-looking thing. "That'll scare the fish away, not attract them!"

Cassie giggled. She couldn't help it. This side of Brannt—this lighthearted, jovial man was a treat she wasn't about to lose, even if it meant accepting a little ridicule. Twenty minutes into this and the score stood as such: Brannt with four beautifully arranged pieces and Cassie a big fat, whopping one (if she could even count it as a fly, at all. It was utterly indistinguishable).

Worse, Brannt didn't seem to be trying all that hard, spending most of his time, apparently, watching her struggle along…

"Don't get cocky," Cassie assured him, reaching for a new set of materials. "I'm just getting my stride."

"At this rate, we'll be up past midnight."

Cassie stuck out her tongue at him. "Bored with this already?"

Brannt stared at her meaningfully. "No," he answered slowly, "but I can think of better ways to spend the evening."

Cassie felt a jerk in her stomach. Without meeting his eyes, she very carefully cut off a piece of yarn. "Oh?"

Out of her peripheral vision, she watched him slip off the couch and come to kneel close beside where she sat, cross-legged on the carpet; a messy arts-and-crafter, she'd preferred the large workspace offered by the floor. Cassie's fingers shook a little as she wrapped the yarn around her hook.

"You're doing that wrong," Brannt told her softly, leaning down until his mouth was scant inches from her ear, the tantalizing smell of his cologne invading her senses.

Cassie rewrapped the slippery filament—and none too steadily, either. The rude result was instantly destroyed when Cassie felt teeth nibbling gently against the outer shell of her ear. Her hook dropped noiselessly from her hands.

"Brannt..." Cassie breathed, her neck shifting, giving him better access.

"Yes?"

"Wha—what are you doing?" she asked, her eyes closing when she felt his tongue flick over the sensitive skin.

"For the best part of an hour I've watched you," he told her, his lips abandoning her ear now to take up residence on her neck. "The hem of your shirt rising ever so slightly when you'd bend forward or twist to the side...your teeth biting down against those lips as you'd complete a knot. Did you know, you make this sound in your throat when you're wholly concentrated on something?"

"No..." Cassie whimpered.

"It's distracting as hell," Brannt informed her, his lips now consumed with the line of her jaw.

"I-ah, I see..."

"I've tried not to notice, but—"

"Clearly, it hasn't worked," Cassie couldn't help but say.

"Not by half," he admitted.

Cassie murmured prettily, her head empty of rational speech.

"And so I figured it was my turn, to divert your attentions."

"Oh yeah?" Cassie murmured, her head falling backward encouragingly when she felt the delicious sensation of biting kisses traveling up, closer, closer...closer to her mouth.

"I thought you might agree."

Cassie barely had time to process this rejoinder before his mouth settled, finally, firmly against her own. Groaning, she twisted her body more fully into his embrace. The sound seemed to only further spur him on. While one hand went to cradle the back of her neck, Brannt's other was busy skimming up and down the side of her shirt, the tips of his fingers just brushing against the material that had been, apparently, driving him to such a frenzy.

With the slightest bit of pressure, Cassie felt herself being pushed backward until she lay flat out on her back. Brannt's strong body, propped on his elbows, hovered just above her. Arms looping hazily around his neck, Cassie's defenses were at an all-time low as she met the insistent havoc of his tongue.

She felt his body shudder in anticipation. Or was that her own?

"Today may not have panned out how I'd imagined," Brannt confessed, pulling his mouth away from hers, his grey eyes staring down into her green ones. "But this is exactly how I hoped it would end."

"Me too," Cassie whispered before lifting her head and catching his mouth. And that was the truth.

# CHAPTER TWENTY-FOUR

"We've been hearing an awful lot about this Brannt person, lately, haven't we?" Abigail Hastings asked, turning to her husband as she dished up their plates for dinner that evening.

Edward Hastings laughed vaguely. "I suppose so."

Abigail went on as if he hadn't spoken at all: "It's not just that, either. It's the *way* she talks about him..."

Edward nodded. "Used to be, she didn't have one kind thing to say about the man..."

"And now," Abigail shrugged. "Now, suddenly, we're hearing of an entirely other half."

Mr. Hastings smiled. Talk of their daughter during supper had turned into something of a habit with the parents. And, since Abigail had spoken at lunchtime to Cassie, she was only too eager to report news of their chat to her husband, and he was only too eager to listen.

"I think I knew something was going on between them even back then," Abigail assured him. "Even when they were enemies, there was something there. It was like, you could feel it. The way she couldn't help talking about him, even when she didn't need to, you know? It was like a compulsion to say his name, even if only in complaint." She gave a superior sigh. "As women, well, we notice things like this."

Mr. Hastings sent his wife a covertly loving look. She had thought nothing of the sort, of course, but to admit anything different would have felt like an insult to her motherly intuition.

"Is it serious, do you think?" Edward asked instead, spearing his fork into the stir-fry steaming before him.

Mrs. Hastings, hesitant of over-expressing her views lest she should be caught unawares (or worse, found to be wrong), merely shrugged carefully. "As to that, who can say but time?" And at Edward's dry: "How profound," she added tartly, "Well, okay, she didn't say anything in so many words, but... she sounded different on the phone. Older. But also rose-tinted, if you know what I mean."

Edward wasn't sure he did, but he kept that to himself.

Abigail. "It's serious enough for the moment."

Edward sighed. "I don't want her to get hurt."

"No. Me neither." Abigail frowned. "After all, this would hardly be an ideal time for her to fall in love."

Edward started. "Who said anything about love?"

She batted at his forearm. "Haven't you been listening to me?"

He gave her a level look. "Love?"

"That's what I'm afraid of."

"Where's the romantic I married?" Edward teased.

"Oh hush," she scolded him, blushing. She picked up her fork. "I only wish I knew what had changed between them. One moment Cassie was cursing him for all she was worth and then, overnight it seemed, their relationship was, well, *different*."

"I suppose we'll know soon enough."

Abigail smiled hugely, tucking into her own meal. "Just under a week."

"Seven days," Edward corrected her.

"Only if you count today. And we're not."

Edward grinned. "Okay."

Clasping her hands tightly together, Abigail breathed: "I can't wait to have her back. I've missed her terribly."

"This Brannt person aside, it's been good for her, though," Mr. Hastings felt compelled to point out. "Just like I said it would be."

Abigail nodded. "I know. Though I hate to admit it, she's, well she's flourishing out there. Finding herself, which I think she needed. She's no longer our shy, innocent baby…"

"But a brave adventurer," Mr. Hastings finished for his wife.

Tears misted Abigail's eyes. Edward chewed thoughtfully.

"Still, I'm counting down the minutes 'til her plane touches down…"

* * *

Cassie, some odd thousand miles away, did not share her parent's sentiment on that particular subject. Indeed, thoughts of her imminent return home had gone almost unnoticed. As unlikely as it would seem now, given just how homesick she'd been her first days in Pantula, Cassie hadn't spared a thought to her departure in weeks.

She had other things on her mind now.

She had Brannt.

And though she desperately wanted to, though her fingers were practically itching with the wanting, she resolutely kept herself from checking to see if he'd called her. Or texted. That kind of behavior would hardly do.

At least, not right now. Not with Andrea and BJ right there, breathing down her neck, just waiting for her give away such a telling move. As they say, any fodder for the rumor mill.

On one topic, however, mother and daughter Hastings' were entirely united in thought: Cassie couldn't keep from wondering at the newfound change in her and Brannt's relationship. If she hadn't gotten drunk at Lucky Lucy's, and if that bartender hadn't called Brannt, and if she hadn't stayed over at his house—one small thing but what a ripple effect! Their closure about the Rachel Thing; Big John's scare; when he'd asked her to *stay*. Two days but by the time she'd left Brannt's everything had flipped. Or, Cassie felt her stomach pinch nervously, at least she hoped so.

But, thankfully, she had neither the presence of mind, nor the peace of mind, to worry the thought just then. No, ironically Cassie was far too busy beating back BJ and Andrea's curiosity-slash-cross-examination, determinedly refusing to either acknowledge or discuss any mention of her weekend, of which both women were deeply, single-mindedly, and almost comically desperate to get the dish on.

"...come on, Cassie, don't hold out on us," BJ whined, coming to stand firmly beside her. Cassie only just kept from rolling her eyes. Her hand scrubbed ruthlessly against the already clean countertop in one of the lab rooms at the Tiamango Veterinary Clinic. Shuffling down the counter, Cassie kept her head bent low. Her hair, swinging gently on either side of her face, shielded her from prying eyes.

"Yeah, you've been elusive all day," Andrea agreed, coming to stand on Cassie's other side, effectively impairing the younger woman's ministrations.

Cassie sighed loudly. She was sandwiched between the two women, with nowhere else to go. "I have not—"

"Have too," BJ insisted. With practiced care, she took the sponge out of Cassie's fingers. "And this just goes to prove it," she insisted, waving the limp thing in her hand pointedly. "This room is perfectly sterile...you've cleaned this counter twice already."

Cassie snatched the sponge back.

"Girlfriends are supposed to spill to one another," BJ continued unabashed. She pressed one hip into the counter, staring Cassie down tirelessly.

Cassie did roll her eyes that time. "Don't you guys have somewhere to be?"

"Yeah. At home, making dinner for my family," BJ answered her. "But I'm making an exception for you."

"Generous."

Andrea grinned. "Oh, come off it, Cass. Everyone knows that Brannt picked you up from Lucy's three nights ago."

"And that your truck stayed parked in their lot until *late* the following afternoon..."

"Yeah?" Cassie challenged them, goaded into responding. "And does everyone also know that one of Brannt's bulls got hurt Saturday morning, and that's what kept me picking it back up?"

"Fair point," Andrea conceded.

"Not so fast," BJ argued.

Cassie arched her eyebrow.

"If your truck was stuck at Lucy's how did you get over to Brannt's to help doctor up that bull?"

"She's got you there."

Cassie opened her mouth.

"You were already with him when it happened, weren't you?" She crowed with delight at Cassie's quick look. "That's it, isn't it? You must have been with him. Otherwise, how would you have even known about the injured animal? It's not like you were on call last weekend."

Cassie set her jaw stubbornly.

"Admit it," BJ dared. "Tell me I'm right."

"I don't think she's going to stop until you answer her," Andrea prompted.

"Fine," Cassie surrendered. "Yes, I was already with Brannt when the bull got hurt."

Andrea grinned.

"And that's where it really gets interesting," BJ continued.

"It's not what you're thinking."

"You mean you didn't get so drunk at Lucy's that Brannt needed to come and pick you up?"

Cassie's mouth dropped open.

"Yeah. I thought so."

"Well," Cassie felt her cheeks twitching. "Now you know. It was nothing more than that."

"Maybe at first."

"Excuse me?"

"I'm more interested in what happened afterward."

"You know what happened afterward," Cassie returned defensively. "Brannt dropped me off at the truck and I came back here to write up an incident report with Dr. Sam. You were here. You know that."

"I do." BJ agreed. Actually, she kind of purred.

"Agreed," Andrea seemed compelled to add.

"So?" Cassie demanded when both women continued to grin in her direction. She tried again: "What's so interesting about that?"

BJ crossed her arms. "What's interesting is that on my way home I just so happened to drive by Brannt's house, and guess what vehicle I saw parked out front?"

Cassie felt her stomach drop. "Brannt's isn't on the way to your house."

BJ shrugged. "Call it a woman's intuition."

"You were spying on me?"

BJ didn't look the least shamefaced. "Playing a hunch."

"Beej!"

BJ grinned at Andrea. "My poor kids won't stand a chance."

Andrea smothered a laugh. Cassie chomped down on her teeth.

Turning back to the younger woman, BJ smiled triumphantly. "Now dish."

Cassie tried not to squirm under that penetrating gaze, but judging by the satisfied looks on the faces of her two friends, she wasn't succeeding very well. Almost against her will, memories of the night before flooded Cassie's senses, like individual film on a movie reel: Brannt's fingers spearing into the hair at the back of her neck; the weight of his upper body bearing down against hers; the splay of her fingers sliding down the length of his back; and then...

"Hello?" Andrea called, waving her hand in front of Cassie's dazed eyes. "Earth to Cassie?"

With a start, Cassie snapped back to the present. "What?" she asked.

BJ chuckled. "All right fine. Don't tell us. I have a good imagination anyway."

Cassie goggled at them uneasily.

"Oh Beej, stop teasing the poor girl. She looks done in," Andrea said then, coming to Cassie's defense. "It's fine, Cass. Don't mind her."

BJ relented with a good-natured smile. "Can't blame a girl for being curious though, can you? I mean, this is Brannt we're talking about."

"So?"

"Honey, he's no rounder."

"I think the term now is player," Andrea corrected her.

"Whatever."

"It's true though," Andrea added. "It's why this town's been so, well, curious about the two of you. Brannt doesn't keep a host of women at his disposal."

"He isn't promiscuous."

"Hell, since taking over the ranch he's hardly dated."

"Not seriously, anyway."

"Not in years."

"Taking you out, showing you off, being there for you...that's serious, you know?"

"He's certainly not hiding the fact that he's seeing you."

Cassie couldn't stem a small, satisfied smirk at their words.

"Look at that grin."

"I see it."

"Girl's bound to burst at any second."

"Oh, stop that!" Cassie insisted.

"Only once you start talking."

Cassie laughed. Holding up her hands, she submitted to their demands "Okay, okay. I'll talk...." But, as it happened, she wasn't given the chance. At that precise moment, Dr. Sam's head poked through the open door.

"Cassie," he said quietly. "Can I have a word with you for a moment, please?" His eyes took stock of BJ and Andrea's presence. "In my office?"

It was hardly a question.

"Of-of course," Cassie stuttered, unnerved at his tone of voice. Without looking to either BJ or Andrea, Cassie quickly went out after him.

## CHAPTER TWENTY-FIVE

Walking briskly toward Dr. Sam's office, Cassie felt a prick of worry invade her senses. What was going on? Dr. Sam had looked…odd. Reserved. She felt her lips twist. Then again, she probably knew what he wanted to talk to her about. Brannt. It had to be about Brannt. After all, he was a big client for the veterinary office. Probably, Sam was concerned that her relationship with him could potentially jeopardize the practice.

The thought rankled.

"Take a seat," Dr. Sam offered, ushering Cassie inside his sparsely furnished office. He shut the door quietly behind her.

Sinking gratefully onto the thinly padded chair, she tried to level out her breath. Though she'd never given it much thought before now, she suddenly realized how much Dr. Sam's opinion mattered to her. She would hate to have disappointed the vet in any way; and yet, her private life was hers. And she'd be damned if she'd allow anyone to say it was interfering with her professional integrity. As far as she could tell, she'd never given anyone just cause to suspect otherwise—not even with concerns to the McDowell Estate.

Fidgeting at the mere thought, Cassie decided to take the bit by the teeth. Before Sam had even taken a seat behind his desk, she was plunging into nervous speech. "Sir, if this is about Brannt and, well, and me please know that I would never let anything affect my ability to do the job—"

Dr. Sam raised one hand, effectively bringing Cassie stumbling to a close. Smiling crookedly, he inclined his head at her impassioned plea. "While I'm delighted to hear of such devoted service, that's not actually what I want to talk about."

"Oh."

"But, since we're on the subject, please let me make myself clear. Your personal time is yours. I have no objections on how you choose to spend it, as long as it doesn't negatively impact this office or anyone working within it."

Cassie swallowed back another, "Oh."

"And, furthermore, if you'll grant me the right to say so," Dr. Sam continued, leaning back in his seat. "I'm rather rooting for the two of you, anyway."

Cassie's face flooded with hot embarrassment.

Straightening suddenly, he cleared his throat. "Now, back to the reason I called you in here…"

Cassie expelled a quaking breath. If it hadn't been about Brannt, then what?

\* \* \*

It was dark in Cassie's small apartment. With only the glow of the living room table lamp, the space was awash with shadows. It looked positively morose, which Cassie supposed only seemed right. That was exactly how she felt, after all.

Morose.

Dark.

After leaving Dr. Sam's office she'd only wanted to be left alone. She hadn't even said goodbye to BJ and Andrea. She hadn't spoken to another person. She'd just left the building, her legs taking her numbly up the stairs.

It was only as she stood there, hidden in the half-light, that she spotted it. The paper chain calendar she'd made upon first settling in Pantula. Walking up to it now, Cassie realized with something of a shock that, somewhere along the way, she'd stopped tearing off the individual loops (each one representing a single day of the week); she'd stopped counting down the days left until she would return home.

With a curse, and feeling oddly out of control—hell, she hadn't known how close her temper was to the surface, Cassie found her fingers reaching out angrily, her nails ripping and clawing, shearing loose the rings from days past. Feverishly. Frantically. Until she stood ankle-deep in a swath of brightly colored construction paper. Breathing heavily, she glared at the few remaining loops she had left on the now up-to-date calendar. Six.

She had six days left in Pantula.

Cassie kicked the paper viciously out from under her feet. Gaining her bedroom, she tried to ignore the pounding in her chest, but at the sight of Brannt's crumpled chambray shirt lying across her bed, tears trickled from her eyes. Snatching it up, she pressed the shirt against her face. It still held the lingering scent of Brannt's laundry detergent.

What a terrible, horrible time to realize she was in love with him.

"Dammit," she cried into the fine material. "What am I supposed to do now?"

Flopping on her bed, the shirt tucked tightly to her person, Cassie's body shuddered violently with the weight of her feelings. Tears leaked out of the corners of her eyes. "This wasn't supposed to happen."

She had it all planned. She'd go back home, graduate from college, and apply for her dream position with the Peterson Veterinary Hospital.

When she closed her eyes she could see herself there, in the small apartment she'd rent down on Bakers Ave, the bright yellow accent pillows she'd use to decorate the living room, the vanity light bulbs she'd always imaged would encase her bathroom mirror.

She could already see herself there, walking to work, her feet carrying her over the cobbled sidewalks as she hummed to the soft sounds of the familiar neighborhood. And when she opened the door the Peterson clinic—

She'd experienced that moment a thousand times.

On Sunday evenings, she'd head over to her parent's house for dinner. They'd talk about their work weeks and she'd tell them about the dog who'd been rushed in after being hit by a car. It had been a large, harried surgery but the animal would live....

She'd meet up with friends on Friday nights, order pizza in from Dino's (they made the best Hot Hawaiian), walk the length of Trinity Park on warm summer evenings, and know, at the end of each day, that she was content. That she was living the life she'd always wanted

She was supposed to go home.

Brannt had never been part of that equation.

Pantula had certainly never been part of her vision board.

Sobs wracked the length of her body. Thrusting Brannt's shirt away, she buried her head in her pillow. She'd worked too hard to throw it all away. She couldn't stay.

She couldn't!

"I lost the thread," she cried into the empty room. "Somewhere along the way, I forgot. And now—oh God, and now...!"

She'd been so wrapped up in the newness of Pantula, in Brannt, in the illusion of it all that she'd forgotten reality. Or rather, she'd refused to remember it. Somehow, somewhere along the way, she'd stopped looking at her time here as transitory. Temporary. She'd never stopped to think about it. How it would feel, what it would mean, when she left Pantula—when she left Brannt.

But she couldn't stick her head in the sand any longer. Her teasing conversation with BJ and Andrea earlier, the butterflies she'd felt in Brannt's arms, the anticipation of his phone call...it all felt suffocated now. Dead. Realized for what it was. Nothing.

"Oh God," she wailed, her head pressing hard against the pillow as the tears fell down. It was over. Just like that.

One dream crushed by another.

# CHAPTER TWENTY-SIX

She'd told herself she wouldn't do this. That she wouldn't see him again. That it was stupid to continue in this ruse. And yet...

"You're not paying attention."

At the sound of Brannt's voice behind her, Cassie's hand jerked. The long, slim fishing pole in her grip flinched with the movement. "Wh-what?"

They were standing waist-deep in the cool water of a river that wound through part of Brannt's property. He'd taken her out fly-fishing. They'd made the plan to go last Saturday night.

"It hardly seems fair," Brannt had told her later that evening, staring down at the assortment of artificial lures strewn on the floor. "To do all the work of tying a fly without actually getting to use it." He'd given her a quick appraisal. "What do you say, Hastings, want to try out your luck?"

Of course, she'd said yes. But that had been then. And this was now. She should have canceled. She should have called it off. Oh, she must've picked up the phone twenty times to do that very thing but, in the end, the urge to see him, to spend a little more time with him had been stronger than her self-preservation.

It was a decision she'd learn to regret. Standing in the water with him, close enough to touch, only served to reinforce what she couldn't have. What she'd never have again. Her stomach ached with the anxiety of wanting to be near him and needing to let him go.

"Deep thoughts, Ms. Hastings?" Brannt asked her now, turning to watch as she attempted to throw her line out in the water again.

Cassie shrugged defensively. "Not really." Nothing she could share with him.

"Don't let the fish get you down," he teased. He gave her a sidelong glance. "Your line is all over the place. Reel it in and cast it again." With a quick movement, he waded to the water's edge, propping his pole against the grassy bank.

"Want some help?" he asked. Without waiting for a response, Brannt came to stand behind Cassie. His right hand moved to cover hers on the rod while the left positioned itself against her hip. Cassie's legs trembled as his body enveloped hers. "Remember how to load the rod?"

She could feel the warmth of his breath against the back of her neck. Smell his aftershave. Her stomach quivered as his left hand tightened against her waist.

"I think so."

"All right, now move your arm back like this—" Following blindly, she felt the pressure of his fingers against her hand. Unwillingly, tears pooled in her eyes as he slowly brought her through the motion.

"And watch it sail," he said as she released the line. He didn't remove his hands. If anything, she felt his body press itself closer to her back. "Don't forget to set it," he murmured absently, his voice a vibration against her skin.

Cassie felt made of glass. Sure that with the tiniest movement she'd break apart into a million tiny pieces. She barely breathed, standing there in his embrace.

And then she felt it. Those lips. His lips, traveling the side of her neck.

Oh God. "Brannt..." she protested, her voice thick.

"Hmmm?" His nose nuzzled against the underside of her jaw.

"I don't think—"

"Good. Don't."

His teeth nibbled against the soft skin there. Cassie felt those biting kisses all over, and without conscious thought, she felt her head tilt to offer him freer access.

Five days. She had five days left in Pantula.

"No!" With the suddenness of economy, Cassie pushed herself forward, her body pitching out of his hold. Her pole dropped forgotten down at her side.

"Cassie?"

"Stop." Her voice was brittle. "Just stop."

Brannt blinked in shocked surprise. "What the hell?"

"I can't do this!" Dropping her face in her hand, Cassie shook her head viciously. "I can't." The last word was strangled.

Gently, he reached out for her. "Honey, it takes years to learn fly-fishing—"

"No." She spun around wildly then, the line tangling in the water. "I mean this." Her hand pointed between the two of them. "*Us.*"

Brannt lifted an eyebrow, but otherwise, his face didn't betray a single emotion. "Care to explain?"

Cassie felt her shoulders snap straight. "What's there to explain?" She laughed without mirth. "I'm leaving Pantula. In a week. Less than a week."

Brannt's eyes flickered across the river. Then, slowly, he nodded. "Okay?"

Cassie bristled, throwing her hair back over one shoulder. "Well, maybe that doesn't mean much to you—"

"It didn't seem to bother you a hell of a lot either, three nights ago," Brannt returned ruthlessly. His grey eyes cut back to her.

Cassie bit her lip. "I know. That's part of the problem."

"I see."

"I doubt it."

"Then fill me in."

"You and I, this, it was never supposed to happen." There was that word again. Supposed.

"That's a bit dramatic, don't you think?" Brannt's voice was the stuff of arrogance.

"No, I mean," Cassie struggled to find the right words. "I didn't expect this to happen. I hardly even knew it *was* happening, not until…"

"Until?"

Her voice cracked. "When I first got here all I could do was wait. Wait until my eight weeks were up and I could go back home. But then, I don't know, something changed. And I—" Cassie pulled a self-depreciating face. "I stopped waiting. I stopped thinking about tomorrow."

"Until now."

She half-smiled. But there was nothing of happiness in it. "Right."

"And once you did…" Brannt took a deep breath.

"Yeah. Once I did," Cassie confirmed quietly.

He pursed his lips. "So now you're doing what you do best."

"Excuse me?"

"Running away." He smiled. It chilled. "Because that *is* what you're doing, isn't it?"

"That's not fair!" Cassie cried. She pointed an accusing finger. "I'm not running anywhere. I'm going home. Home, Brannt. In case you've forgotten, I was only here on an externship. It's done at the end of the week." And then, for her benefit as much as his, Cassie reminded them: "So that's it. I'm leaving."

"Ah."

"What did you expect?" Cassie spat, churning her hurt into a much more manageable anger.

"Probably nothing."

Cassie shook her head in exasperation.

Brannt laughed. "But hey, at least be honest about it. The end of your externship is only an excuse."

"I don't understand—"

"I know about Sam's offer."

Cassie stilled. Her mouth formed silent words. "But how…?"

"I take it you turned him down." It wasn't really a question.

The fight knocked itself out of Cassie; she nodded solemnly. "I can't stay."

He pursed his lips. "You won't stay."

"No. I can't." Cassie felt her shoulders tense at the damning silence beside her. "This is my future we're talking about, Brannt. Everything that I've worked for all these years, it's back at home. I can't just throw it all away…"

"Pantula was nothing more than a stop-gap." Brannt's voice was even, conversational.

"I wouldn't put it like that," Cassie hedged.

"Hell. Put it however you'd like." With a half-step back, he reached for his fishing pole again. Without glancing at her, he set the rod.

"Please..." Cassie pleaded softly, her eyes large in a pale face.

He glanced up at her dismissively. "Please what?"

Tears blurred his image.

"Please what, Cassie?"

Her chest heaved. "Please don't be mad at me."

He sighed. Then he turned back to the river. "I'm not. I'm just stopping while I'm behind."

His line twitched on the surface of the still water.

"But know this, you run away this time, Cassie, and I won't chase after you."

She felt those words. She actually felt them. "I know that."

He reeled in his line. "Have it your way." And with a snap of his wrist, he was casting off again, his attention on the task at hand. He didn't even offer her a last look goodbye.

Turning numbly, Cassie stumbled out of the water and up the creek bed until her feet hit solid ground. From there she did exactly what Brannt had predicted: she ran. And she didn't stop until she reached Dr. Sam's work truck.

\* \* \*

When she showed up at Andrea's house ten minutes later, tears streaking down her face, that woman didn't need to ask what was wrong. Cassie told her in one, heaving breath.

"I'm leaving," she cried, standing there on her front porch without preamble, without warning. She wiped her wrist under her nose. "And it's stupid because I kind of forgot."

"Oh babe," Andrea said, pulling Cassie into her arms.

"It hurts."

"I know," Andrea soothed, running her hands down Cassie's hair. "I know, baby."

"I didn't know!"

"You didn't know what?"

"How it would feel to...to say goodbye. I didn't kn-know!" she wailed, her fingernails digging into Andrea's shoulder.

"Shh," Andrea soothed.

"I wish I'd never met him."

Andrea closed her eyes. "I know. I'm sorry."

"I'll never see him again."

"Cassie."

"I can't breathe. When I think about that, I c-can't breathe!"

....

They didn't speak of Brannt again after that night. Cassie made Andrea promise her. It wouldn't change anything. She had to go. She had to let him go. So the next day, she showed up to work dry-eyed and resolved. If the rest of the staff noticed she was the first to arrive every morning and the last to leave at night, they chalked it up to last minute cramming. If they thought that she smiled too often, laughed too loudly, and yet seemed oddly absent in the midst of conversation, they told themselves it was all the nerves of her approaching graduation.

Cassie had never been so glad to allow them to believe a lie.

After all, it would have been pointless to continue on with Brannt. It would have only created a larger heartache in the end. And yet, knowing this, she was still excruciatingly aware every evening as she sat up in her apartment of the time she could have been spending with him. Her last moments in Pantula, slipping by, wasted.

Of him, there was no sight. He didn't stop by the veterinary office once that last week, didn't set up any last minute appointments to see Dr. Sam. If he went into town at all, Cassie wasn't aware of it. She told herself she was glad for this, and then she cried herself to sleep. It was funny when Cassie thought about it later. When she'd first arrived to Pantula she'd frequently cried herself to sleep, wishing herself back home, gone from the small Texas town. And at the end, she cried because she hated the thought of ever leaving it.

# CHAPTER TWENTY-SEVEN

Cassie took one last, lingering look around the surgery room at the Tiamango Veterinary Clinic. Shutting the lights off for the last time, she braced one hand against the door. This was it. Her last day at the office. Five o'clock, the end of her shift. She'd fly out early Sunday morning, and then it would all become a memory. Swallowing past the thought, she closed the door quietly behind her. With hard-won composure, she took herself down the hallway and toward the main lobby where she knew they'd be waiting.

And sure enough, there they were. BJ and Andrea, Dr. Stevens alongside Dr. Riley; Simon Brown, the vet tech, besides Kalli and Mara, the two part-time office girls—but they weren't alone. Standing smashed together in the cramped space, Cassie also saw Mr. and Mrs. Tubbs, the latter of which was holding out a pot of chili that Cassie wouldn't have the heart to tell them couldn't go on the plane with her. And there was Ben, Andrea's husband, standing by Bev Hickley and Mr. Bergen. Taking it all in, Cassie counted a number of other people waiting there, as well, customers of the clinic who'd come to send her off.

Stopping short at the sight of their faces, Cassie felt the tears she'd forcefully held at bay rush to her eyes. Her stomach felt constricted, weighed down by the tangible expression of everything she'd be leaving.

Though she told herself not to bother, she scanned the crowd for a glimpse of grey eyes. But Brannt wasn't there. Not that she really thought he would be. They'd already said their goodbye. She'd made sure of that, hadn't she? Her last memory of him would be on that riverbed, his back turned to her. Chucking that thought to the back of her mind, as she'd learned to do this last week, Cassie felt her lips trembling at the group huddled before her.

Spotting Cassie first, BJ rushed forward, her arms almost strangling as they reached around her neck to hug her tight.

"Oh!" she breathed into Cassie's ear. "I'm going to miss you girl! It just won't be the same without you; I've rather gotten used to your Northern blood."

Cassie smiled in a watery sort of way.

"Here, here!" cried a Dr. Stevens and Dr. Riley, pushing themselves forward to pat her awkwardly on the shoulder and offer clichéd words of goodbye.

"To your future success!"

"We've loved having you here."

"The stuff of a brilliant vet..."

Cassie swallowed with difficulty. "I'm going to miss you all—!" Putting a shaking hand to her mouth, Cassie stopped to compose herself.

"You were a true asset to the team," Dr. Stevens said gruffly. While he and Cassie hadn't spent undue time together, he'd frequently offered her exposure to interesting or tricky cases he was working on, encouraging her to investigate all avenues of the business.

Not a man of many words and none of them flowery, Cassie took his parting words to heart: "Should you ever require it, you'll receive nothing but a glowing recommendation from this office. That is if you decide not to...." Faltering a little, he coughed. "Er...that is—"

Cassie nodded. She knew what he was trying so hard not to say. "Thank you."

"We'll miss you too, love," Bev called out. "You've been a real joy to get to know these past weeks."

Heads nodded in agreement.

"You stuck up to these stubborn cowboys," Mrs. Tubbs said, pushing the crock of chili in Cassie's hands. "And it looked good on you."

Cassie laughed. It had a sodden sound.

"Hey. No crying." Turning at the command, Cassie saw Andrea standing behind her.

"I can't make any promises."

Andrea glowered. "If you start then I'll start and pretty soon we'll both be holding BJ."

Cassie let out a watery giggle. "I can see it now."

BJ, taking that moment to relieve Cassie of the heavy crock of chili in her hands, harrumphed. "We'll just see who's calling who a cry-baby in a couple minutes," she muttered.

Andrea wiggled her fingers. "All right. Come here," she said, her arms gathering around Cassie. "What's it they always say, don't be a stranger?" But Cassie saw right through her attempt at flippancy.

Still, she tried to respond in kind. "You either."

"Promise."

Cassie's arms squeezed once, hard, around Andrea's waist. "And thank you. For always being my friend."

Andrea nodded sharply before letting Cassie go. "It was easy."

Ben moved forward then. He had something in his hand. "Andrea."

"Oh!" Rushing forward, she took it from her husband. Then she turned to Cassie. "It's nothing much..." she said shyly, before shoving a small present into her hands.

Stunned, Cassie's eyes latched onto a thin, rectangular object, wrapped in pretty purple and white polka-dotted paper. "I—what?" Cassie fumbled.

"Just a small memento, something to remember us by," Andrea said, looking a little embarrassed now. "You don't have to open it now..." but she might as well have not spoken for Cassie's hands were already greedily ripping back the wrap.

Inside was a gilded picture frame holding a photo of the entire staff—including Cassie—that someone had snapped earlier that summer. They were all standing outside the office, smiling into the camera for the annual Staff Appreciation Day. Dr. Sam stood a little off to one side, as he was ought to do, a large chef's hat perched jauntily upon his head, and a grilling spatula held mightily in one hand.

"It's perfect," Cassie whispered, staring fixedly at the still photo. Her voice was eloquent. "Absolutely perfect."

Everyone smiled nicely.

At long last, Cassie found herself staring into the etched lines of Dr. Sam's face. BJ took that as her cue to announce that refreshments were located in the back of the building if people wanted to head that direction. The room, feeling as though they were intruding on a private moment, didn't need any further encouragement. Shuffling quickly, they called out last goodbyes as they followed after the receptionist.

"And you," Cassie murmured, only half-aware of the sudden hush in the room. Her attention was on the wizened face before her. "Thank you for giving me the best...the best days of my life." It sounded corny, contrived but she meant every word.

Dr. Sam smiled crookedly. "I could say the same to you, my dear, but then, there's been enough tears already, huh?" He laughed quietly. "I'll spare you the sight of an old man's moping, shall I?"

Cassie blushed, wiping her cheeks dry at his words. "It's funny, you know, when I got here, I thought I'd never stop being homesick and now... it's so hard to leave." She tried to pass this off casually, but the hitch in her voice gave way to the heavy truth of her words.

Dr. Sam gave her a knowing look. "That's because it's the goodbye that's tough."

Cassie nodded, though she wasn't entirely sure she knew what he meant, or if she even agreed with him. But it didn't matter.

"Can I—can I hug you?" Cassie asked instead. Dr. Sam wasn't a sentimental man, she knew the sight of her distress caused him discomfort, but she couldn't help the plea that rang so pitifully from her mouth.

However, Dr. Sam didn't look the least put out by her request. He smiled gently and opened his arms. Without a word, Cassie fell into his embrace, her arms snaking around his middle tightly. "Think about what I said Cassie—take all the time you need to form an answer. I won't change my mind," he said softly.

Cassie's head bobbed. She couldn't pretend she didn't know what he was talking about. It had consumed her all week, always there, at the back of her mind. That sudden, determined request to see her in his office seven days ago…the shocking, elating words he'd spoken. And to think, at the time Cassie had been worried he'd called her in there to reprimand her over Brannt.

At the thought of Brannt, she bit down on the insides of her cheeks. She felt half strangled at the thought of never seeing him again. It had been the only thing that had gotten her through the last week: the hope that he'd be there. Somehow. Waiting for her.

But he was a man of his word, wasn't it? He said he wasn't going to chase after her and he hadn't.

Pulling away, Sam saw the fresh tears spilling down her face. "No more of that," he admonished. Retrieving a hankie from his back pocket, he handed it to her. "There's a party in the back. Tonight, we celebrate."

Cassie nodded.

"At the airport," he informed her. "Then we cry."

"Fair enough."

So once again, Cassie willed thoughts of Brannt to the back of her mind. Pinning a determined smile on her face, she refused to let his absence matter. It didn't work, of course, but then that's what pretending was all about.

# CHAPTER TWENTY-EIGHT

Abigail Hastings sat down with a plop beside her husband at the kitchen table. "I'm worried about Cassie."

Edward glanced over at his wife. "Yeah."

"She's been home for almost six weeks, Edward."

"I know."

Abigail shook her head. "Something's not right."

"It's been a big change. Graduating…"

"You mean, coming home."

Edward murmured. "That too."

"She's not herself."

He looked at his wife tenderly. "I know."

"She's—despondent."

"It's an adjustment. Give her time."

"Did she tell you, she got a call from Peterson's clinic yesterday?"

That got his attention. "No."

"They offered her the job."

"But that's great!"

"She told them she needed to think about it."

He paused. "That's—"

Abigail smacked her hand down hard on the table. "It's what she's always dreamed of. That job. And now, suddenly, she needs to think about it?"

"Well, she has gotten other offers."

"Those were safety applications. Back-up plans. You know that."

He did. "Have you talked to her?"

"I tried. But, you know how she is lately. She just got that far-off look in her eyes. Told me she wasn't sure anymore."

"What changed?"

"She said she just kept waiting. Throughout the interview process, she kept waiting for the clinic to feel like home."

Edward raised an eyebrow.

"I know," Abigail said, just as though he'd spoken. "How could she possibly know what that would feel like?"

"What did she say?" But Edward was pretty sure he already knew.

"She said it would feel like Tiamango."

"I see."

"She's lost weight."

"You mentioned that the other day."

"She's lost too much weight."

Edward reached over and patted Abigail's wrist. "Don't push her."

"Me?" Abigail looked affronted. "Never."

"She needs to figure it out on her own."

Abigail sniffled. "She fell in love with him."

Edward didn't need to ask who. "I know."

"It changed her." Abigail looked through the kitchen window. "She won't even speak his name."

"Losing someone is hard."

"This is different."

"No, I know…"

"She cries herself to sleep." She bit her lip. "I could almost hate him for that."

Edward was slow to answer. "I don't think it's just him."

Abigail swung her eyebrows together. "Excuse me?"

"I think there's more to it than that."

"Such as?"

"What was the first thing she said to you, the morning she came back home. When you took her outside to drink coffee out on the patio?"

Abigail sighed. The patio led off from the kitchen. Situated on the second floor of the house, it offered a sweeping view of the trees and cityscape. "She told me that BJ would love it up there."

"And what was the first thing she did that Sunday when you took her out shopping for her graduation dress?"

Abigail nodded. "She bought a pair of horse-shaped earrings for Andrea."

"And isn't that who she's talking to right now, up in her room?"

"Lord knows, she's not talking to me." Abigail returned her gaze to the trees outside.

He gave her a look. "Abigail…"

Abigail sniffed. "We're going to lose her, aren't we?" She turned pleading eyes on her husband.

He smiled gently. "Isn't that the whole point? In a way, we already have."

\* \* \*

Up in her room, cocooned against the backboard of her bed, Cassie listened to Andrea's chatter.

"…snapped the growth plate clean in half."

Cassie winced. "How is he?"

"Sedated now. But Sam did excellent work on that leg—with any luck, the cat will have little more than a slight limp."

"I wish I could have been there."

Silence. And then: "Yeah."

Cassie bit her lip.

"Would you listen to me just going on," Andrea asked. "How are you? Doing anything fun on your Friday night?"

Cassie pulled a face. "Besides talking to you?"

"Please. That's supposed to be my line."

"Do I need to have a talk with Ben?" Cassie teased.

"Go ahead. That is if you can actually get him alone for two minutes. Lord knows, I can't."

Cassie's eyebrows lowered. "What's going on?"

"Brannt. He's got them all working overtime."

Cassie felt her breath still. It had become an unspoken rule between her and Andrea and BJ—there was no talk of Brannt. "Oh."

"I swear, he's going to be the death of me."

Cassie nodded slowly.

"Or the death of Ben." Andrea sighed. "He's pushing them to the extreme."

"Busy time of the year?"

"Not particularly." Andrea was quiet for a minute. "No. I think it's something else."

Cassie narrowed her eyes. There was something she didn't quite trust in Andrea's tone.

"I think he's trying to forget."

"Stop."

"I'm just saying…"

"I'll hang up if you do."

Andrea sighed. "Okay, okay. I'm sorry. Oh. Hey, how's the job hunt going?"

Cassie would almost rather talk about Brannt.

With a sideways glance, she looked at her computer. A stack of resumes sat beside it.

"It's going."

"Get any offers?"

"A few."

"Still waiting on the Peterson Hospital?"

Cassie stalled. "Well, no…."

"No?" Andrea's voice was hesitant.

"Actually, I heard from them—"

"And?"

Cassie blew out a breath. "And I got the job."

"Oh my God! Talk about burying the lede. Honey, that's great."

"I'm not sure if I'm going to take it."

"What?" Andrea sounded genuinely confused. "Why?"

"It didn't feel the same."

"The same?"

"As what I always imagined."

"Oh."

Cassie took a quick breath. "It didn't feel the same as Tiamango." And then an even longer: "Oh."

"Don't laugh," Cassie begged her, pulling her knees up tighter to her chest. "But I always thought I'd know. When it was the right fit."

"And this wasn't?"

"No."

"And you've set Tiamango as your barometer of sorts."

"I guess." Cassie shrugged.

"Honey, that's ridiculous."

"Why?"

Andrea laughed. It had a rich sound. "You know why."

Cassie licked her bottom lip worriedly. "You think I made a mistake."

"No. No, I didn't say that."

"What if it's just that I miss you?"

"That could be."

"What if it's just that I'm scared?"

"Could be that, too."

Cassie felt oddly soothed by Andrea's lack of answers. She glanced at the resumes again. They looked both exhausting and pointless suddenly. A resolve she hadn't been aware of started taking root.

"I don't think that's it," Cassie said. "I mean, I do miss you guys and I am scared. But…"

"But?"

Finally, she spoke the words she'd once been so terrified of knowing: "I miss home."

\* \* \*

It was Monday morning. Her first day on the new job. Walking nervously toward the back door of the clinic, Cassie stopped for a moment to catch her breath. When her hand reached forward to grab the door handle, she hesitated—soaking up the moment.

Her first day on the job.

Walking through the back door, she'd hardly had time to let her eyes adjust to the fluorescent lighting when a voice broke out.

"Well. It's about damn time you showed up!"

Cassie laughed at the short woman standing just inside the room, her hands pinioned on her hips. "Sorry I'm late."

"Oh shoot," BJ gushed, rushing forward, her arms slipping around Cassie, bringing her in for a hug. "I forgive you."

"Dr. Hastings. Welcome on board."

Cassie looked over BJ's shoulder. Her grin widened. "Dr. Coleman."

"From the sounds of this back room, I take it she's arrived?" Coming in on the heels of this question was none other than Dr. Sam. At his entrance, BJ reluctantly let her go.

Cassie smiled. "I'm here."

"Good." He winked. "It's been quiet without you."

"Never heard you complain," BJ teased him.

"Get in all right?"

"Yes," Cassie assured him. "And thanks for letting me use the apartment upstairs until I get settled."

"Take all the time you need."

"Ready for today?" BJ asked, grinning excitedly.

Cassie took a deep breath. "I think so. A little jittery, I guess."

"I know what'll help. Follow me."

"Where are you taking me?" Cassie teased, allowing herself to be led down the hallway.

"Just wait and see."

Bringing Cassie out into the front lobby, BJ stopped. Andrea smiled. "Over there."

Following her gaze, Cassie gasped. Hanging up on the wall with all the other staff photos was a picture of Cassie on her college graduation day—the same picture she'd sent to both Andrea and BJ. Set directly above it was a sign that read: Congratulations, Cassie!"

"But…" Cassie turned, stunned, to look at her friends.

BJ beamed.

"Obviously, you'll get an official picture taken soon," Andrea assured her.

"But we thought for now, well, this would do nicely."

Cassie swallowed. "Thank you."

"See? Nothing to be nervous about," BJ assured her. "You're already one of us."

# CHAPTER TWENTY-NINE

It was on Cassie's third day that Dr. Sam made the request. She'd been standing up at the front desk, just finishing scheduling an appointment with Mrs. Bausch when he'd come out of Examination Room One.

"Cassie," he said. "Hold up a moment, will you?"

"Sure. What's up?"

"I just had a call from Mrs. Jennings. She's got a colicky horse."

Cassie's face turned sympathetic. "Oh no."

"Yeah. I'm going to head over there now, but I was hoping..." he paused.

"Yeah?"

"I was wondering if you could take over my next appointment for me?"

She nodded automatically. "Sure. Where's it at?"

He made a show of running his finger down his appointment book. "The McDowell Estate."

Her voice faltered. "Where?"

Glancing down at his watch, Sam noted the time. "I'm set to be there in half an hour but, at this rate, I don't think I'll make it."

"Wouldn't it be better if you just rescheduled?" She hated the desperation in her voice.

"Well, it's rather late to do that," Dr. Sam pointed out. "And anyway, you know how Brannt gets..."

"I also know how he gets when someone other than you shows up." There. That was a solid point.

"It's not like you haven't worked on his horses before," Dr. Sam reminded her. "Besides, this isn't anything you can't handle—just a general check-up on Berma and her foal."

Cassie gulped. "Oh."

"So? Can you take care of it?"

"I...uh..."

"I'd ask Dr. Stevens, but he's in surgery and Andrea's out on another call." He waited a moment. "I could really use you, Cassie."

She opened her mouth. She'd have to tell him no. Politely. Respectfully. She couldn't do that. "Yeah. Yeah sure."

He smiled. "Great. Thanks." When she didn't immediately move, he nodded toward the door. "Better get moving. You'll need to load up the truck."

She nodded robotically. "Yes. Okay. Right." With stilted movements, she turned and left, her feet taking her limply to the supply room.

"I know what you did just there," BJ said to Sam once they were alone.

He turned an innocent face in her direction. "I'm sorry?"

"Dr. Steven's finished up his surgery fifteen minutes ago, as you well know." She smirked. "And Andrea's half way to the McDowell Estate now. She could have made it there in plenty of time, if you'd bothered to call her."

Dr. Sam grinned, but all he said was: "No reason to overwork anyone."

"You're not fooling me," BJ assured him. "You old romantic, you."

"Now BJ…" Dr. Sam's voice lowered.

"Oh, don't worry," she promised him. "Your secret is safe with me."

Twenty minutes later, with something less than grace, Cassie brought the work truck to a stop outside Brannt's barn. For a moment, she remained behind the wheel, her eyes gazing unseeingly ahead. But she could only stall for so long and, soon enough, Cassie found herself getting out of the vehicle. Her legs trembled just slightly as she gained her feet. Shielding her eyes against the blinding sun, she didn't have to look far to find Brannt.

He was standing with his back to her, his arms crossed over the top of the riding arena just right of the barn. It was the same arena that had once housed a bleeding, angry Big John. Shucking off the memory with a force, Cassie grabbed for her supplies. Silently, she walked toward him.

He never turned around, but he must have sensed her approach. She could actually see his shoulders tense as she came closer. He kept his eyes trained straight ahead as she brought herself to a halt beside him.

"So," he said, his cowboy hat pulled low over his brow. His eyes never once strayed from the horse getting worked in the round pen. "I heard you came back."

Mirroring his pose, Cassie was careful to keep her voice neutral. "Yup." Her fingers tightened against the medical bag in her hand. She wasn't sure how to proceed. She wasn't sure what to say.

He made a half strangled sound. "I hope you weren't expecting some grand welcome?" He did glance her way then, a mere flick of his gaze. There was mockery in those eyes.

Cassie blinked. "Hardly."

His arms dropped away from the fence. "Good." A muscle twitched in his jaw. He curled his fingers around the metal rails. "What happened?" He asked scornfully. "Lose out on your dream job?"

"No. That's not it at—"

"Then what?" His gaze returned back to the horse.

There was so much suspicion in that question that Cassie laughed. It had a raw, unhinged quality to it.

Dangling the heel of her boot against the bottom rung, she shrugged. "I doubt you'd believe me if I tried to explain."

He nodded once. "You're probably right about that." With a swift movement, he pulled himself away from the gate. "And, anyway. I don't have the time to hear it." He glanced pointedly toward the barn. "I'm actually waiting—"

"For Dr. Sam," Cassie finished for him. He turned to look at her, his eyebrows raised. She nodded meaningfully. "You got me instead."

His chest expanded on a breath. "Great." He turned toward the barn. "Well, come on then. I haven't got all day." He didn't wait for her.

Cassie wheeled after him. It wasn't the right time. She knew that and yet, seeing him, she couldn't help the words from bubbling out of her mouth: "You were right!"

He stopped walking, but he didn't turn around. Cassie was almost glad for the reprieve from those grey, grey eyes. "When you said I was running away…"

"Ah hell, Cassie," he cursed. "I told you, I don't have time—"

"But I ran back." The words came out torn, echoing around them. "I ran back."

Brannt was silent for a moment, his shoulders so straight they looked about ready to snap. "Good for you," he offered, and with that, he started toward the barn again.

Hot tears rushed to Cassie's eyes as she watched the proud lines of his back walk away from her. He'd warned her, hadn't he? What had he said, that he was stopping while he was behind? That he wouldn't chase her anymore. Her shoulders shuddered on the realization—the hope that had kept her going all these weeks lay crumpled at her feet.

"Jesus!" With a jerk, Cassie felt her face being pulled up. She hadn't seen him turn around, hadn't heard him stalk up beside her. She only felt those fingers curling under her chin, tilting it up to his face. "Are you crying?"

Cassie jerked free from his hold. "Never mind," she muttered with as much pride as she could.

"Well, what the hell did you expect me to say?"

She averted her eyes. "It doesn't matter, does it? You didn't say anything at all."

His nostrils flared. "I tried. Once. But it wasn't enough."

"I was scared, Brannt," Cassie cried, her arms swinging out at her sides. "It was my life you were asking to change!"

"And yet here you are," he reminded her. He paused, and then: "Why did you come back?" There was something different about the way he asked it that time.

Still, she tilted her chin. "I thought you didn't have the time?"

"I'm making it now."

She sighed, her eyes looking down at the dirt laid track. "I'd been so afraid to try something new, to stray from the path of what I'd always thought I wanted." She pulled a face. "So I left."

Brannt made an impatient gesture. "Yeah, I know that part already."

She ignored him. "But it didn't work."

Brannt didn't say anything to this.

Cassie's tongue smoothed over her teeth nervously. "I think I had to go back to realize—"

"Realize?"

Cassie could feel his eyes on her as she stared out over the pasture. "Just what it was I'd left behind."

"And what was that?"

Turning her head, she looked at him. Her eyes never wavered. "Besides you?" She asked conversationally. "Easy. I left behind my home, my friends, everything I—"

Brannt took a short step closer. "What did you say?" The question was quick, hard.

Cassie didn't pretend to misunderstand him. "Why else would I be standing here, making a fool of myself?"

She felt his hands reach for her shoulders. But they didn't pull her closer. "Cassie…"

"I'm sorry," she said into those grey eyes. The words were pleading, small. "That I pushed you away. That I wasn't listening. I'm just sorry."

"Hell, I don't want your damn apologies."

She stared up at him. Her mouth trembled. "What *do* you want from me?"

Brannt's eyes narrowed on that trembling lower lip. "Now there's a question," he murmured absently.

"Whatever it is, I'll give it to you." She took in a breath. Held it.

His eyebrows rose up. "That's a hell of a proposition, Cassie." His thumbs rubbed circles against her shoulders.

She felt that caress everywhere. "I mean it." She bit her lip. Her eyes lowered to his big boots. "I understand if I ruined everything between us."

"Always the histrionics with you," he said, but the briefest of smiles was tugging at the edges of the words.

"And I'll leave you alone if that's what you want."

"Did I say that?" He asked quietly, bringing her closer.

"But if I didn't—" her mouth quivered. "Just know, I'm willing to chase after you this time—!"

Cassie wasn't allowed to finish. Before she could take in another breath, Brannt's mouth bent, taking hold of her lips. Tripping into his embrace, she didn't stop to think. Twining her arms around his neck, she sank into the sensation of his lips, the abrasive texture of his stubble as it razed against her jaw.

She forgot everything in that kiss. She wrapped everything in that kiss.

Brannt slowly lifted his head. "That's a tempting offer, Ms. Hastings," he murmured against her mouth.

"Don't stop now," Cassie whimpered, tugging his head back down.

He smiled. She could just make out the curves of his lips before they descended on hers. Her stomach dropped out when his tongue darted inside her mouth.

And then a horse whinnied loudly into the still morning air.

Lifting his head, Brannt swore under his breath. "Dammit Tagger," he said, glaring after his horse, who'd come nuzzling up beside the fence to watch them.

Cassie giggled. She couldn't help herself.

"What's so funny?" Brannt said, but there was nothing of anger in his voice now.

"We have our very own chaperone."

"Damn pest is more like it."

"He's probably got a good point," Cassie conceded reluctantly, shifting her head toward the barn. "I am here on official Tiamango business, after all."

Brannt narrowed his eyes. "It'll keep," he assured her. His mouth bit down against hers.

"I love you, Brannt," Cassie whispered.

"Took you long enough to get here."

She pulled her head back just slightly. "Here?"

"Where I've been all along," he promised her. Drawing her close once more, Brannt showed her exactly what he meant.

\* \* \*

# Amber Laura

Author | Romance | Women's Fiction

## NEWSLETTER

## B&N NOOK

## AMAZON

Made in the USA
Monee, IL
24 June 2025